My thanks go to Silvia De Laude and Davide Tortorella, who guided me through the labyrinth.

Thanks for invaluable criticism and advice to Stefano Agosti, Patrizia Cavalli, Christopher Gibbs, Marc deí Pasquali, Roberto Peregalli, Walter Siti and Aldo Tagliaferri; thanks for botanical advice to Hadj Mohammed Temsamami and for medical advice to Edoardo Moor. Thanks to Stefano Zucca for the care and attention with which he deciphered, typed and retyped the manuscript; finally thanks to Stephan Janson, my excellent walking companion.

THE AGE
OF
FLOWERS

UMBERTO PASTI

THE AGE
OF
FLOWERS

Translated from the Italian by
Alastair McEwen

PUSHKIN PRESS
LONDON

© Il Saggiatore, Milan, 2000

English translation © Alastair McEwen, 2002

This edition first published in 2003 by
Pushkin Press
123 Biddulph Mansions
Elgin Avenue
London W9 1HU

British Library Cataloguing in Publication Data:
A catalogue record for this book is available
from the British Library

ISBN 1 901285 47 2

Frontispiece: © Leonardo Cendamo/Grazia Neri

Set in 10 on 12 Baskerville
Designed by Blacker Limited
and printed in Britain by
Henry Ling Limited at the Dorset Press, Dorchester

THE AGE
OF
FLOWERS

THERE IS A FIRST SCENE. The boy and the girl are on the cliffs over the Atlantic. The light is that of spring, but of a pre-industrial, prehistoric spring, and thus stronger and more extensive, of a spring that bites in winter or in summer, and lasts as long as it wishes: the light of spring has instantly infiltrated this slumberous film, it pierces it, blurs it, makes it crackle. The ocean is flat calm, green as a lawn. In the sky clinging to the horizon falcons describe overlapping circles. Down below, big black rocks herald the Cape.

She is wearing her pretty skirt, a taffeta print with bunches of poppies, one of those flared, mid-calf length skirts they used to wear in the fifties, made up at home by a seamstress friend. It is the most elegant item in the wardrobe she has brought with her to the White City for the no-frills holiday of a secretary living in a two-room flat in a northern city. The skirt is her stand-by. Marta is a little tipsy, and swaying, and she is leaning on him, and looking at the ocean without really seeing it. She is not used to drinking. Perhaps this is why, in her honest face hollowed by scrimping and saving (it is a folly, this holiday, a folly to be recounted to acquaintances and friends for months, for years), her eyes hold the same watery melancholy, the Semitic grief, as those of goats—a goat at someone else's sabbat.

He too hails from the north, but from a north farther north than hers. From a snowy north, of moorland and dog roses, of hunting parties on horseback in the oak woods and long lunches with porcelain and silver in square houses built of red brick. Mortimer is not on holiday because he doesn't work. He travels, amuses himself, studies. He is a gentleman, with centuries of wealth in land and animals, grain and milk, women and books behind him. His forebears were brigands. No one in his family has ever worked. This is why he never has a penny in his pocket. It had been he who, on seeing this pretty, petite girl walking along the boulevard, had drawn up in his car at the pavement. But when, after the invitation and the lunch at the restaurant that she, instantly in love, accepted straight away, the waiter placed the dish with the bill before him, he had to pretend that he had left his wallet in his hotel room. The bill, a steep one, was paid by Marta. Then, the run in the car. The eucalyptus trees, the minarets, the villas, the palms. All so obvious, like an amateur film over-exposed by the searing light. All so like a Sunday, so cruel.

He takes her hand and she abandons it to him because she had decided to—or so she thinks—right from the moment she saw him at the wheel and got into the car. Mortimer does not have to insist in order to persuade her to go down the path that cuts diagonally across the cliff face, through the rock roses and the juniper, down to the beach where they will take their siesta. Although she has made love only once before, Marta has already given him her assent, unspoken but unconditional. They come down, through the hot rocks and the bushes. He stumbles, grabs onto a thistle, and curses in his language. She laughs but stops immediately, because she fears she has offended him. They come to a crag. The throat of a lizard pulses. The lizard darts off. They are on the beach. Marta slips off her sandals, pulls up her skirt a little, and goes into the water, which is cold and still as crystal. Foolish girl, drunk, she walks in the sea parallel to the shore, and in this moment she is happy because he is looking at her: she is aware of the gleam that the whiteness of her calves, the white of her feet, has kindled in his eyes. But all Mortimer has to do is call her. Even their first kiss on the water's edge—behind Marta's closed lids—is not a kiss: it is as the sea was before, from the cliff top. A poor postcard to be kept.

They find a sheltered nook in the cliff, a cramped space, but enough for them, protected by a large projecting boulder. A young fig tree is growing there. They sit down. Marta is so excited—the sea, the holiday, this man, the wine—that she would have done without the jacket he has taken off and laid on the dust, to prevent her skirt from getting dirty. She doesn't care a thing for her stand-by skirt, not now. At the end of the second kiss—he is already inside her blouse, calmly caressing the breast that has always been his—Marta sees the flower. It is a little wild iris peeping out, brownish and violet, bearded, from between two rocks. She stretches out her fingers and plucks it. He takes it from her hand. Observes it. And as wild flowers are his passion (since he was a little boy he has kept a membership card of the Royal Iris Society in his wallet): "*Iris lutescens*," he says. On saying it, he is already taken by a whim, by a fantasy.

Marta is naked, outstretched on the jacket. But Mortimer is still dressed. Only his erect phallus sticks out from his open trousers (although she cannot see it, because she is keeping her eyes closed, he has asked her to, and she has obeyed). With a slight pressure of his hands, Mortimer has her open her legs. He contemplates the girl's sex, the parched tuft, her labia, the reddened skin of her perineum. He draws a breath of desire. In his other hand—his right—he clutches the flower. With his right hand, he slips the stalk into Marta's vagina; she gives a shudder, like the thrill of a tickle, but notices nothing. Mortimer looks at the iris peeping out of the vagina as if it had been born in this girl, as if she were giving birth to it in this instant. He leans over and looks at it from closer up. Then he begins to lap, with the large confident tongue of the master, petals and epithelium together. He licks and nibbles. He grunts. She, who was no knowledge of such foreplay, gives a little laugh of shame, of discovery, of pleasure.

Mortimer breaks off. He kneels down between Marta's thighs, points his phallus, approaches, and with his glans he pushes the flower—he pushes it inside her, and now she feels something ... but already she feels it no more, because his phallus fills her. They are not using any of the contraceptive devices people used to employ in the fifties, the years of this poor over-exposed film. Mortimer comes inside Marta. Then he withdraws. He is already bored. She notices this—she is sitting up once more, covering her breast with one hand—by the way he runs his hands through his hair, sprucing it up before going somewhere else. Marta gets up, dresses herself once more. He has buttoned up his trousers. They climb back up in silence.

They go away, leaving the landscape there, almost intact. Perhaps because he is sorry for her—he has persuaded her to confess that she is staying in a Spanish boarding house where there is no hot water—Mortimer invites her to have a shower in his hotel room. Marta accepts because she accepts everything that comes from this man. She is not drunk any more. She knows that this is the way things are.

After the shower, Marta emerges from the bathroom wrapped in the white terry-towel bathrobe with his initials embroidered on it. Mortimer is lying on the bed. He is sleepy, and has no desire to take her home. In any case, he will not see her again. He tells her the bathrobe suits her, and that she can keep it, as a present from him. She is so glad to have something of his to keep that she does not even try to demur the way bourgeois people do when they receive a gift. After their farewell, it is with the white bathrobe folded over her arm that Marta, the nanny goat in her Sunday best (but she is vaguely aware, only vaguely, that the party isn't for her), walks back down the boulevard towards her destiny. Again, a dusty postcard. The iris, the lily, is still in her womb.

to another species

Potresti essere mediocre e ignavo,
e molto meglio che tu sia schiavo.
MARIO MIELI

You could be mediocre and shiftless,
a far better thing to be a slave.

PART ONE

IRIS LUTESCENS

I

A CENTURIES-OLD mass of refuse, the exploded cesspool of millennia, debris accumulated by an idiotic fate—this was the hill. Among the goat droppings and the brushwood, amid the tufts of wool and the rags, beneath the sun-bleached mounds of tyres that look like dead pachyderms, cetaceans, the embers smouldered. Fire did not break out because everywhere, squatting behind the palings, against the sheet metal panels and the walls of the hovels, on the cardboard boxes, on the straw, on the shards of glass and the plastic bags and the rusty cables and the ropes and the wood shavings and the girders, men would urinate. Thanks to the corrosive effect of this collective urination, sometimes a spurt of relief sometimes a discharge impeded by the smart of prostatic hypertrophy or urethritis, thanks to the relatively vigorous distillate of the kidneys of thieves and vagabonds, smugglers and glue sniffers, Berber peasants, soldiers with gonorrhoea, of old marabouts dripping gout, and of young boys engaged in a merrily coarse challenge to see who could pee the farthest—target the cat—the most disparate materials decomposed and blended into one another in the sometimes greasy and friable, sometimes compact ground of this mountain of refuse glued together by piss. The air smelled of piss, and of burnt rubber. At times, the breeze brought whiffs of bad but innocent smells: of sweat, frying, dung. Peddlers chanted the price of their wares, T-shirts printed with messages like *Danger, Chanel, I am a killer*, and *Niño peligroso*, bric-a-brac, synthetic carpets, effigies of Saddam Hussein with black beret and raised fist like Che Guevara, Korans bound in metallized plastic, cheap radios and stereos, bunches of peacock feathers, piles of boxes of expired medicines, sheep, rabbits, poultry, and the bodies of dead hedgehogs broiling under the hot sun. Then, as the summit of the hill gradually grew nearer, while the crowd thinned out and voices and cries merged into a hum, another odour seeped through, insolent:

the smell of the sea. As if, on climbing this mangy slope, among the thistles and the dog turds, on drawing nearer to the sheet of the sky, the White City had vanished: vanished along with the suburbs and the featureless tenement blocks with their tarred roofs bristling with antennas, vanished along with the cafés and the *madrassehs* and the boarding houses—Rembrandt, Sevilla, Paloma, Centrale, del Mar, Mar y Playa—in whose rooms family men in singlets took their afternoon nap alongside señoritas who could open bottles of beer with incisors made of gilded lead: the *hammams*, vanished; vanished along with the local shops with the mounds of dead flies in the windows among the bottles of Johnson's Baby oil and the biscuits; vanished along with the mosques, the garages, the stony and uneven streets like dried-up riverbeds; vanished along with the avenues, the squares, and the flower beds. Here, while Luca and Irene, young, hot, and bronzed by the days spent on the Atlantic beaches, were setting foot on that summit open to all breezes, one got the feeling that the White City had never existed. The peak of the anthill was its lowest point. A submarine world with no memory. Prehistory. A Pleistocene in which sounds were faint: the gurgling of molluscs, a dispirited rasping, a voiceless rumbling in the bowels. Everywhere, arcane life forms. The man-hermit crab dozing in the dead shell of a washing machine. Globular eyes like those of a scorpion fish peeping through a slit in an overturned cabin, spying on the blonde foreign woman with bare arms. Beneath the debris of a shipwreck—the bonnet of a car held up by the frame of a bicycle—among strips of canvas blooming with mould, a swollen leg protruded, a moray eel lying in wait. From beneath the parasol of the jellyfish lying open on the ground with its tentacular fringes sunk in the mud came a thirsty cheeping— chicks, a new-born baby. This underwater world was slower than the other. Nocturnal, it lay hidden by day. But of an evening its denizens would climb back up the ladder that from the invertebrates leads to the mammals, the primates. At night, the molluscs come out of their shells. In a flapping of rags, among boxes that open out like the corollas of nocturnal flowers and coral reefs of scrap metal dislodged by their inhabitants, the gastropods would come out. The metamorphosis they underwent was always the same. They would get to their feet. Arm themselves with sticks. Then—lycanthropes, vampires, hyenas, wolves—they would fall on the leftovers from the market, gather in packs in the city dumps, the remotest ones, ready to vie for any remnants they could possibly reuse. These people were the lowest rung, the untouchables, the pariahs: Irene called them "the antique dealers".

"Spider! Look! The glory of the Andalusian tavern of the fifties!" Her harsh voice, the lines of tension between her eyebrows, the curl of her lips, betrayed strain, enervation. Bent over a jumble of pans, handles, valves, and springs, she pulled out a couple of wrought-iron lanterns the sight of which filled Luca with melancholy, for him they conjured up the dinners with solitary tourists in the dives overlooking the city beach, the slow silent chewing of hairdressers from Liverpool and window dressers from Düsseldorf on half-board in some hotel in the *medina* for a week of couscous made of human flesh seasoned with sun tan oil: the sighing and peering into the shadows lurking between the bathing huts and the showers, the clash of spoons on zinc bowls made in China, the thump and sizzle of the insects that managed to fry themselves on the very panes of the lanterns that his wife, wearing the grim smile of a medieval sexton ringing the passing-bell, was brandishing. Irene woke up the slumbering shadows of this lazaretto. Everyone knew her as "*la chattarrera*"—the rubbish fancier—here in hell. She would haggle over the price, pay, then leave her purchases. Later she would come back with a bearer, who would load them onto a handcart and carry them down to the car. Walking fast, she came to a pile of debris and lumber. The skeleton of a screen from some sailors' brothel, with its panels reduced to satin cobwebs the colour of grape pomace, it had already been promoted from "straight out of Balzac" to "Odette: pure Odette de Crécy". Lying stretched out in the dust, the seller was observing her darkly. Luca tried to catch his wife's eye. He cherished the fond hope that, if he caught it, he would have managed to make her see the absurdity and the danger of these prospecting trips. Not even the police came up here, among the damned. But Irene was looking elsewhere, into the distance, her mouth set hard, concentrating on a hunt that was an escape. She had been like that since the beginning of the summer, when they had moved into the new house. As if possessed by an idea that made her movements mechanical, and her words a flickering knife blade. In Europe, in her consultancy office, she sold pictures, furniture, sculptures and antiques, here in the White City—where they had come, for the first time, years before, by chance—she was furnishing the two pavilions bought with money supplied by her father, the Great Widower; it was a mania, an obsession. "*La decoración, la decoración*" she would repeat in honour of the place's Hispanic past, roaming through the dismal rooms wild as a drugged tiger (and if he approached her, if he tried to stop her, to fondle her, she would go rigid like an animal for which contact with man is the most terrible outrage, then she would regain her control, and mocking, almost voicelessly, she would spit a leaden volley in his face, "Don't touch me"). Luca would never forget the night on which, in a fairground that stood on some waste ground among the building sites where they were constructing summer residences for families from the torrid hinterland, packed in tight against each other in the car of the rollercoaster as it climbed to the top of the first slope, just when they got to the top—a bird's eye view of the city and the bay, the pitch black sea, the glittering lights of distant ships—she had given a wriggle, unbuckled the safety belt, stood up and spread out her arms—Redeemer of Rio, Let them come, let them come unto me—from down below came whistles, the laughter of young kids, applause, howls of encouragement, then dismay, silence. With a jerk he had managed to drag her down just as the abyss swallowed them up at a hundred an hour, only to hear her say, at the end of the run, with his legs atremble his stomach inside out and his heart in turmoil: "Did you crap yourself? Get ready. One of those days I'm going to fly away". (And his heart had stopped. For those were the very words, the same words that had been uttered years and years before—

perhaps by a friend of the family, perhaps by a neighbour—in front of the bed on which there lay a great empty chrysalis: "Look how beautiful your mother is, Luchino! Marta has flown away." Were women all butterflies, then? Why didn't they let themselves be loved in peace, like doves, why did they flutter about lugubriously, these harpies?) Now, on watching her fingers sliding along the scrollwork of a wooden shelf supported by a carved swan, and on observing her fingertip as it lingered, the fingernail scraping away the crust of caked mud to reveal flakes of gilt work on the surface of that object, which must have belonged to a Nazi who had taken refuge here after the war ("*Grottino Wittelsbach*" croaked Irene, her gaze already casting about elsewhere) he thought back to when—they had been playing with some local kids on the foreshore—he had seen those fingers squeeze the breast of a little girl, those nails clawing the tender flesh. The little girl's cry—pain, bewilderment. Luca had turned round. Only then did she realize what she had done. That's why she had released her grip a fraction too late. They had confronted each other. Never as in that moment had Irene been so close to breaking down, to confession: "She threw sand in my eyes, the little shit". And stiff with shame she had stalked off—slim legs, a heron's legs—leaving him to console the little girl—who nonetheless, for the rest of her life, would have thought that it was true what people said: that *nazrani*, foreigners, were bad because they did not know the laws of Allah.

Irene had vanished: all it had taken was to let her out of his sight. Luca glanced around, aware of the need to conceal his anxiety. An old man sitting on an oil drum winked at him. He felt a presence behind him. A man with a face furrowed by fistulas had crept to the door of his hut. He was staring at Luca open-mouthed, a gleaming thread of saliva hanging from his lip. Through his trousers, ostentatiously, he rubbed his sex. The old man's laughter exploded like a coughing fit: "*Loco!*" he bayed asthmatically, tapping his temple with his finger. "*Esta loco de tu culo! Amigo! Loco!*" Luca sprang forward, mastering the impulse to run. He had to find her, take her away. The foetid air was saturated with the exhalations of their dog-like drooling:

the white woman all milk and honey, the gazelle, the hind, skinned like a deer hanging from the butcher's hook. They would have sent her crashing to the ground. They would have come over her, they would have attacked her mercilessly like clusters of crabs and snails on the corpse of a drowned man. A hand seized his calf. The other was stretched out: "*Allah ou akbàr* ... God is great". He wrenched himself free. Down there, on the other side of a barbed wire fence, he caught the swerve of a familiar T-shirt, long arms in the sun. He caught up with her at the end of an open space where a sheep was grazing on waste paper. "Now, isn't this just Sissinghurst? Isn't it ideal for our Sissinghurst-*sur-mer*?" She was pointing to a scratched leather armchair whose seat had caved in: "It belonged to a very old Englishman with a passion for roses, cats, and pricks: want a bet?" The usual machine gun. Imperturbable, the dealer was smoking his pipe of *kif*. No. Absolutely nothing could happen to her. Her recklessness protected her like armour. A full suit of armour. Luca again tried to comfort himself. Although months had gone by since Irene had last wanted to make love with him, he tried to convince himself that she was the same as before, the same as ever, his girl who smelled of mushrooms and beaver, the girl who had crossed the Sahara on the roof of a lorry without complaining so much as once about the heat and the jolting, discussing cattle and crops with their travelling companions, an old Fulani and a Hausa ("Hausa, nothing to do with Tuaregs, love"), the seductress who at the table of a fancy restaurant, amused by the head waiter's embarrassment, had reeled off all the things she was going to do to give him pleasure, between the *soufflé Rothschild* and the duck *en croute*, closeted in the toilet "or right here, give me your foot, hurry it up, spider". Then, he gave up. It was the fixity of these library pictures—and the mawkishness of the holy image they were making of them all—that revealed the truth. Pointless to stare with this superstitious insistence at the photo on a grave. The two children in love were dead. It was a dull pain, the heaving spasms of a sterile birth. They could not—Irene could not—have children. He was exhausted. The chirping of the cicadas grew even shriller, a screeching climax of sistra. The sun was a white ball in the sky. And already she—avid as a housewife in a flea market poking about among the remnants of wretched domestic existences foolishly convinced that they are the bits and pieces cast off by others, whereas they already belong to her, have always been hers—was rummaging on her hands and knees among a landslide of newspapers, books, and photos compressed into compact lumps by the mud. Don't do that. Madwoman. Luca felt a thrill of disgust. Then pity. He asked the dealer's leave to go inside his hovel. The other nodded.

The relief was immediate. It was a sort of warehouse, larger than one would have guessed from outside. The half-light smelled of fodder. Enjoying the cool, he made his way through sacks of grain and piles of furniture—a forest of tables and chairs piled up in towers draped with cobwebs that stretched as far as the corrugated iron roof. More and more distinctly, he heard a sound, breathing, coming from the back of the shed. Afraid that it might be a dog, he stopped. Outside, in the brutal light, the man was still sitting. The buzzard was still raking about with her talons.

Through the doorway he could see only her arm, her shoulder, the contractions and the carnivorous darting of the biceps beneath the naked skin, then her hand seizing a book, opening it, and disappearing again. It could not be an animal. Regular, deep, the breathing came from the other side of a blanket nailed to the wall. He lifted up a flap. It screened a cavity that gave on to a little room. The smell was of damp wool. In the middle, in the faint shafts of sunlight that filtered through the irregular planks of the walls, there lay a voluminous object, a dark mass, a rolled-up mattress, black. Then came the gleam of the eyes—African. In the mahogany of the flat face, the only other colour was the pink of the gums. The old black woman was lying in her basket, hidden like a scarab beetle in its hole. Swathed in black rags, smiling, she beckoned him to come nearer. He noted her feet, bare, calloused, the lighter-coloured sole furrowed by deep gullies like those of an eroded landscape and the toes crushed by going barefoot. He felt dizzy. The impulse to run away. But it was pointless—useless to cling to the fading holy image that was the girl-bird outside. His cock, already erect, was hurting him. His throat was parched. He knelt down like an automaton. He ran a hand over her foot. She let herself be caressed, the she-panther. Here, the truth. It was not because, as perhaps it had been with Irene, that the seed of obsession was germinating in him too, there in the desiccated land of their spent passion. The phantasm would have materialized in any case. Even when he was a boy there could have been nothing fresh about the breath exhaled by the hairy moths that emerged from the chrysalides of his clandestine nights of drunkenness, of error, of blunders made by an orphan on the hunt. Recently, since they had been here, with growing frequency his eyes had alighted avidly upon strange creatures, followed the hypnotic unfolding of a fabulous bestiary made up of mermaids that were hippopotamuses, hippogriffs like hollow-flanked horses, swollen chimaeras, lame unicorns, indolent, prolix basilisks. Now, on caressing the wrinkly skin of the paw of this otter—its hardnesses, its thickenings, its wrinkles—for the first time he sensed the truth: it was in the distorted form of monsters that he felt the throb of emergent life.

Touched by Luca's youth, the old woman stretched out a hand in her turn, running it over his cheek. But the breathing of the foreign boy had already become a pant. Then, in the business-like manner of a queen obliged, during some medieval carnival, to give herself to one of her subjects, and rummaging through the rags that covered her, the witch began to extract a breast made of chocolate; long, terribly long, it was a convoluted blackish serpent whose spires, uncoiled, now hung, floppy, with its little head resting on her thigh. The ostension of the body of the sphinx fascinated Luca.

She—omniscience of the simplest of gestures of love—lifted up all she possessed. Trusting, without saying a word, she proffered it to him and it flopped down again. In her smile there was an age-old resignation, that of a monkey who cannot speak. With both hands he grasped her breast and brought it to his mouth. He had never felt as he did in that moment, the moment in which his lips repeatedly took in the tip of that nipple hard as horn. It tasted of dust wetted by the rain: behind his closed eyelids a scrap-iron sun kindled amid the flashing, the gleaming, the leaden splendour of a skin that was a sky at the first lightning flash, at the first thunder clap, at the first barbarous cry of the she-vandal: "A Savonnerie! Luca! A *Savonnerie*!"

He came in his pants, an overwhelming gush, without even having touched himself. He jumped hastily to his feet and searched in his pocket for a banknote. With a grunt the old woman snatched it and spirited it away. Turning her back to him, she pulled the blanket back over herself and stretched out—amorphous once more. Staggering, Luca made his way back through the forest to emerge into the sunshine. With her face sweating, flushed with excitement, the madwoman was brandishing a piece of cloth: "Louis-Napoleon! Better than an Aubusson!" Luca's head was spinning. Suddenly, he felt like taking her by the hand and leading her into the depths of the hovel: "Let me introduce you to my new lover". Instead, he took the fabric from her hand. Before the avid gaze of the seller, he pretended to examine the discoloured garlands of roses and violets that gave off the smell of urine, in order to conceal, behind that shroud, the still-fresh stains of life on his trousers. There was no need to get the bearer and his handcart for this, he said. He would wait for her at the car, he was bone-tired. "Is there anything, inside there?" "No. Nothing of any interest." And shielding his genitals behind that rag, in an unconscious re-enactment of the maniac who has cut them off in self-mutilation, he headed off down the slope, through the thistles, the waste-paper, and the turds.

As he gradually made his way down, his face took on the hardness of a medallion—Luca was conventionally handsome, chiselled Alexandrine features, with curly hair that would have been chestnut but was bleached by sun and salt (but not Irene's pure Byzantine gold) and a large, full mouth. His eyes, usually of a muddy green, in this moment were too light, too ardent, dazzled by a vision. From below, among the cadavers of the elephants, columns of smoke were rising, they shredded in the air and fell back in a haze to stagnate upon the silent crowd below. The stridulation of the cicadas was like the rumble of this immense silence: black pythonesses who, brandishing their sistra, proclaimed to the multitudes the end of the rite, the rebirth of a man, and they howled his ineffable name—the name of a lily.

Full moon. Howling of dogs. Against the liquid sky, a little funereal among the other trees, towered the cypresses of the garden that surrounded two pavilions in the Moorish-floral style built in the early twentieth century: crenellated roofs, arched doors, and windows framed by multi-coloured ceramic tiles, the tower of the upper one was meant to resemble a minaret, but looked more like a dovecote in Portugal or Andalusia. (Irene, on visiting the house for the first time, to the American who was selling it to her: "An excellent example of the respect the colonizer has for the traditions of the colonized". And while the American's smug smile was freezing into a polite mask: "Building newspaper stands, villas and public toilets in the style of their cathedrals. That's eclecticism for you, my dear chap".) Now she was not there. They had argued. She had locked herself up in the bedroom. But the light filtering through the curtain drawn across the window suggested that she was still awake, still reading, sucking on a lock of her hair. All Luca had done, as he had often done in the past—but in imploring tones that depended on his awareness that he had reached a point from which there might be no return, or possible redemption, either for him, or for her—was to suggest that she adopt ... "Do you want to go shopping directly in shanty town?" she interrupted him, mockingly. (—And where do *you* buy, where do *you* grab the stuff, you bitch?—) "Look, they've already thought up the multi-racial family, you know, to sell pullovers." She got up: "I hadn't realized you had become so illustrious or so rich that you needed an heir, poor spider". (When she wanted to be nice, or nasty, that's what she called him. Luca wasn't skinny, but he looked a bit short compared to her friends, who were all tall: as if physical stature betrayed his origins in a *lower* social class). She had gone off, leaving him sitting on a wickerwork chair on the lawn.

To Luca, despite the fact he was almost thirty-one, none of this was very important. It mattered nothing that the money was always his wife's (or rather the Great Widower's): that she kept him. How could you make an advertising man out of someone who, when he had to promote a brand of lemonade, could think of nothing other than how fond the Fatimid sultans had been of lemon sorbet? (Even though the owners of the agency were friends of Irene, after a couple of months they had explained to him kindly but firmly that ...) For how much longer could he go on proof-reading cheap novels, he who was ardently fond of fine books? Could he perhaps become a doctor merely because he had a passion for anatomical classifications, this boy who had lived in terror of illness ever since his mother had died? Could he? But Luca's mind was far from these worries. The summer was over and he had made up his mind: he was going to stay here. Here lay his task and his destiny, his work. Not in the city (down there lights gleamed, a mellow, almost fake phosphorescence, vain promises, boundless flattery, a hall of mirrors at the end of which swayed the moon). Luca's work was in the garden. It was the garden. This first garden that he felt was entirely—that is to say in its totality, as a whole, right down to the last leaf, right down to the smallest lump of earth—his.

He had worked hard on it, with the dogged passion of the neophyte, all summer long, together with Mohammed, the deaf-mute gardener who lived with his family in a little cottage inside the property. Neglected plants, plants that had been mutilated and tortured for years (the American, afflicted by a phobia, thought they were "dirty", and periodically told the gardener, who against his will was compelled to obey him, to "clean up that disgusting mess"—the shears of those beringed fingers were unequivocal, ruthless), trees with trunks scarred by the cicadas, and whose poor branches were too thin to bear fruit, were healed, resuscitated, strong, and grateful. Luca gazed pensively at his garden. And he felt a happiness that was pride, and peace. He looked at the sloping terraces, the pergolas with jalap and jasmine, the lemon trees in large pots lined up under the new dry stone walls, from which the plumbago was already falling in bright cascades. Under the hostile sun of June, July, and August, he and Mohammed had dug deep holes at the bases of the trees—Brazilian pepper, banana, jacaranda—then they had filled them with cow dung. They had scattered liberal handfuls of humus over all the flowerbeds. Early in the morning and late in the evening the beds had been given an abundant watering. They had sown. They had planted and transplanted. They had hoed, weeded, and thickened. They had pruned and mulched. More water, lots of it, streams of it, to soak, to quench the thirst. Luca explored every nursery in the White City. He knew few names of plants, for the time being: here an oleander, a datura, or an acacia to fill the gap in a bed, and climbing pelargoniums of all kinds (he called them "geraniums") to run, tutored, along the bridges of wood and wire that united the old quince trees and the apricots, the pomegranate and the peach. Then, roses. Rock rose. Broom. Clumps of strelitzia like multicoloured crested birds (you again, sterile girl, sister). Fuchsias. Day lilies. Love-in-a-mist. Zinnias and cosmos. A village fête of dahlias. And other shrubs, other bushes, with unknown names. Covered with orange flowers. Whites and yellows, scatterbrained as butterflies. Luca got up. In him, in his movements, there was a lacustrine calm. The September night, clear and still warm, granted him this. Today he had come home with a little pink hibiscus. With its roots compressed into a clump inside a plastic pot, it was already in the place where it would be planted the next day, in the last bed, at the base of the *olea fragrans*. Luca went to the tool shed and emerged clutching a spade. He walked down the path. His shadow, that of a rather short boy, of a spider, was gigantic in the moonlight.

Tranquilly at first, he began to dig the hole. From the damp earth there came a good smell, which excited him, urged and spurred him on. Now Luca was digging with the fervour of prayer. The hole was deep enough. He took the plant out of the pot, put it down taking care to let the roots spread out like fingers, tamped down, scattered a bit of earth, tamped down again, and then, with his bare hands and not with the spade, he topped up the hole with earth, tested the suppleness of the stem with a flick of the finger, and ran his fingertip over the lowest leaves to clean them of any remaining soil. He was sweating. An owl hooted. Luca unbuttoned his shirt and took it off. Bare-chested, he lay down with his belly on the ground. He was not wholly aware of what he was doing. But if anyone—Irene, or Mohammed, or one of his children—were to catch him lying down there like that, he would know how to explain, he would say he was resting. As if to make himself more comfortable, with a rotatory movement of the pelvis, he penetrated a bit more into the womb of the earth. He was only at the beginning. He was a healthy, tired young man resting in his garden. His eyes were closed.

Luca, however, sensed something strange about this. At first it was a glimmer. But lying there stretched out, hard and naked on the earth, the feeling became precise—acutely precise. He felt his body growing. Growing beyond measure. It was then that he was transfixed by the exactness of words. They were so many pins, they were the spears and the arrows of the denizens of the mysterious island where this slumbering giant was stirring. It had been after his mother's death. Every day, for years, at school, he had spent hours poring over anatomy books, taking from them one after another the stones with which to build his dyke, his protection, convinced that these very names could exorcise things. There in the earth, the discharge of taxonomies that coursed through him was electric, it seared him. And it was, in the vivid and utterly beautiful words for the muscles and the organs and the bones—his bones, his organs, and his muscles— an epiphany of soma and semen, a ravishing light. As it had been when he caressed the old black woman's deformed feet. Luca sensed himself, and sensed the whole world. He was on the earth, and at the same time he found himself at stratospheric heights and abyssal depths, he glided down and soared up again, and he could see all that he wished. He saw the watchman huddled in a corner of the entrance hall of a city-centre building look up, suspiciously at first, and then with instant lust, at the young heroin addict who came every night to give him a blow-job for a few coins; he saw children sleeping the sleep of the blessed alongside mothers who were forever girls (forever girls like his girl, like your dead Marta, Luca); he saw other mothers, wrapped in the embrace of the family men who in the lumi-nescence of this black-cat night mistook their softness for that of the señoritas with whom they took their clandestine siesta; Luca saw those señoritas sitting as if enthroned in the doorways of the boarding houses, wigs like towers, painted faces, bodies heavy with certainty and *cerveza* and squeezed into imitation leather girdles from which Baroque volutes of fat overflowed—they called to the passers-by in angry tones, the imperious orders of queens: "*Aquí, hombre!*" "*Vente, amigo!*" "*Mira, chico!*" Luca saw the lost boys, the *peligrosos*, the dangerous ones, emerging from a showing of the latest chop-socky movie and, athirst for fame ("*Bruslí ... Bruslí ...* Bruce Lee ... "), finally facing one another and duelling in an Elizabethan glittering of blades among the hovels of shanty town or in the depths of the alleyways in the casbah—yes, they were heroes—he saw the window dresser from Liverpool and the hairdresser from Dusseldorf accost, trembling, with a wretched wrinkled smile that revealed the fangs of a weasel, the body-builder who had stopped to wait for them (he was a pro): "You're looking fit! What line are you in?" "*Y tu?*" "Me? I'm a sort of artist ... "—they were heroes too, heroes. Luca saw the fishermen brandishing their useless assegais coming in Indian file down the path that led from the mountains to the sea (the dynamite is in the sack, it would be a massacre); he saw, on the shore, the butcher of human flesh like Polyphemus counting his flocks: "*Veintinueve ... Treinta ... Treinta y dos ...* " (and the patera of the clandestine emigrants set sail, the ghost ship of real poverty set sail, in dream this raft of the Medusa set sail, a raft that would never land on the other side of the Straits, on the diseased body of the siren who uses her dartling and her blandishments to deceive these heroes old and young—heroes, heroes all). He saw the taxi drivers wandering around the station, leaden with fatigue, he saw the undertakers' carts moving off, the werewolves rummaging through the dumps, the drunks vomiting, the madmen howling—heroes—he saw, in a shanty, the figure of a strange heroine, part woman and part iguana, snoring fully clothed in her bed, her paw still clutching the empty bottle—he went closer to her, the bags under her eyes, the cysts, the smell of sweat and garlic—something shone whitely, it dazzled him, like a moth against the glass of a lantern he bumped up against this thing—body, or object—that was hard, white, and gleaming. He fell. (What made him fall was the reflection of a neon light on the ceramic tiling of a bathroom oozing cleanliness and poverty, but Luca could not remember this any more, he cannot know it yet.) He was on the ground. He was afraid. The moon had set. It was dark. He got up. He buttoned up his trousers, rubbed his belly, chest, and arms. He put his shirt back on and went back up, leaving the spade where it lay. It was as if he were simulating these acts, as if they were those of another, of a ghost that moved, slowly, against the murky background of a dream. He had gone out of his body. He had lost it.

Luca entered the doorway of the upper pavilion, went to the bathroom, undressed again, completely this time, and took a shower. He dried himself. Not even tonight would he put on the man's bathrobe that was a precious memento of his mother. He appeared at the door of their bedroom. Irene, lying down on the bed, regarded him from over the book. She had been crying: "Tomorrow there's the last rodeo of the season at Dar Sultàn," she said. She bit her lip: "I'm leaving the day after tomorrow, Luca". She was on the point of adding something, but fell silent. She held her fear inside herself like an injured migratory bird, which flies as best it can, but still flies and does not give in and does not alight on anything. This phoenix flapped her gaunt wings in the ashes of disease: "The farce is over," she said.

II

THE TRAGEDY was brewing behind the backcloth of the stage on which the foreign residents performed their summer operetta. It was brewing in the enormous auditorium, in the amphitheatre, in the gods, in the stands, in the suburbs with no sewage system and no schools, in the prisons and in the worm-infested condominiums, in the fields castrated by drought, in the dusty villages still without a name and in those with sweet, extravagantly ancient names redolent of Phoenicia (Ashakkar, Char Ben Dibbane, Djebila). The tragedy was looming, and already you could sense the eruption on the scene of the barefoot unshod public who, after spending centuries watching the foreigners' performance, was shaking off its torpor, and like a boy awaking from an overly long sleep, could feel the bite of hunger in the bowels. But the farce was not over. The White City was close to the hearts of the Generals in power, who on account of its geographical position kept it crushed in an iron grip. It had sprung up, this innocent city, at the foot of mountains on which blond Berbers have cultivated since ancient times almost all the cannabis for smoking consumed in all the world. Only the Straits separated it from the European coast. The repression of Islamic fundamentalism went hand in hand with the prosperity of the Generals thanks to commercial activities that a revolution would not have interrupted, but would merely have made profitable for the new masters. Yet, despite the relative "political stability", the life of the foreigners, the *nazrani*, as they were referred to by the locals, was no longer that of the good old days, when the White City, Villeblanche, Weisstadt, Medinablanca, a free port governed by an international commission in which all currencies circulated and no one paid taxes, had been the mecca of businessmen from all the world over, as long as they were persona non grata north of Tunis and Alexandria. From being the Levantine cousin of Montecarlo, packed with banks and bureaux de change open twenty-four hours a day, and casinos and brothels in which musical ensembles strummed away all night long, after almost thirty years of annexation to the country the city had been transformed into a Third World town, dirty, idle, violent, in the hands of drug traffickers. Traces of its former splendour were scanty. The palaces on the promenade—in whose suites widows of Ottoman khedives whose breath smelled heavily of anisette lived next door to German gentlemen with Argentinean passports whose swims in the freezing waters of the bay reminded them of plunges into the Rhine, while they tried to forget many other things—were collapsing before the bulldozers. By that time you could count on the fingers of one hand the Rolls-Royces, driven by chauffeurs in tarbushes, which would drive back up the deserted boulevard at night towards one of the villas on the Vieille Montagne, where finally Madame, or Señora, or Milady, having left her embroidered—and mended— dress in the hands of a maid, would digest dinner in solitude aided by two fingers of Spanish brandy. Almost all the old lux- ury cars, reduced to wrecks, with no tyres and windows smashed in, lay among the weeds behind semi-dilapidated houses, where they served as a refuge for cats. Life for the survivors— Uncles and *Oncles*, Nannies and Aunties, Grand Duchesses— was hard. You needed a certain sangfroid to carry on with a performance grown dissonant while pretending to ignore the fact that the theatre had become immense. Fortunately for the Uncles and Aunties, there were the Pigeons, which descended from the skies every summer. Every year, between July and September, the residents made themselves up, donned their masks, and trod the boards of their eternal theatre, scattering about an inexhaustible supply of mouldy corn and stale bread: it was important to persuade the birds to nest down there, at least some of them, as many as possible, and not because an ill shared is an ill halved, but because the ills shared helped per- petuate the illusion that good does not exist.

That evening in front of Dar Sultan, a massive stone con- struction overlooking the square of the casbah, there was a throng of guests, between two wings of local children kept at a distance by some policemen who, although they brandished their truncheons from time to time, were laughing up their sleeves at their witticisms and their cracks about the *nazrani*— none of whom, luckily, had been so incautious as to learn the language of the country. "Aren't they delightful?" a lady perched precariously on high heels asked her husband, returning the smile of a bigger child that was instead the boy's response to her husband's looks. The man, inured to the funambulism of the faint-hearted, forever on the razor's edge, squeezed her hand and had her look away just in time, before she saw the urchin's unequivocal gesture: "I'm wearing the emerald! You're hurting me!" "Sorry, darling. Yes, in their own way they really are delightful".

"Better than a rodeo! It's a solemn requiem! With a bit of luck the Cardinal will kick the bucket tonight!" Irene cackled, arm in arm with Luca, in line with all the others. Just then, a few explosions sent a thrill of excitement running through the queue, but before one of these words—Algeria, Dynamite, Terrorist Attack—could finish taking shape in their minds and emerge on their lips to disperse the queue, to break it up, the fireworks exploded in the sky, where they shed a livid light on the cupola of Dar Sultàn and the rooftops of the neighbouring houses, from which at the same time, among the washing lines hung with clothes, the women, who had assembled up there in order not to miss the spectacle of the foreigners, raised their trilling cry of *you-you-you*. Even the police were distracted for a moment. "Señor, what is your name?" A little boy was hanging on to Luca's trousers, and he had responded by caressing the boy's head. "Want chocolate to smoke? *Primera calidad?* A prick *más grande?*"

"How sweet he is! Does he want a bonbon?" the lady who had spoken before inquired, snapping open the catch of her purse. "Irene! My angel!" exclaimed a woman from behind them: as everyone turned round, a policeman shoved the little nuisance away before he had the time to grab the lady's gold compact case. "Still with us, in our paradise!" "Huguette!" "Have you met … "

But it wasn't a favourable moment for introductions: a man had got in between them, then a second man, a couple. The crowd was pushing them against the barred main door. Only the little door at the side was ajar, to allow one of the Cardinal's major-domos to check the invitation cards. Beside him, two youths wearing turbans, with scarlet waistcoats open over bare chests, were standing with arms folded, and in obedience to orders received they did not bat an eyelid if one of the guests, under the pretext of the crush, and in order not to be bowled over, were to cling to their biceps, or their shoulders, or at least tried to do so, since, anointed from head to foot with aftersun cream as they were, their muscles would have slipped out of less furtive grasps. "They've done things in grand style," commented Huguette, who lived between the White City and Chile, where she said she had an old, extremely rich husband, while she got by, unmarried, on piano lessons: "Hans Peter and Isidro are still the absolute tops".

Inside, in a corridor illuminated by torches, they were inundated by the rose petals that another two young men, bare-headed and wearing transparent djellabas, scattered over them in generous handfuls. The heels that had made heavy going of the cobbled square sank voluptuously into the soft floral carpet.

It was a grand finale, Luca thought: in reality, as far as he knew, the Cardinal's servants were faithful old retainers stiffened with arthritis. These lads must have been the sons and grand-sons of some of them, or temporary staff hired at the last moment for their good looks. Working this kind of substitution was one of the commonest theatrical devices in the repertoire employed by the residents in the summer. And it worked: "My God, how ... turgid they are" a Parisian pigeon in the city for the first time cooed into his companion's ear. A selection of *Oncles* and Aunties had already had the newcomer visit, over a couple of weeks, at least ten houses and a similar number of estates on sale, "because you would fit in divinely here: it's obvious that you're one of us ... "

Beyond the bend in the corridor an adolescent dressed like the shepherds of a hundred years ago welcomed the guests by playing on his flute. "*Et in Arcadia Ego!*", Irene said in a very loud voice, careless of the fact that the others could hear her. They came out onto the patio. It was a vast rectangular court-yard surrounded on three sides by a loggia, and occupied in the centre by a swimming pool at whose corners truncated pillars were crowned with enormous Chinese vases. All around the swimming pool, under the arcades from which hung crystal chandeliers, the guests, two or three hundred of them, chatted in groups, sitting in wickerwork armchairs but more often standing, raising their voices to carry over the sound of the Arab orchestra that was playing in the background.

"The same old wine in new bottles, treasure." Isabel, a buxom brunette who had moved here thirty years before follow-ing a jewel robbery in London, threw herself on Luca. She stank of vodka. "Thank God, it'll all be over in a few days." "Isabel, darling, what are you calling yourself this time?" inquired Irene, after having allowed herself to be kissed on both cheeks by Hassan, Isabel's fourth husband, but the first native of the series. She was alluding to the law that obliges the bride, whatever her religion may be, to convert to Islam and take a Muslim name. "Little scrubber!" the other had smiled. And raising her glass high: "Fatima! Fatima Bouchalef! Your good health!" With a swaying of heavy thighs swathed in a flower-pattern dress she vanished into the crowd, followed by her husband. "Did you see that floral print?" Irene asked Luca. "Irises the size of barbecued chickens? Isn't it unbelievable that at her age and in that state she can still find someone to screw her for free? So it's true that they like cellulite round here!" Luca restricted himself to a shrug.

The Cardinal was on the other side of the swimming pool. Impossible not to see him at that distance. He was wearing a djellaba in turquoise silk, with a skullcap of the same colour on his head. Skeletal, bent over, almost blind, yet hieratic as an old sovereign, he was supported on one side by Danae Pompes Funèbres, in black lace and with a corsair-style felt hat, who owed her nickname, and the chance to be a paying guest for the whole summer at Dar Sultàn, to the showers of gold that fell back down from the clouds that formed above her incinerators (she owned the most fashionable crematorium in New Orleans). His Excellency's other arm was leaning on that of Isidro, his secretary-factotum, who was sporting gold lamé mechanic's overalls with pantaloon trousers.

"Their own designs", a Grand Duchess was saying to a female pigeon who was staring at the trio in amazement, but for entirely different reasons, and that is because at their feet there was a little boy in his underpants, his legs dangling in the water of the pool, who was trying to persuade an ape bigger than he was to take the banana he was offering it. "And so wearable! I'll have to find a moment tomorrow or the next day to take you to the boutique. Only hand embroidery: the cost of labour, round here ... "

Although the Cardinal was past it by now, and Isidro, recently, had also stopped going to the shop—after having harboured for decades ambitions analogous to those that had made his companion a cardinal, he had opted for the temporal aristocracy, and lately he had been demanding to be called count because on his mother's side he was descended from Montezuma—the couple's luxurious lifestyle still depended, in good measure, on the takings of a bazaar in the *medina*, where the pigeons could find local-style clothing, but modified and improved thanks to the inspiration the creators gleaned from the illustrations in a couple of books on Hollywood hidden in the back shop. "Poor old man! If anyone tried to screw him all the straw would fall out!" Irene exclaimed. And since Luca, for she knew what he was like, would have tried as he usually did to hide himself among the guests in order not to have to cross the patio and pay his respects to the master of the house, she said: "Don't be a shit. It's time for a laugh, spider".

It was a torment for him. In town Irene had a name for being capricious, but she was generally loved—the news of the Grand Widower's wealth, and her mother's reputation "a saint, and always dressed by Balenciaga", had reached even here. Every two steps she stopped to respond to a greeting: Luca who, he knew, was considered an inferior by those people

("the drone", the "kept man", the "escort"), usually avoided
these gatherings. Why had he agreed to accompany her? To
spend the last evening together with her? Fortunately, the presence
of the pigeons also prevented the worst of the Uncles—*Oncles*
like Sir Everest—from giving free rein to their perfidy. "Old
gymnastics still doing the trick eh, you little blackguard?" the
old soldier limited himself to asking Luca, with a wink and a
nod in Irene's direction, convinced as he was that the duration
of their marriage depended on the amatory talents of this boy
who was so dull, but attractive. After which—and still owing to
that conviction—bending over him until his nicotine-stained
moustache brushed Luca's cheek: "One of these days you'll
have to watch one of our artillery competitions: war is war, my
child!" And he patted him on the shoulder. Like everyone,
Luca knew about these gatherings, farting competitions between
local boys in the presence of a jury of elderly foreigners who,
after having provoked their intestinal colics with secret recipes,
would award the winner the most obvious prize. Luca's heart-
felt gratitude went to Harold, the painter who specialized "in
turqueries and singeries, in chinoiseries and in tromp-l'oeil",
who came up in a gardenia-scented cloud: "*Ciao* Luca! My dear
General!" he exclaimed. And waving his hand with a tinkling
of bracelets and chains: "Still busy organizing your barrack-
room entertainments?" Sir Everest replied with a snarl and
turned his back: not even during the pigeon hunting season did
the precarious truce between *Oncles* and Nannies, between
Aunties and Uncles, transform itself into peace.

Lady Weathergood, the doyenne of the English colony, was
holding court at the foot of one of the Chinese vases, surrounded
by her most stalwart followers. But although she was talking
with the usual fervour about her project—a museum devoted
to the famous women of the White City—nothing escaped her
eagle eye: "Irene! Love! Come to your Priscilla!" Her listeners
turned towards them. Avoiding tripping over the train of a
lady's dress, Irene limited herself to pointing, down there, at
the Cardinal. "They'll never learn any manners", commented
Dolores, the proprietrix of a downtown boarding house, in a

voice loud enough for Luca to hear. "The poor dear", replied Perla Lytton, the writer of love stories, giving Irene a look veiled with tenderness and regret as the girl made her way through the crowd: "Such a boring husband ... how sad!" "My children! How nice of you to have come! Irene, you are stupendous! Here are our little friends, Hans Peter!" Isidro was bent over the old man's ear, whose lobe hung down like the wattles of a cockerel. And shouting: "Irene and her husband. Do you remember them?" The mummy remained motionless.

Luca was observing the life-size portrait hanging on the wall at the back of the loggia, behind his hosts: it was common knowledge that it had been that Hungarian prelate, Mephistophelian in his Cardinal's robes, who had moulded Hans Peter in the days when he, a young boy, had been his protégé. "At twelve years of age he could give a corpse a hard on" the gossips used to say. "He already had an outstanding talent for Greek culture." The fact remained that after a half century of official activity as an antiquary, interior decorator and dress-designer in places that, owing to the increase in his unofficial activities as a spy, smuggler and blackmailer, changed often and whose location moved gradually farther and farther south, the gigolo of those former days had been transformed into a faithful copy of the model in the picture, a quasi-identical replica of the original.

"Irene! The *muchacha* who bought the villa from that ghastly American!" insisted Isidro, and he carefully pronounced the name of the previous proprietor of their house: "The rich girl!" At these words, the old man, half-closed his mouth and held out his claw to be kissed. Irene grasped it and shook it without ceremony: "Magnificent party, Hans. Big success". But Luca brushed the walnut-sized amethyst with his lips. "It's nice to see that a young man has a little respect for the traditions of our city" Isidro sighed, with eyes moist with satisfaction and approval. And while the Cardinal plunged back into his catalepsy: "Your wife has aged, the poor thing. Is she ill, or is it the drugs?" Irene had already moved away among the guests. "My dear *Maestro*! Our Great Designer!" Isidro shouted: pouncing on the most appetizing of the pigeons to arrive that summer. So saying, he pushed him towards His Eminence, who, deprived of his support, was swaying dangerously on the arm of Pompes Funèbres. "You too a victim of the magic of Villeblanche! *Hans Peter esta encantado!* You don't know what a pleasure it is, an artist like you, with your talent!" And the secretary-factotum once more grasped the arm of the old man, who, because of the shock he had sustained, was trembling from head to foot. "Stop it, Hisham! You little monster! You're wetting the gentleman!" Isidro said to the little boy, who, tired of playing with the monkey, and having thrown the banana into the swimming pool, had begun splashing them. "Let him be, my dear count! What a handsome little boy! Oughtn't he to be in bed?" In that moment a splash struck the Cardinal full in the face, and he burst into beatific laughter, careless of the drops that, running down from his forehead and along his cheeks, were tracing leather-coloured lines in the face powder. The running make-up revealed what lay below the copy of the portrait, in other words a toothless old man of peasant stock, his skin baked by the sun, left quite gaga by drugs, alcohol and arteriosclerosis, but still capable of feeling pleasure. "He adores children", Isidro cut him short. "Tell me, dear *Maestro*, have you found the house of your dreams?" And lowering his voice, while rummaging in his pocket with one hand in search of a handkerchief with which to effect a rough and ready restoration of that disaster Giampiero's make-up (Hans Peter was a stage name): "Your little love nest? Keep me informed. It is not beyond possibility that one of these days ... Our beloved one hides it but he is very, very tired ... Dar Sultàn might be available ... only for someone with taste like yours ... without the furniture and the porcelain ... "

"Uncle Isidro! I have to do poo-poo!" the child shrilled. Having got up, he had one hand inside the elastic of his underpants. "Come on, treasure". Danae Pompes Funèbres leaned forward opening her arms with their burden of lace. "No, not with you, you're ugly. I'll go with Pepé who is hungry." Little Hisham took the Cardinal by the hand, and he, docile, albeit with hesitant little steps, had allowed himself to be led to a door. The monkey followed them, capering. "Is it a dinner or a cocktail party with buffet?" a voice asked. "A Eucharist", a second voice replied. "Black mass or black wings?" "In Spain we say '*beso negro*'." "In France it's '*nègres en chemise*'." "Negroes in shirts? I have always preferred them without", shot back the first voice.

On looking inside the house, through the French windows that gave onto the patio, Luca realized that there were lots of children, in Dar Sultàn. In a salon in which the lights were out—but where the glow of the candles in the chandeliers in the loggia, reflected towards the interior, kindled reddish-yellow highlights in the giltwork of the furniture and the picture frames, making the shoulders and the buttocks of the bronze ephebe on the pedestal glitter, and bringing out the gleam of the opalines and the porcelain on the bookshelves—five or six of them, all in pyjamas, kneeling or lying on their bellies, were playing with an electric train. In that pale glimmer, absorbed, distant, they struck him as the inhabitants of another planet intent on planning, on a model in miniature, the destruction of our world. Hunkered down against the wall, at the feet of a bench as tall as a throne, two barefoot women were peeling oranges.

Luca refused the glass of champagne that a waiter was offering him. At the bar, he poured himself a glass of whisky, and made for the steps that led up to the big terrace. The women invited to the party were almost all elderly, carefully coiffed and made up. But the silks, the flounces and the furbelows made their evening dresses seem impersonal, professional, like those uniforms with frogging and gold buttons worn by hotel doormen and waiters. At first sight more at their ease, in mufti, the men were dressed in a variety of styles, in djellabas or with tunics held at the waist by scarves, or by sashes, some in tee-shirts and others in pastel-coloured dinner-jackets—one man, to tell the truth, down there, was wearing a red and black fringed hussar's cloak draped across his shoulders—while the female half of the assemblage was dressed as if resigned to carrying out a chore, the tiring drudgery of the social whirl; in contrast to this, the men's outfits conjured up a carnival procession of little boys that had grown old but were still anxious, thus betraying the expectations, the illusions, and the solitude of those who wore them. It was no accident that the few locals, impecunious youths, were almost all wearing jackets and ties, in the most incontrovertibly Western style. As Luca gradually made his way through the knots of people, his impression of sadness grew more distinct. In the glances, behind the panes of alcohol, there was a fuddled angst. The faces, greenish on account of the suntans, seemed on the point of falling apart under the assault of volleys of tics. Immediately afterwards they would stiffen into evasive, grimacing masks whose wrinkles and puffiness were like landscapes no longer inhabited. Below the toupees, bald heads gleamed with sweat. Stomachs dilated by food and the sedentary life, held in for too long by abdominal contraction, ended up yielding, sending out rumbles of relief that filled and deformed the hang of the fabrics.

As often happened on these occasions, and ever more frequently since he had begun to cultivate the garden, Luca felt ill. It wasn't a social complex—or not only that—nor did his affliction (cold hands, breathlessness, and that pressure on his shoulders, that weight) depend on shyness or on his judgement of the persons in whose midst he found himself. He did not judge. He felt that he was different, but in a way that frightened him. A member of another species, landed here by chance. The terrace dominated the city—the rooftops of the casbah, the domes, the harbour and the gradual curve of the bay marked out by lamp-posts. From the patio—as if from the bottom of a well—scraps of talk floated up to him, words, phrases: but they were the moans and gasps of a suffering that was not his, that excluded him.

"... *ask her to show us the label of the chinchilla* ... "

"... *all stolen when they were deported to Dachau* ... "

He stared at the city, the seafront with its lime and salt, the crumbling buildings of the *medina*, the blocks in the suburbs on the hills and the spurs of the steeply climbing slopes of the mountains, like dice scattered in angry handfuls by a child who did not know how to play, or to count ...

"… *Bingo! Did you think he bought the villa on the strength of a legacy from his mother, the concierge in Belleville?*"

"*Villa Danube? Daisy? Ginette?*"

"*It was the husband who reported them to the Gestapo! It was Gestapette!*"

"… *a battalion of Negroes bivouacked in the park, and the little mongoloid got herself pregnant after a couple of months …* "

"*Just imagine the newspaper headlines: 'Grandson of a Peer of the Realm a mulatto …' *"

Even though, with imploring gaze, Luca explored this broken city that he felt was his in a mystery, despite his yearning for transformation, for transfiguration, he could no longer take flight and see, the way he did when he lay down in the earth.

"… *and what's more they would be first cousins to the queen …* "

"*Straight out of Firbank …* "

"*But it was a hysterical pregnancy, like the cat …* "

Insurmountable, the White City, like the walls of a bathroom in which together with the lapping of the water there also resounds a tuneless ditty that goes over and over: "My little spider … my clean little spider … clean inside too … " Once more he heard Marta's voice as she washed him.

"*Pussycat, pussycat …* "

The flight would have been the fall from the terrace—the body found, lying shattered on the travertine in which lay the foundations of Dar Sultàn, this old stone house that resounded to the wailing of the witches assembled in their sabbat.

"… *Wasn't he the papal nuncio to Prague?*"

"… *The one with the dalmatics by Worth?*"

"… *He started going to Dior afterwards, for the chlamyses, when they elected him the Fon of Bafut in Cambridge!*"

"Luca, where have you got to?"

Harold, the painter, was coming towards him: "Have you heard too?". He leant against the parapet. He was moving his head jerkily, looking around nervously; the golden crest of his hair, trembling, made him look like a crowned crane. Like Isabel on their arrival, his breath stank of vodka. "Myriam told me, she had it from Donna … the other night, after they stoned those whores on the Qsar el Hamsa road ... you and Irene are still in time. If only I too could leave for good and all ... " Luca was surprised by this tone, since it presumed an intimacy between them that didn't exist. But Harold raised one arm, let it fall back again, and after a sigh, with bitterness: "I'm sorry, I've had too much to drink and I had a smoke beforehand too". Luca resigned himself to listening to his rambling account, putting its dramatic character down to that need for emphasis that on the third or fourth drink assails those who do not have a good head for alcohol.

Harold was talking of knifings, of wounds, of blood pouring in great gouts, wide-eyed, almost as if he were watching, there and then, the massacre of the two Germans among the graves of the old cemetery. "The bodies in the mortuary" he concluded, struggling to emerge from his waking nightmare, "were identified by that whore Isidro, who in any case won't talk." He adjusted his crest, more erect than ever, making the gold trinkets at his wrist tinkle. "The authorities will not give the news until these beautiful people have left ... my God, in their cemetery of all places ... those boys, Luca, those innocent, pure boys ... " His voice grew shriller and shriller until it cracked in a sob, and in the meantime, with his arm outstretched like Cassandra, he pointed at the city at their feet, before them and around them: "All because of a few fundamentalist hotheads those boys have lost their heads ... "

"Hot-headed boys? Lost their heads? What on earth is all this nonsense?"

Richard Springsummer, the old expert on fleas (*springsummeriana* was named after him) caught them by surprise: "The Nescafé society is a bottomless pit. I have a couple of things to say to you, Harold. Goodbye Luca".

Luca noted Harold's expression: terror and happiness in lightning-fast succession. He watched them as they moved off arm-in-arm, before disappearing beyond the top of the steps. In the event of a prisoner being taken in the war between *Oncles* and Aunties it was possible to have recourse to torture: mysterious laws were in force, among the castaways clinging to this drifting launch. Who knows what those two Germans had felt—Luca could recall their faces, he had seen them around on various occasions—as the blades of the knives hacked them to pieces. How much physical pain can a consciousness take—how much, before the stolid awareness of the solidity of one's own being dissolves and merges with the world's breathing? Luca's neck and back hurt—the sternocleidomastoid and the splenius, in that moment, the atlas and the epistropheus vertebrae. He went back down to the terrace. On the other side of the swimming pool, Irene was talking to the French consul and his wife. "An Aladdin's cave, a wonder", a woman who was in league with some antiquaries was saying to a couple of pigeons. And, ably plucking her birds: "Hamidou has the trust of the members of the old local families ... the other day the duchess found a little Syrian occasional table that came from the living room of the Princess Royal ... no, there's no point in my giving you the address, you couldn't find it, an alleyway that is a corridor between hundreds of others ... "

"Let's go together, it's better to have an introduction ... it wouldn't be the first time he has refused to open to strangers ... "

Luca wondered why it was that the residents had never tried to lure them into their traps. Irene maintained that it was because they didn't have any good enough to catch them in. They were younger than the pigeons, less conformist, less biddable. And especially because they were not attracted by lures like the low cost of servants and boys. Luca was convinced that it was because such traps were not needed: whatever the reasons may have been, after having rented houses for several summers on the hill that dominated the White City, they had bought one, and although they seldom took part in assemblies like this one, and even more seldom invited *Oncles*, Aunties and Grand Duchesses ("Bric-a-brac isn't always amusing" Irene used to say), by that time they were a part of the foreign colony: marginal members, less integrated than many others—especially him— but still members. On the face of it, like all the others.

A belly dancer began her show in front of the band. At first only a few pigeons paid any attention to her. But when, on the invitation of the dancer herself, specially instructed by Isidro, the Great Fashion Designer set to imitating her, wiggling his hips and tracing sinuous patterns in the air with his arms, the guests gathered round. Plates and glasses having been set down, they beat out the rhythm with handclaps: "Bravo! Bravo! *Muy bien! Ole!*"

And in low voices: "It's the same thing every evening … " "Worse than a hairdresser, a window-dresser … " "A better odalisque than a designer … " "It would appear that he is suing his Japanese backers … " "Not a word to Isidro, let him dream on." "Do you know how much they're thinking of asking him for the place? Five million". "Dirhams or francs?" "Dollars, *querido.*" "Is he going to throw in his title as a descendant of Atahualpa?" "Wasn't it Montezuma?" After, when the designer, his face dripping with sweat and an ecstatic smile on his lips, grasped the dancer by her waist and obliged her to follow him in a travesty of the tango: "*Ole maestro! Che viva l'Espagna! Vive la France! Muy bien!* That's the way!"

Luca moved away. He couldn't take it any more. Behind a column, Sir Everest was talking to a young local boy. "You little rascal!" the old soldier suddenly exclaimed: thinking he could not be seen, he slipped one hand between the buttons of the boy's shirt and pinched his chest. That gesture again. Irene on the beach, that little girl. But the other remained impassive. And, as if reciting a nursery rhyme: "I am only a baby, *mon général*" "What the devil are you?" "A dirty little baby, *mon général.*"

"You must see the marvellous swimming pool", an *Oncle* was telling the Parisian pigeon who, when they had arrived, had shown himself so sensible of the turgidity of the muscles of the boys who were scattering the rose petals. "Moorish, in a cloister, at the end of a garden out of the Arabian Nights. If it's all right with you we could visit the villa even tomorrow … "

"It's a pool of water in which the goldfish have gone grey owing to the lack of sunlight" whispered Isabel, staggering, into Luca's ear. "Not to mention the anthills in the bathrooms." And, exhausted, she slumped into a deck chair.

Luca observed the swimming pool illuminated by the

spotlights. The flesh of the banana had come away, and the skin was floating on the surface of the water. "What with vipers and vampires, did you manage to save your skin?" a new voice laughed at the nape of his neck. Irene was almost touching him: despite what Isidro had said, she seemed younger, with eyes shining thanks to the champagne. "How beautiful you are." She frowned, surprised: "Did you see the show put on by that flabby queen of a designer who thinks she is a houri? Enough is enough. Let's go home to bed."

They headed for the exit without saying goodbye to anyone. They were holding hands. "She may well be very well off, but I find her common" said Isabel as she watched them moving off; she belched, stretched out her legs, and then yawned. "He's much worse, even though he was born poor", pointed out Sir Everest, who after making a date for the following day with that agreeable young man, so quick on the uptake, had come to relax on the deck chair beside his friend.

"Going around bragging about the size of his equipment, if you don't mind ... In my day ... "

"Really?" the woman interrupted him, suddenly interested. And after another belch: "I was sure that drink and drugs had reduced him to a vegetable!"

"I think that, in some senses, he is to be admired."

This was Huguette, the unmarried pianist. She had sat down only then, but she had been listening to them for a bit: "They tell me that he is of really humble origins, the son of a domestic even, that he was orphaned very young, and keeping up with her ... "

"Don't be petulant, darling," Isabel cut her short. "Have you seen my husband? He must have fallen asleep somewhere, the poor treasure."

" ... but on mature reflection, you are right: if he weren't so bad-mannered he wouldn't always be ... " Huguette would have added "alone and friendless" had she not noticed that the other two had dropped off. She brought the glass to her lips. The taste of the champagne was enough to make her think how much she would miss the White City once she was back in

Chile, and all these elegant people, these magnificent parties, all these good things to eat and drink ... there was little help for it: the season was over. Heaven knows what those two Germans had got up to in order to get themselves killed that way. They had probably been fondling some disinterred corpse, the two fools.

III

L UCA WAITED until Irene disappeared behind the partition separating customs and the boarding lounge. She didn't turn round for a final wave of farewell, not even a nod. The taxis outside the airport, ramshackle Mercedes in line one after the other, made him think of the wagons of the little train that used to rattle along in the park behind the institution in which he had spent his childhood and adolescence, starting from the wooden station surrounded by oleanders, before crossing the bridge over the pond—the smell of detergents, the plunge of a rat—that reflected the urinal around which certain old men spent the summer afternoons. They were always the same, melancholy slugs that concealed the forbidden sweet in pockets deformed by habit, among coins and pieces of soggy bread. It was an attack of migraine: perhaps the heat, the sun. He gave himself a shake. He had a couple of condoms on him. He was travelling along the coast road at the foot of the mountains. Sitting at the side of the road beside their metal pails, some peasants were selling Indian figs. The flesh of the peeled fruit, arranged in pyramids of pieces of plastic, was of a colour that ranged from raw liver to gold. Like mirrors, the pails reflected the sunlight, sending it flashing into the air. In the mica sky, oppressed by the heat, falcons flew.

He stopped in the middle of a bend, at the top of the cliff, before the Cape. Those black rocks had been attracting his attention for some time. But Irene had never wanted to come to this beach, which was frequented in summer by good-for-nothings, fishermen, prostitutes and by family men who swigged whisky and beer among the dunes (given that they were about to disobey one religious precept, then they might as well break another two or three at the same time). When he had suggested to her that they stop there, she had replied: "It's dirty. It's a place where single men take their siesta". Having locked the car, Luca began making his way down the path that

49

cut diagonally across the cliff all the way to the point. Among the stones and the scorched rock roses shards of glass glittered. The crevices spewed forth beer cans, strips of toilet paper imprinted with the kisses of dirty arses, potato peelings, dung beetle balls, and tufts of dry seaweed like the pubes of old men glimpsed through yawning flies in the entrance to a pissoir. He leaned out over a spur. A light blue lizard darted away. On the waterline, towards the left, two boys were playing football. In the distance, where the beach finished at the base of a hotel under construction, there were several people, but rendered innocuous by the distance. She was right below him, a bit to his right, in a bikini, leaning against a rock: big, brown and sleek as a whale, she was looking at the sea from which it seemed she had just emerged.

Luca quickened his pace. He slipped, grabbed hold of a bush, and swore. It was a thistle. Then he made his way down, treading circumspectly with feet made heavier by the scorching sand that found its way into his sandals. His hand was throbbing. At the entrance to a cave on the promontory a couple were making love: two hairy buttocks contracting—the spasms of a rat too big for the hole in which, half in half out, he had been trapped—as if the man yearned to disappear altogether inside the supine woman. Luca ran to the sea. Immediate relief of cold water on his feet, and his hand. Sucking the fleshy pad of his fingertip, he managed to extract a spine. In that moment, the drone that had been growing louder and louder became a roar. A steel cicada, the aeroplane that had swallowed Irene, was crossing the sky, scattering nectar on the ocean as it banked, dwindled to a pinpoint, and disappeared. To each his destiny. A second Jonah, he was going to end up in the soft belly of the whale.

Who, when the *nazrani* passed in front of her (she had unobtrusively observed his approach manoeuvre) felt a pang of disappointment. He was badly dressed, and too young to be one of those aid-workers who, when they were not constructing dams or roads, would invite girls to the bars of the luxury hotels, where they would guzzle bottles of brandy and then flake out as soon as they hit the bed. But he was still a foreigner: therefore a thousand times preferable, as a client, to any local man, especially after those poor girls had been stoned on the Qsar el Hamsa road, damned fanatics. But he was good looking, and he seemed shy. Instead of coming up and asking her the price, he had gone to sit down farther away, among the rocks.

The girl went into the sea, where she walked up and down swaying her thighs, with the water up to her knees. In the meantime she checked to make sure no one came near. Having brought up one hand to the strap of her bikini top, pretending to adjust it, she lowered one of the two cups a little, revealing a crescent-shaped segment of skin that was lighter than the rest of her body, the colour of damp straw. Luca got up, smiled at her, and held out a packet of cigarettes. She came towards him. When she stood before him, with her raven hair hanging over well-turned shoulders, her breasts constricted by her costume, her belly, prominent but tight, as if made of rubber, he realized that she was little more than a child. What had deceived him was her size. Although her eyebrows were plucked, and her swollen, reddened lids bore signs of lack of sleep, her young cetacean's body glowed with energy and health. Now that she was sitting beside him with comradely nonchalance, inhaling and exhaling the smoke of the cigarette that she held between two stubby fingers, whose nails were painted bright orange, she really looked like a little girl hunkered down in the doorway of her home, bored by the sight of the neighbours' comings and goings. He ran a hand down her hair, heavy as wool. And while the vile fancy that he was a corrupter caused a shiver to run down his spine, he turned to point towards the cliffs, thus avoiding her gaze: "*Mademoiselle,*" he proposed, foolish and gallant, "shall we take a stroll?"

The big girl contemplated him with diffidence. She crushed out her cigarette in the sand. "Hotel," she said, trying to refine her voice, but it came out harsh, guttural. "Hotel," she repeated, aspirating the "h", when the *nazrani* laid his hand on her knee. But since that hand, after some hesitation, was now trying to work its way up her thigh like the hands of her usual

51

clients, to extinguish the hopes aroused in her by that sobriquet, "*mademoiselle*", often heard in the Egyptian plays they showed on television, which she was passionately fond of, she uncere-moniously grasped the hand in hers and laid it on the sand: "One hundred dirhams and the room" (she normally got thirty). "It's dangerous here." Luca took a hundred dirham note out of his wallet: "It's nicer in the open air. *L'oxygène*. If you are nice to me I'll give you another two hundred".

The girl folded up the banknote, and slipped it inside her bikini top: "What's your name?"

"André," he lied.

"Are you married?"

He shook his head. Then, staring at him with suspicion: "Are you a *maricón*, a gay?" She had already had a nasty experience with a tourist of that type, who had forced her to do a show with three men, who afterwards, every time they met her, by threatening to tell the whole story down at the café, obliged her to satisfy them wherever they happened to be, behind a wall, up against a tree, one time even in the toilets of the central post-office, and gratis into the bargain.

"No, I like girls. Pretty girls like you."

She smiled at him: "André. Will you take me to Europe with you?"

Like all *nazranis*, the *nazrani* told her that this was not possible: the visa, the work permit, the crisis … She got to her feet, shook some sand off herself, and resignedly she led him along the path. The stones were scorching, but she, barefoot, walked along calmly. When the going became difficult, she bent over and clung on to the handholds offered by the uneven ground, and she did this as if she knew every inch of the climb by heart. To Luca, she seemed a prodigious amphibian accustomed to passing her days on the sea floor, and to emerging at twilight to take shelter in her lair among the boulders. He followed this Atlantic creature—the oceanic ornithorhyncus—with his eyes glued to her sea-lion's back, to that backside made for incubation, to the nape of her neck that, when her mane fell to one side following a sway of the head, revealed itself to be even lighter than the crescent moon of breast that had escaped the cup of her bikini top, of a silvery olive colour, a burnished and oleaginous silver like the scales of certain fish.

They took shelter beneath a boulder that protruded from the cliff face to form a niche. The entry was screened by a fig tree. Here too the ground was covered with litter. In a corner were the ashes of a fire, and a white, desiccated turd. "*Ici c'est bon*," puffed the girl. Still short of breath from the climb, without hesitation she pulled down her bikini-bottom. Luca fell on her and placed both hands on her sweat-chilled buttocks, which shuddered at the contact. The gluteus medius, contracting, took on a peasant compactness that was almost masculine. But the gluteus maximus, supple and soft without being flaccid, was protected by a layer of adipose tissue that trembled. Immediately below, where the elastic had pinched it, the skin was irritated: little pimples over which his fingertips could run, tickling and goose flesh, the prickling of tiny parasites in the folds of the fish-queen's body. The girl eluded his grasp. Her lip was beaded with pearly drops of sweat. Her eyes were empty, and the lids seemed puffier, swollen: "You have beer? whisky? Gordon gin?" Luca said no. With the resolute gesture of a mother helping her little boy to urinate, she pulled down the zip of his trousers, forcing him to take a step backwards because an unmistakable stiffening of the penis made him fear he was going to melt already. He knelt down, saying: "Come here, beautiful, come here, my treasure". He pulled her to him (now her buttocks were dry and warm), he laid his head on her belly, pressing against it, then he began to lick her. But in spite of his tongue, which had descended from her navel to her shaved groin, and was lingering there trying to make its way even lower, or if anything, *on account of* this homage that struck her, not much accustomed to foreplay, as injurious, an act of violence like the ones in the blue video-cassette that she had seen, while still a child, in a Saudi's hotel room, the girl had welded her thighs together, transforming herself into an idol that was all contours but devoid of fissures. Luca tried to force her to open her legs, but the buttocks became granitic, and the girl wriggled free.

"*Ahshouma*," she hissed like a wildcat: "For shame".

He looked at her, naked and sullen, her back to the rock: his genie of the lamp. He begged her to be kind, he didn't mean to hurt her, only to kiss her there, then he would do everything possible to take her to Europe, did she or didn't she want the money he had promised her? Now she despised him the way she despised all the others. Might as well get it over with quickly. Hunkering down, she shot him a defiant look. He nodded, nodded again, his eyes wide, a madness in his look. The girl lay down in the dust, stretching out her legs until her feet came up against the trunk of the fig tree. Arching her back, applying leverage with one heel and throwing her head back, she raised her pelvis. With her hands she spread her thighs.

He squatted between the legs of his Herculean girl-child, he looked at her and now he was looking at her from close up, bearing down on her with the weight of his chest to make her spread her legs even more. Out of fear, the girl giggled. It was in that moment that Luca saw it. It was behind her. From the cliff top, from the road, came the sound of a motor-cycle, then the crackling of its exhaust dwindled away. A small, purplish flower, which protruded from the sand, an early sea iris, perhaps because in that point the spilt remains of a bottle of drinking water brought along for a picnic—a barbecued chicken, there among the rocks—had awakened the rhizome before its time. He lowered his head. His tongue licked the dragon's clitoris, insistently lapping away, making the sound of an old man guzzling soup.

The taste, at first, was of sun cream, then of bitter almonds, finally of metal, of a lighter alloy that ran molten inside that hot body, almost a residue of infant quicksilver, an indelible trace of the acidic sweat of adolescence, puss-in-the-corner in front of the garage, skipping rope, siestas, mammals, menses, raw liver and milk—the pails employed by the peasants at the roadside were the type used for milking—the flesh of an Indian fig . . . He thought again of the two Germans slashed to ribbons by the knives: in a blinding light, the connection between their bodies, him, and the girl was revealed to him. It lasted a fraction of a second. Then a cloud cast a shadow. He came as soon as he touched himself. The sun came out again, but the air had a different smell. He felt supremely unhappy. A swivelling movement uprooted him, left him outside. With a shove, the girl had pushed him to one side. She was still dry. But out of habit she looked around on the ground for something to clean herself with. She plucked the flower, ran it over her vagina, threw it away, and pulled up her bikini-bottom. She hadn't even removed the top. "Is that what you do, you *nazrani*, to avoid having children?"

Hurt, Luca gave her the other two banknotes. "My mother is ill, Monsieur André," she said, suddenly supplicating, her hand still outstretched. "She is in hospital, the medicines ... nine little brothers ... " He added a third note.

Aware of the fact that the customer would have given her no more, and that it would have been useless now, to bring up Europe again, and wishing to get back into the cool water, she bounded down the slope, the black crest of her hair in the breeze and the little paws that from up there seemed too small to bear her weight. Luca watched her dive in. He looked at the flower reduced to a clot of petals at his feet. In an unconscious gesture of exorcism he touched his pocket containing the condoms in their plastic wrappers, intact. He began the climb back to the cliff top. The falcons flew in the white sky, there was the smell of melting tarmac, flies buzzed around the body of a dead dog; a ramshackle bus rattled past like a train, the outgoing tide left gleaming pools in the sand, the two boys were still playing football, the whale was swimming calmly, parallel to the shore.

All that lapping and licking had stiffened the fraenum of his tongue. He stood in front of the bathroom mirror, after a shower, naked, reddened by the hot water. His tongue felt like sandpaper, it hurt. Someone was knocking at the main door.

The knocking rang out again, after a few seconds there was a fresh hail of blows on the door, intimidatory, like a police raid. Luca decided to don the white bathrobe that he always carried with him and never used, leaving it hanging in the bathroom (three letters embroidered in sky blue thread over the heart, three initials mysteriously connected to his mother, M R T ... but why a man's bathrobe? Why?). He ran out, down the stairs, crossed the lawn, towards the main door—where had Mohammed's wives and daughters got to? He stopped, inhaled, exhaled. The only person who knocked that way was the sky-jacker, the terrorist with machine gun at the ready, in other words Irene, when she forgot her keys on going out. He opened up. The man crossed the threshold and looked around with eyes as cold as those of a blind man: "Dear boy! Still struggling to find the words for the soap powder adverts?" Gordon Ritts-Twice, the novelist, with one small, pink, pudgy hand holding up the hem of his djellaba, was already advancing at a brisk pace despite his bulk and his age, imposing as a Roman in his toga but swinging his hips like an old Juno accustomed to her role as a diva among the gods. He went up to the little wall at the base of the palm tree. Lowering his hoary head in order to clasp the chiton with his chin, he opened his legs and began to piss, making sure that the stream did not wet his buskins. As he finished shaking off the last drops, he turned round, his large thighs glabrous as those of a baby. And, making his pig's tail comfortable inside briefs already adorned with yellowish stains, he said: "Are you a lover of the open air too? Shitting among the buttercups has inspired my best stuff. You look in excellent form, treasure". He was dying to visit the new house, to know about Hans Peter's party, to get up to date with the latest gossip from the White City; what a pity Irene had gone away; he had arrived that very morning—all this in a uniform tone of voice with only a trace of a slur, while the level of a certain little pool that had formed in the space between two stones gradually descended as the earth absorbed the juice of kidneys wrecked by gin.

They were in the living room. Ritts was saying that he had just come back from a fruitless trip to South East Asia. The antiques dealers sold junk, and as they made love the little boys grimaced like professionals. "Prehensile as leeches, treasure, and always glabrous, like slipping it into a boiled hen." He stank. That he didn't wash much was no secret to anyone. During his stays in the White City, where he said he was searching for the "ideal home", he, the collector, the owner of one of the finest castles and one of the finest parks in England, would refuse the invitations of the members of the English colony, who would have fought for the honour of having him as a guest, and lived in a downtown boarding house with no bathroom ("At nights my friends the whores light fires on the floors. The aborted foetuses resemble in a curious way the births of Christ as depicted in Italian paintings of the *trecento* and *quattrocento*.") Luca, who unlike Irene, a friend of Ritts for years, felt ill at ease on the rare occasions when he saw the novelist, asked him if he had already visited the house in the American's time there. No, was the reply, that creature had a name for being incommensurably dull, and the idea of forever traipsing about between the two cottages, at a certain age … He laid his hand on the boy's bottom and through the bathrobe he palpated the muscle that contracted out of surprise, testing its consistency the way people do when considering the purchase of a horse. In that moment—as, getting excited, he was squeezing the boy's flesh—Ritts noticed the initials. But, maintaining his bored expression, he concluded by remarking that it was an ideal house in which to keep the muscles firm. Unfortunately, in his case, it was too late: "Want to touch, treasure? Worse than a blancmange. Or would you prefer a taste of the cursed croissant, which if you apply yourself can still rise a bit?" He crossed the room letting his djellaba flutter, and turning round after having looked out of the window (he had had to swallow something, certainly not a hiccup, the blood that had issued from a broken capillary, one of the symptoms of his disease): "I admire Irene's courage enormously". He paused in order to finish swallowing, and in the meantime he assessed the snot-nose's reaction. Then, with a mocking smile: "Courage in the choice of fabrics and colours, of course". He kept his eyes fixed on Luca's, trying to understand if the girl had stuck to her guns, and had spared her husband the confession that she had made to him—to him of all people—over the telephone even before the summer had begun.

After the inspection of the two pavilions—they were on the lawn, on the verge of "moving on to serious matters", that is to say visiting the garden, Ritts asked Luca if he and Irene had decided on the corner in which they would be buried. He hastened to add that it was a custom, when people came into the ownership of a piece of land. The human body, on decomposing, was transformed into ideal nourishment for the plants and flowers. Luca was put in mind of the sinister legend according to which, before setting fire to the room in the boarding-house in Iran that he was sharing with his brother, Gordon had beaten the latter bloody. They said that his brother had been the real author of the travel journal that was to become *The Road to Kabul*. Perhaps only because of the book's enormous success, the gossips had insinuated that the charred remains of the young man bore the marks of strange fractures. But the affair had been covered up by an accommodating consul, intimidated by the important connections of the novelist's family. Gordon had saved himself by diving out of the window onto a mound of snow. Luca observed the fat, incendiary vestal. He saw an overgrown child running his tongue—his tongue—over his lips. Nero. He screwed up his courage and preceded Gordon along the path, and down the steps.

The fading light made the greens even darker, but it lingered on the corollas of the hibiscus, on the golden ones of the Mexican sunflower, making them look like little Japanese lanterns hanging from the branches—a penetrating, Asiatic scent rose up from the flower beds—while the rustling of the birds among the branches seemed to herald an ambush, as if the shadows surrounding the garden, like Khmer killers, were already digging their own mass grave in the mud, with their nails; the heads of the trees, imposing and black, brushed against one another and overlapped to form a curtain, a shroud draped around the outskirts of the White City. Gordon was astonished by the beauty of the garden, a revelation. Too improbable even for a novelist, but it would have been funny if the son of one of the many bitches ... he didn't have the time. The doctors had been clear.

Luca began to show Gordon his marvels, his treasures, with the modesty of a Republican mother showing her sons off to a crumbling whore of the Late Empire, a mother so proud that she did not realize that the raddled old courtesan, at the sight of a couple of fresh and well brought up little boys, would immediately feel the desire to get her hands on them: "See how well they're doing?" he said pointing to the pelargoniums (yes, he still called them geraniums) falling in cascades from the earthenware jars standing at the base of the arch up which the solanum climbed; then he ran a hand lightly across the cosmos among the asters and the roses, pointed out the globes of the oranges overhanging the festoons of convolvulus; that one, the bush covered with a coral-coloured inflorescence, was new ... ("*Browallia*", the old Syrian Poppea had hissed angrily from behind him): he told Gordon of the state in which he had found the garden when they had bought the house, of the lorry loads of manure that he had had brought in, of the work that ... There was a sound. Luca turned round. Big and fat in his outsize tunic, wearing a cruel grimace, the giant was clutching an uprooted plant, a petunia, whose roots were brushing the ground. Careless of Luca's expression, he bent over again. Grunting, he uprooted another, and another again, until in the corner where there had been clumps of flowers the earth appeared naked, churned up, as if it had been trampled by a herd of wild pigs. "Where do you dump the rubbish, treasure?" This time the drop of blood, black then instantly red, had fallen from his nose.

They faced each other. Luca was on the verge of ordering him to leave the house. But Gordon beat him to the punch. Mellifluous, dabbing at his face with a paper handkerchief, he corrected himself. Those horrible petunias should not be thrown away, they should be burned forthwith, because they were infested with a parasite that could have spread to the other plants. Having completed massacring the flowers he rolled them up into a ball and tossed them, along with the

Kleenex, over the garden wall. The haemorrhage had ceased. White fly, he explained, was a pest. Unfortunately, it was time for him to go back to town; kisses and hugs to the enchanting Irene. On looking at the boy moving around the garden, observing the gestures with which he pointed out the plants— movements of an unconscious, quasi-vegetable ease and tender- ness—the memory had become unbearable. His plan would have to start from the objective. He couldn't kill him. Really, this time, couldn't he?

They passed in front of the caretakers' lodge. Rose branches intertwined with those of apple and olive trees. Together with the honeysuckle, the Mexican ivy, the *podranea*, and the chalice vine, they created a vault beneath which, like raw meat on the grill, the fleshy leaves of the beefsteak plant blazed in the gloom, the Chinese lilies grew hieratically, and the standards of the datura nodded in the breeze. Even the scent was that of meat, slightly off, and of fermented fruit. Ritts was now absorbed in the elaboration of his plan, just as it had been when, on following along a corridor the old chatelain who was showing him round his castle, he suddenly saw hanging on the wall an Italian terracotta from the Renaissance, an Egyptian mask, a spectacular relief from Gandhara, and overcoming a dizzy spell, he had murmured: "Strange object, odd," eyeing his generous host to gauge his reaction. ("We put it up here because it is merely a souvenir of a journey made by an eccentric great-uncle.") An *hortus conclusus*, a garden of delights, a Persian miniature . . . Iranian . . . Yet again the creator was unaware of the miracle he had brought about. He could not wait—he had two, maybe three years left—but he knew that trying to speed things up by telling Luca of Irene's condition—by then he was sure that he was unaware of it—would have produced the opposite effect: the young man would have borne him a grudge. Pointless to offer him money: he was too enamoured of his garden. At the door, Ritts complimented Luca on the civic sense he was showing by staying there alone, without yielding to the pressure of the growing hatred of the locals. Had he heard of the end made by their two German sisters? A good-natured old fellow who wanted to entertain the youngsters with the tale of his happy years, he began to call up the White City in its heyday, when he used to spend long holidays there with his little brother, who was mad about botany; with colourless eyes he watched Luca's every gesture, while he crammed his discourse with terms and expressions "Mediterranean patriarchate", "the innocent blooming of the senses", "paradisaical pricks, treasure, they smelled of narcissus, of bread" that on his lips, with that voice, sometimes sounded incongruous, other times mocking. "Are you complaining," Luca interrupted him "because the boys have put up their prices too much?"

Ritts gave the bastard a humble smile: "Old fashioned, your bathrobe. Did you buy it at the flea market?"

"It's a memento of my mother."

The novelist's eyes narrowed to slits. The image was crystal clear. The little fair-haired boy was waving a card and saying happily to him: "Gordon, look! I've joined the Royal Society!" Clearing his throat, he advised Luca to get busy in the garden. Why did he content himself with creating corners of what a station master's wife would call "a feast for the eyes", such an inhibited, municipal garden? The area was renowned for its volunteer plants. Would it not be interesting, advised perhaps by a civilized person—that's how he put it, a "civilized person"— to collect wild flowers, mix them with the others, and thus make those beds a bit less vulgar? He could have passed the time exploring the environs of the White City. As far as he knew Luca was not an indispensable figure, on the local social scene.

He was going to have to get the boy out of town. The oldest way was the best way. Then a lady friend of his would show him the other face of things.

It was dark. A dog barked, echoed by another dog, then there was a chorus of baying. A massive sixty-year-old, ill, disguised as a local, and a youngster fresh from the shower, ill at ease in his bathrobe, were standing in a doorway, enmired in a protracted farewell that was the beginning of a war. Luca felt an urge to punch Ritts in the stomach, to bring Goliath crashing to the ground, to blind with kicks that greedy Polyphemus of mud who pissed where he felt like it and tore up his little plants. Instead he said that that very day, among the rocks, near the beach, he had seen a little iris. His tone was humble, sorrowful, that of a son whose ignorance was a source of guilt, a son who by confessing hoped to obtain clemency. Gordon had triumphed. Breeding will always out. Was it brownish and purple, bearded? Certainly a *lutescens*: "You are lucky, dear boy! Very lucky!" he concluded. It still grew on the Atlantic cliffs, but it had become extremely rare. All you had to do was look at him: he was hanging on his every word. Encouraging, paternal (it was only a coincidence that those initials were the same as the only writer in the family, his brother, who as he read him that journal, and in response to his amazed expression, had asked him candidly: "What's the matter, Gordon, am I boring you?") Ritts-Twice suggested that Luca go to see Madame Martinez, Señora Jaima Martinez, a most delightful woman, the greatest expert on the indigenous flora, especially on the iris family, the ideal guide for the realization of their project. He would hear all sorts of great stuff about those old dotards who called the *Moraceae*, the "flowers of the east wind!" He wasn't to be put off by her appearance—a tiny little creature that any cardinal or margrave would have willingly displayed in one of the cabinets of his *Wunderkammer* (Luca shot him an interested look). It was easy to meet her. Every afternoon, towards dusk, she went for a drink in the Casino Judio. But perhaps, beforehand—and he had smiled—Luca ought to have a word with Irene. To the best of his knowledge, she was the one who made the decisions.

Luca reassured him. The garden was his—his province, he immediately corrected himself, ashamed. They embraced. There was the creak of the opening door, the thud as it closed, the sound of a car door slamming, followed by the purr of the engine. While an overexcited Herod at the wheel of his car raced back to town to inform a lady friend of the role he had assigned to her, to discuss cash with her and to give her a down payment straight away—a green light, another light, empty pavements, the rustling of the eucalyptus trees already autumnal; his love, the love of an impostor who had never had any story to tell, lay in the fire of the humiliation upon which he had based his life, in his doom to play the usurper—shivering in the bathrobe saturated with moisture that was his only memento of his mother, the little child contemplated the terraces of the garden. Now, goodness knows why, the trees and the bushes, reduced to outlines, struck him as being laid out symmetrically, conventionally. Perhaps that idea about the wild flowers was not as absurd as he had thought earlier. Gordon owned a famous park, and as far as gardens were concerned he certainly knew more about them than he, Marta's son brought up in an institution. To realize the satisfactions to be had from gardening, however, he didn't need that old cynic. He was tired. Telephoning Irene could wait until the next day. The moon had half completed its climb across the sky. Down below, the lights of the White City glimmered like those of a crèche. Among the stones, at the base of the wall that buttressed the bed with the palm tree, there was a dark stain. The sign of a dog's piss, left there to mark the limits of his possessions.

The telephone message—terrible Annunciation—was preceded by days during which Luca frequented the beach and the nurseries of the White City, buying more plants to be planted in a garden in which no white fly flew, no matter what that bird of ill omen had said. He had tried on several occasions, and at different times, to speak with Irene. At the office, there was the answering service, and at home there was the odious Maria, the domestic who had brought her up. Miss Irene had gone out, she would say, stressing the title to imply the regard she had for his existence. No, she did not know when Miss Irene would return. Luca would have begun to worry. Were it not for the fact that at dawn of the eighth day—he was counting them by then—while he was in bed, half asleep, the annunciation arrived. It was not accompanied by the beating of an archangel's wings, and the only ray of light was the one that penetrated the room slantwise from between the drawn curtains to fall on Irene's pillow, revealing its immaculate and clinical rigidity.

She was pregnant. This was Luca's first interpretation as he hung up the receiver, from which her voice, sounding like that of a person miraculously saved and made guttural by a sob, was still emerging. He had assured her that he would return that very day, or the following day at the latest—for he, in some way, would save his girl-bird and free her from her cage—but now he realized that he was in the grip of a fear so great as to be unreal. He understood her anger, her obstinacy, and her folly over those months. But he was powerless. He was stuck in the centre of a maelstrom of images all of which portrayed the Virgin nursing her child. Why adopt one, when their heir was already growing in her breast? Irene had known it for some time. Before talking to him about it she had waited the outcome of further tests, made in another country, the country of banks and doctors. She hadn't wanted to ruin their first holiday in the new house. It was a nodule, a pea then a cherry that was growing in her breast, a crab that was eating at her tissues, snipping away with its pincers, from the inside. A carcinoma. Like Marta. Both dead. He could not get his breath.

The system of nomenclature with which for years he had been exorcising his deepest terror—disease—collapsed over the hours that followed. The dyke crumbled before a wave of milk. On emerging from the travel agency with the return ticket in his pocket, he could not say whether the cramps in his stomach were vascular, muscular or osseous in origin. He allayed them by getting drunk on whisky in a bar that stank of fried fish. Vomiting on the deserted beach of the city (window dressers gone, body builders elsewhere), he had the feeling that his retching was a symptom of the labour pangs of his gestation. He too was pregnant, he too was with child, ill.

The sun was pale, a firefly in a glass box. He slumped down onto the sand. The bay, the harbour, the *medina* pierced by minarets that ended in a concrete tongue lapping at the sea, the ferries at anchor, the boats, the barges, everything expanded and contracted to the rhythm of a dilation followed every time by a contraction. The world was breathing, the world was suckling like a new born child. When its little chest stopped rising and falling, when its little belly exploded, the milk would gush out everywhere, pouring through the air in dense acid cascades. He fell asleep.

It wasn't a dream, or even a vision. Although the white creature had come out of the sea of milk, immediately huge, covered with the fleece of a mouflon or an Afghan hound, as if curious, as if to sniff him, the brontosaurus-like neck craning over him topped by the thin and sunken head—a few centimetres from his face—of a grazing goat, its existence was manifested in the sound that it was producing: what Luca was having was an *auditory* hallucination. At first it seemed to him that the monster was expressing itself in rhyming couplets, then he realized that it was always repeating the same word. But it wasn't a word. Its coarse tongue, devoid of syntax, was so compact that the light of no vowel could penetrate it. Connected to one another to form a wall, were blocks, massive boulders of consonants: the muffled lowing—*mdr, mtr, mdr*—of a herd of bovids with neither herdsman nor cattleshed. But Luca was not afraid. On the contrary, he felt a sense of peace. He laughed. And Marta smiled at him in response. Then the creature turned round. Its rump swaying, it moved away until it was immersed in the milk once more. "Smothered." He woke up with this word in his ears. The rest, all forgotten.

Quite a bit of time must have passed. Luca was cold. He had heartburn. Staggering, he went to buy a Coca-Cola from a street seller. After guzzling it down he began the climb back up to the city centre. He had a goal. Avenue d'Espagne, rue Cervantes, calle de la Constitution, place de France, the boulevard with a wan sunset pasted to its farther end, a youth who gave him a smile of invitation while squeezing his tool through his trousers, a patisserie from which people emerged eating little cakes topped with fluffy squirts of cream, children with shaved heads blooming with scabs, a group of peasant women selling goatsmilk cheese round as holy wafers taking them from milking pails, rue du Portugal, the synagogue, the Immeuble Beethoven, calle de Hollanda—immobilized against the trunk of a linden tree by a twinge of the prostate, an old

Greek Italian or Turk, impeccable in his cream-coloured suit, was looking in the direction of the sea—a barefoot boy who was urging a donkey laden with panniers full of cement up the hill yelling "*Burro! Burro!*"; a beggar woman disfigured by eczema who, hunkered down on the pavement, exposed by the shower of light from a lamppost, was nursing a skinned plastic doll, singing it a lullaby. A metal plaque was affixed at eye level on the façade of the building: Casino Judio, *troisième étage*. The door gave on to an entrance hall full of sacks: Luca crossed it without hesitation, went up the stairs, through naval rooms (a bar in the form of a prow, stools in tubular steel and skai, wainscoting painted to look like mahogany) in which old human relics were playing cards, talking in low voices, sipping drinks, powdering their faces, and exchanging smiles under the neon lights. He walked on heedless of the suspicious looks that rose up to greet him.

Obviously she was in the last room, alone, sitting on a gilt settee, between two vases of *monstera deliciosa*, relict and reptile (iguana enthroned). Obviously they recognized each other at first sight (she recognized him thanks to Gordon's description, and he had understood immediately that she could be none other than Madame Martinez because she was the mummified version, worthy indeed of a *Wunderkammer*, of a certain cetacean, a sperm whale in oil, purple eyelids and yellowish shadows under the eyes set in the big square head from which the chops hung like empty saddlebags, and in her hand, like a sceptre, the straw through which she was in the habit of drinking her sherry on the rocks). Obviously at the announcement of Irene's illness— "My wife has cancer," said Luca, slumping into an armchair— Jaima heaved a sigh of relief (the fact that the girl had decided to put him in the picture made her task easier), feigned surprise and compassion, and after having him tell her about the house she urged him to sell it, to return no more to Medinablanca, unsuited for the young, unhealthy, and destined to fall into the hands of the fundamentalists. And obviously, faced with Luca's reaction, she maintained she had said these things just to put him to the test, causing a shiver in the loins of her future proselyte, who was already longing for his initiation. *Las flores*, then. Now she talked to him of the indigenous irises, *unguicularis, filifolia, latifolia, battandieri, forrestieri*, and lastly *lutescens* (she had committed the names to memory over the previous days, one hour in the evenings before going to bed), and she alluded to the difficulties involved in finding, identifying, and uprooting them without damaging them, before transplanting them and fertilizing them in a suitable fashion. ("The Nazis, *niño*, discovered the secret.") Of course, as he listened to her (she had a cavernous but soft voice, moss between stones) Luca kept his eyes fixed on the sagging breasts below her little angora sweater, as he imagined sucking her nipples, which he felt would be hairy as big warts. What was less obvious was that, under the lustful gaze of that handsome boy whom she had been told was virtually an idiot, a means with which to have the living room redecorated, the go-between found herself repressing what she had tried to write off as a pang of compassion, but it was an impulse of another kind. It titillated her *amour propre* to list the characteristics of the bulbs, some the size of peas, others of cherries, others again—the biggest—the size of apricots (finding these terms of comparison had been a stroke of beginner's luck), and in describing their need for warmth, nourishment, and care. Perhaps this was why her eyes, between those reptilian lids, lost their fishy fixity, outside the jar of formaldehyde, and were now shining with a ferocious and sensual light, a sated lioness rolling on the savannah. Luca swallowed. He was trembling. Jaima called the waiter: a glass of warm milk, right away, for the young gentleman.

There was a cloudburst, brief, violent. The old mammal slipped off one shoe, there was a smell of talcum and feet, of damp rags, of garlic. She muttered something about a *paella*, and spruced up sparse curls of a courageous carmine *encendido*. Her tongue made a flickering appearance in the fissure of her mouth, the swollen foot in its cotton sock girlishly brushed against Luca's knee, so that when the milk arrived he swallowed the contents of the glass in one gulp, without noticing that a little spider was still wriggling about on the surface. Licking her whiskers (she didn't bleach them any more, lately she had been letting herself go a little), Jaima urged him to come back soon, together with Irene when she was better, in order to transform their garden into a blooming oasis of wild irises threatened by the pincers of progress.

"Wipe your mouth, *niño*, you look like a suckling."

Her smile was warm, extremely close, without her having moved. At least it seemed so to Luca, who was feeling the need to be washed again by a hand that would give him a good rubbing down … "Will you really help me to look after the garden?" Without realizing, he had shifted to the intimate form of address. She opened her arms wide, a lioness on the cross in the centre of the arena. That was what she was there for, she roared, they would do great things together. He wasn't her cub. Let that vulture Ritts tear him to shreds if he wished.

PART TWO

IRIS FLORENTINA

I

IRENE WAS FINISHED. She had realized this right away, on the first evening. She no longer smelt of mushrooms and beaver. Her clean smell was that of the seriously ill, who conceal, by turning to disinfectants, soaps, and perfumes, the stench of the secretions of glands made hyperactive by the struggle. She was ashamed of the wretchedness of her body. She was already decorous. She was doomed. Sitting on the bed in her pyjamas, the tan yellowing under the eyes and around the fine, bitter mouth—girl-bird no longer, because already similar to a freshly captured and shackled monkey, liable to start screeching at any moment, squirting out the juice of its fear, soiling itself— she told him with a catch in her voice that after the operation she would have breasts like a Picasso from the mid-twenties or the late thirties: did that idea turn him on? In ninety per cent of cases, upper external quadrantectomy guaranteed a complete cure, half of the remaining ten per cent allowed for a second operation, a mastectomy, while the other wretched five per cent concerned no one ... Luca gave her a hug. Freeing herself from his embrace, Irene slipped off her pyjama trousers. She lay down on top of him, resting her head on his chest with her buttocks sticking up in a pose expressive of faith, abandon. He slipped a hand into the cleft, the little girl was dry, he brought his fingers to his mouth, wet the tips with saliva, deposited this offering on the lips of her vagina, massaging them gently. Irene murmured, she squatted over his sex, engulfed it, she lay still for a few seconds, eyes closed, then she began to sway a little from side to side, pauses, deeper thrusts, her breath coming only a little faster as the rhythm became more intense and she swallowed him with increasing avidity, opening and closing her mouth all the while, jaws clacking, a female orang-utan who had learned to stay in the saddle by dint of electric shocks to amuse the circus crowd, masturbating herself as she galloped by rubbing her clitoris against the coat of the nag. Luca clawed at a breast, the breast, the entire audience got to its feet and laughed, even Irene was laughing, the drooping penis slipped out of her vagina, only one little boy had stayed in his seat without applauding, terrorized by germs, by the idea that the monkey might infect him, give him cancer: he was on the verge of tears, but no one noticed. "Do you think you're screwing a dead woman? Buck up, spider, where's the harm?" She got up and went to take a shower—the third or fourth of the day.

During the days prior to the operation, Ritts-Twice had telephoned. Irene was in hospital for a check up: Luca had spoken to him. The Englishman asked him to pass on his best wishes to Irene. He had known of her illness for months, he had not mentioned it on the occasion of their meeting in the White City out of respect for her desire for secrecy, touching for the generosity it revealed. On the subject of the White City, had the dear boy given any further thought to the idea of collecting wild flowers, or had he dropped the notion? Had he managed to get over his reluctance, typical of beginners, in order to plan the changes to be made in the garden? Was he studying? They said goodbye without either one of them having mentioned Señora Martinez. Luca got into the habit of taking long walks. The house stank with that smell from his childhood, of Marta's last months, of the medicines and the soups brought by neighbours, of his own body, dirty, since mummy no longer bathed him. He went out as soon as he woke, in the mornings. He had to breathe. To free himself from the past that had pierced the present like the tongue of a reptile sucking the egg from which it is emerging—and biting its tail. One afternoon, walking through a district he was not familiar with, he found what he was looking for. It was a bookshop specializing in botany. He bought some books. Sitting down at a table in a bar, he began to read.

With the same avidity with which, had he been able to, the little boy of an earlier day would have collected information on the mysterious illness that was making his mummy grow thin, transforming her body into a skeleton, paring away a face grown nasty until it was a skull, with the same ardour with

which a man in love would have fought side by side with the
woman he loved, consulting texts, comparing statistics, question-
ing the doctors who were treating her, Luca set to studying the
habits, the needs, and the geographical diffusion of *Iris susiana*,
an *oncocyclus*—the root of the name of this species, like its common
name, mourning iris, struck him as being anything but fortuitous—which prefers alkaline soil; of *bucharica*, an iris native to
Tajikistan that had settled around the Mediterranean and was
a member of the *scorpiris* family; and of *filifolia*, a *xiphium* that like
all its kind needs a long rest over the summer. While Irene, without ever complaining (protected as she was by her armour),
went in and out of hospital alone or accompanied by Maria for
the umpteenth X-ray, for a scan, to undergo the trauma of a
bronchoscopy, the torture of a needle biopsy, sitting in a café or
on a bench in the public gardens (a children's mini-train rattled
past, the cast iron urinals had been removed a long time since),
a terrified young man learned the names of flowers as in far off
years he had learned those of bones, muscles, valves and arteries.
Everything twice. *Solanum* and *solandra*. *Pubescens* and *lutescens*.
Now as then. The delicate *Narcissus elegans* bloomed in November,
as did the autumnal variety. The *tazetta* and the late narcissus in
December. In January, in the wet fields of certain temperate
regions, came the extremely rare *viridiflorus*. When, in the
evenings (but only at first because she soon gave up), Irene
would tell him the results of her tests, or talked to him about
hypothetical post-operational therapies, of alternative cures
aimed at reinforcing the immune system, radiation, he would
listen to her without understanding. Words and formulas like
undifferentiated carcinoma and metastasis, systemic disease,
nodule, and hormonal regimen no longer had any sense. He
was obsessed by the difficulties he would have to overcome in
order to transplant a Peruvian squill in bloom, to fertilize in a
suitable manner the bed of loam intended to accommodate the
Assyrian fritillary or the orchid known as *Serapia cordigera*, lost in
a maelstrom of doubts as to how to create the drainage indispensable for the growth of *Crocus sativa*.

Irene was admitted to hospital. Maria took her. Alone at last,

Luca threw open the windows. He could read at home, in peace. On the day before the operation something happened of such importance that the following day, instead of rushing to the clinic and waiting outside the door of the operating theatre to bombard the surgeon with questions as soon as he emerged, he limited himself to telephoning. Having learned from Maria that the operation had gone well, he refused to speak to the Great Widower, who had rushed to his daughter's bedside: Luca felt ill, he had had to take to his bed with a fever. In reality, on a high shelf of the bookcase, between a publication on bonsai and a paperback titled *Household Plants*, he had found an old volume whose cover bore the legend *Fleurs de Villeblanche et de sa Région*. He read unremittingly, for hours and hours, filling a notebook with lists of names, memorizing the details of scientific illustrations in black and white that reproduced the appearance of the flowers with an exactitude that put the colour photos in more modern books to shame.

Maria had not lied to him. Everything had gone well. When, two or three days after the operation, having torn himself away with a painful effort from his studies, Luca washed and dressed, and went to the hospital, the Great Widower and the maid gave him a cold welcome. Irene, lying in the bed, had a rested look. In reply to his small talk she said that the anaesthesia, like the hard drugs she had used from time to time when she was younger, had done her good. Her father shook his head and continued staring out of the window. Only then did Luca notice the tubes of the drainage system and the catheter that emerged from the blankets like epiphytic roots and wound their way down to a point below the metal bed, where they disappeared into mysterious bags. He was on the verge of fainting. He left the room. But the diseased part of the rhizome had been cut away. Irene would bloom again with the beautiful urgency of a miniature iris.

After a couple of weeks—he could have told an *Iris pumila* from an *attica*, a *paradoxa* from its *forma atrata*, a *juncea* from its *mermieri* variant, and this last from a *numidica*—the convalescent had still not returned home. Maria explained to him that she was undergoing intensive chemotherapy. He did not attach excessive importance to the news. Once back in the White City, he uprooted the plants from their beds, the roses inherited from the American, and those that he now knew to be banal jasmine, solanum, begonia, aster, datura: he prepared and fertilized the ground, because irises love rich, loose soil. He had forgotten the allusion to the Nazis made by a certain lady (the encounter with the dwarf with the iguana eyelids and the magnificent sagging dugs, if by chance he thought of it, struck him as having happened in dream). But the mere idea of digging, of breaking up, of opening the ground and of adding organic matter, decomposing leaves, pieces of leather, food leftovers, sent him into a febrile state of agitation similar to the one that had formerly possessed him, when he used to make his nocturnal expeditions, a cannibal greedy for fat chrysalides and plump pupa.

There were moments in which he thought he glimpsed an analogy between flesh and flowers. He recalled the little brown iris peeping out from a cliff that dominated the Atlantic ocean. To collect and set out in good order what were none other than the genital organs of the endemic plants of the White City—a gaping vulva here, a little farther back a little clump of turgid clitorises, and behind them a bunch of pricks into whose meatus the hornets would slip their proboscides—would have meant creating an Eden, a personal paradise in which he would have wandered, tranquil as a god. Cutting back and uprooting, transplanting and fertilizing, watering and pruning, were the magical acts with which, like a shaman within his circle of fire, he would exorcise Irene, cleanse her of disease, and restore her whole to the cycle of growth, bloom, and pollination. Never, not even in the months of work together with Mohammed, had Luca been so passionately absorbed in his project.

Irene returned home, and with her returned the smell: human, laden with frustrations. Yet, she seemed in good spirits. In the clinic she had had her hair cut. Luca noted that her straight, vibratile mop and her thinner face reminded him of the blooms of certain bulbous plants, rosy garlic or flowering onion, *muscari*, or agapanthus. This resemblance made the senile caution of her movements, caused by the tight dressing over her bust, look even more incongruous. She was talking about Alfredino. Listening to her, Luca realized that the pro-liferation of cruel cells inside her mammary glands had aroused, through a certain law of compensation, her maternal instincts, which converged on that sick young man, barely eighteen, who was being treated in the room next to hers in the hospital for a tumour of the bulbs, the testicles. Or was it not, rather, the excess of life that is in cancer, which made her feel the need—she the barren one, she the sister—to be a mother like all women, but the mother of another man, like all wives, in the insipid betrayal and in the trap of deceit thanks to which the human species reproduces itself, as it forever plays out the same drama? Predictably, when he suggested it to her, Madame (a bird? anything but) croaked that she had no intention of returning to the White City. And since he insisted on explaining, albeit with prudence, his project to her, she added that she was worried about his garden mania: "You're going mad, spider".

It was in those months that Luca refined his skills as a dis-sembler, skills that were later to become indispensable if he was to procure manure. Ignoring the coming and going of the nurses who came to the house for injections, he spent the days outside, dragging around bags full of books that he opened in the bars, because the cold kept him far from the public parks and gardens. The desire to get down to work was becoming obsessive. He needed to fly. Ever more frequently he imagined delving into the rich soil of his garden, clutching it between his fingers, sniffing it. But since Irene, in recounting her telephone conversations with Ritts-Twice, told him, just as her father had done, that the Englishman had also advised her to get rid of a house that was so awkward to reach, so far from good doctors and efficient hospitals (and it was obvious that this was a lie, since Gordon himself had been the first to show him the path winding its way though the Elysian Fields of botany), he became convinced that she was jealous of the passion that filled his life, and that she was threatening him in this way because she felt excluded from it. He began to lie to her. He was reduced to giving the concierge the bag with the books and the notebooks, so that Irene would see him leaving empty handed. He carefully avoided talking to her about the plants and flowers that were proliferating in his thoughts, and invading—tangles of convolvulus in light and shade, cascades of clematis and waves of nasturtiums—his dreams (once he got lost in a sea of Dutch iris ruffled by the wind, the first time he wet the bed back at the institution). As the darkness favours the germination of a seed, so did clandestinity and secrecy lend vigour to his passion, intensifying it until it was painful, transforming it into the physical pressure of something in his body, in his breast, in his groin, something that was pushing to come out. Accompanied by the first chills of spring, this sensation made him feel dizzy. Ever more frequently he could not get his breath. Sometimes, when walking, he would stagger. Pimples blossomed on his skin. One evening, on looking at himself in the mirror, he noticed that the little veins that had appeared on his sunken cheeks, below the shadows under his eyes, were the veins of sepals, of petals, and that his hot, fevered brow was violaceous, while there was a silken beard around the anther of his mouth, and when he opened it he could see the pistil of the tongue—then the iris, the iris swollen with sap, dissolved, leaving him trembling with the violence of the revelation. He had to get back into the ground. He needed an excuse, a pretext, to leave Irene and go back to the White City. An excuse and a pretext that presented themselves in the form of the adolescent he bumped into, on returning home one evening, in front of the lift door.

Not only did Luca realize immediately who he was, but as he furtively observed him while they were waiting for the cabin to arrive at the ground floor, Luca sensed that the youth, skinny as a twig, in the leather bomber jacket that was too big for him, with the shock of tousled hair and the face tensed in an expression of embarrassed awkwardness, would prove to be his salvation. A couple of times, in rapid succession, the boy snapped his fingers as if exasperated by the slowness of the old lift, and it was obvious that that cool, disco-type gesture was intended not only to conceal his shyness in front of a stranger, but to buck himself up, to keep up his courage. The peripheral sapling of the species *Alfredinus salvificus* was in bud again even though it had been pruned to the bone. He could have sworn it: this first gallant visit had been decided on without his wife's knowledge—a surprise. Luca had had no need to invite the other to enter the lift first because the boy dashed in as soon as the door slid open. "Are you coming to our house?" he had asked, artfully, as he pressed the button for his floor. The snotnose's discomfiture had sent him into raptures. As the lift began to go up the lad had spread his legs, almost as if he wanted to cushion the blow he had taken: "Shit, you must be the flower guy! Pleased to meet you. Iris talked about you a hell of a lot, in hospital!"

The possibility of this extraordinary pet name had never even crossed Luca's mind. The theft of his most secret possession. He could have broken it in two, this sapling who was stubbornly budding despite the removal of one of his bulbs, or had it been both? He couldn't remember: he could have uprooted it, torn it to shreds, a petunia in the hands of the ogre. But the fit of hatred was a brief one. After a few minutes, his initial intuition was confirmed by the enthusiastic welcome that a certain girl accorded her little pal as he entered the living room. The pleasantries with which, on realizing that this last was followed by her husband, poor Irene had tried almost immediately to conceal her happiness—her cheeks were peonies of embarrassment and pleasure—were so clumsy, so revealing, as to exceed the gardener's most optimistic expectations: trapped in the city, but not for much longer.

From that day on, Alfredino's visits became an almost daily occurrence. Madame, who appeared to be on the mend according to the most recent check ups (and it must have been true, since the Great Widower had gone back to his place in the country), had reduced the number of chemotherapy sessions. Her strength was returning, and with the patches of alopecia hidden beneath the kerchief she wore knotted at the nape of the neck—patches like exfoliation, which in Luca's eyes made her small head resemble a lily bulb—she would go out with her young suitor, the first times using him as a prop. Both of them avoided Luca, and if they happened to find themselves face to face with him they would look away as if from a distressing sight. But the botanist, who had let his beard grow and who, in order to spend the least possible time in the apartment, had recently begun to dress as soon as he awoke before dashing out without even brushing his teeth, was convinced he was hiding his obsession. He would work in the house at night only, when Irene slept, exhausted, and her cadaver stink obliged him to get up and leave the room. He would close himself in the study and fill page after page of notebook with maps, plants, and lists of names. Until the day came when his patience was rewarded.

One happy afternoon—one of the two every week during which the servant Maria took advantage of her freedom to go to the hairdressers or to visit a friend—Luca returned home from his peregrinations from bar to bar earlier than usual. Events unfolded with the predictability of a soap opera, heralded by clues—a leather jacket on the armchair in the hall, a cigarette end smouldering in an ashtray, the pillows crushed as if there had been a brawl on the couch—so obvious as to oblige him to play the role they were suggesting with such insistence. He slipped into the shoes of the jealous husband who tiptoes along the corridor, puts his ear to the door, holds his breath, lowers the handle and opens the door to reveal the mother of all scenes, a real classic. The putrid mother and her castrated son were in bed, naked. She was licking his arse.

They were enchanting. Two stunted little plants clinging on to each other, united by an imaginative graft, with the excised parts swathed tightly in bandages of the same yellowish colour. The spectator had the time to note the speckling on the boy child's back, the steel buckle of the bandage that was supposed to ensure that the elastic band between the potatoes of the buttocks was kept taut, held to one side by the fingers of the leading lady on whose face he was still sitting, so that her tongue was free to dart among the tubers, the grass, to the root of that *salvificus* trunk open in two. "Taste good?" Luca inquired (his tongue suddenly began to hurt him, his mouth suddenly filled again with the taste of raw meat and metal of a splayed Atlantic girl, which was why his voice sounded a bit too urbane, a bit too lounge lizard). Alfredino hopped off the potty, and lay on one side, the big worm of his penis outside the dressing wrapped around his empty bean pod—and since the invertebrate was there but the beans weren't he tried to call them up by invoking their name: "Bollocks, bollocks, bollocks". For her part, Madame, who had sat up while keeping one modest hand over her bandaged bosom, was staring irately at this person who had dared interrupt her savoury repast, and it seemed as if she had absolutely no intention of providing an answer to that indecorous question. Luca approached the trough. The mother speedily covered up the child: she laid her other hand on his stalk. She did it with a protective gesture, as if the intruder intended to bite it off. Both of the Madonna's hands were now covering a wound. Luca stifled a yawn.

Irene, who must have interpreted his hesitation badly, asked him with a rather worried smile if he didn't feel like stripping off and resting between them. She was sure that Alfredo too— she did not use the diminutive—would have been glad to get to know him better. The *salvificus* nodded energetically, shaking his shock of hair. The intruder replied that he was unable to accept. The stench they both gave off, of rottenness, of disease, had spoiled his appetite. He left the room careless of Madame's expression, he went out of the house, and walked for a long time thinking about his irises.

Two days later, despite a final argument during which Irene had alternated insults and blandishments, accusations and tears, Luca was on board a plane. After having called him a coward, maintaining that only a madman could have let himself go like that, to become so obsessed with plants, spending his days holed up in bars memorizing books on botany, and his nights filling up notebooks with rambling gardening projects instead of staying by her side when she needed him, his wife went so far as to apologize: "I swear to you, spider, it was the first time", declaring in concerned tones that she had sensed his suffering, she had imagined the re-emergence in him of memories of the death of his mother. But he didn't have to worry, the crisis had passed, the disease was vanquished. These inferences and these conclusions, so stupid, so beastly, left Luca unmoved. Luca who now, as the aeroplane began its descent towards the silvery and violet fields that surround the White City in springtime, felt his heart pounding madly, as if it wished to rip open his breast and let the happiness with which it was overflowing gush out. Something, in his appearance, persuaded the customs officer to make a meticulous check of the luggage he had with him. Obediently, he pulled the bathrobe with the light blue monogram out of the suitcase. While the policeman's hands palpated the terry towelling, he had to make an effort not to punch him. He found himself outside. Awaiting him was the supreme realm, which is not of the heavens nor is it of the animals, but here, at hand: a paradise in which flowers feed on dead bodies, distilling and transmuting putrescent matter by virtue of the miracle that is their nature. Under the illusion that he was free, the boy conceived on an ancient cliff—he, the son of the lily, stood at the beginning of his Calvary.

II

NEVER HAD THE OUTSKIRTS of the White City seemed as beautiful to him as they did in those first days, spent in the non-stop baptism of *lithosperma*, calendulas, *crispum*, rock-roses, sweet alyssum, Star of Bethlehem, and adonis—every time he recognized an exemplar of a new species he would bend over to caress it, pronouncing its name, and he himself was amazed by the sound he had emitted, at least as much as the peasants or the shepherds who chanced to witness these ceremonies, without the officiant's noticing. Perhaps because he had adopted an exploratory strategy right from the start—he did not make his search by taking the usual ways, paths through the forest, ledges carved out beneath the ridges, trails, tracks, but by following unexplored routes, up and down the slopes, penetrating the thick of the undergrowth like a wild boar until he was bent double, until he was moving forward on all fours, his face and hands bleeding from the scratches of the brambles—perhaps it was a matter of a new point of view, or perhaps the botanical flavour and the excitement had opened his eyes, but even the best-known landscapes seemed different to him. From a distance, the bay on which the city stood was no longer a smiling mouth, but a worm-infested mass of stalagmites in whose meanderings beetles and ants followed one another. The grassy cliffs that plunged down into the Straits, strewn with lavender and juniper in bloom, were the ribs of the blind reptile, which, with its incongruously minute head swaying under the water to the rhythm of the ebb and flow, was swallowing clouds of plankton. There were places, after he had pushed the curtains of cobwebs to one side, where the forest opened up before him like the nave of a cathedral. From the capitals of the columns he was observed by owls, dormice, cuckoos, and geckos. Hundreds of thuribles in the form of pine cones wafted incense fumes, and sunbeams the colour of beer darted in through bullseyes open to the skies. Once out of the thick undergrowth, the faded mountains on the horizon were a yawn. Colossi waved their light blue crowns. Limping, the moon scaled the heavens. That was the hour, dusk, in which Luca returned home, and got down to work.

The choice of the first iris was inevitable. Ever since he had learned from books that Muslims, accustomed to burying bodies without coffins, but simply wrapped up in a piece of cloth, had since ancient times planted in their cemeteries certain spontaneous white irises native to the Mediterranean region, known as *Iris florentina* because in the city of Florence their violet-scented rhizomes had once been used as a cosmetic, it had struck him as a good omen to begin with a few exemplars of a species so emblematic of the supremacy of the vegetable world within the cycle of transformations. His destination was the old cemetery. A plan not unconnected with recollections of the slaughter that had occurred there the previous summer.

Before telling Señora Martinez of his decision, however, he wanted to be prepared. The flower bed from which he had determined to begin, the biggest one, on the first terrace, on the edge of the lawn that separated the two pavilions, contained the roses inherited from the American. His attention became focused on that point at the very moment in which Mohammed, with a sigh of pride, had pointed out to Luca those bushes heavily laden with triumphant blooms, in colours that ranged from a venomous pink to the yellow of certain powdered soft drinks. Hard to imagine anything farther removed from the shy, retiring flowers on which he intended to lavish his care. But the whole garden, after the winter rains, had exploded: the wisteria ran from one tree to the next, its flowers with their nauseating scent hanging down, the plastic jasmine and the *podranea* covered the dry-stone walls, the arrogant strelitzias stuck out their tongues among the arum lilies similar in their turn to rubber funnels, and the bushes of *Browallia* were already ablaze with thousands of orange blooms, a portent of the purifying flames in which they would soon end up.

Just as soon as the gardener retired, Luca, wearing his gloves and armed with secateurs, got to work. The thorns pricked him through the cloth, the branches got tangled up in his clothing, the roots put up a surprising resistance, the extraction of every trunk required an effort that left him panting for breath. Despite this he waded in and cut back until the darkness prevented him from continuing. When he went to bed, the path was blocked by a heap of severed branches. The flower bed, the other one immediately below it and the verge of the lawn were strewn with rose petals.

He slept better than he had done for months. On the following morning he was wakened by a racket, someone was shouting, running, as if the house itself were on fire. Mohammed was at the foot of the bed. Extremely agitated, he was beseeching Luca with guttural cries to get up and follow him. Once outside, in his pyjamas, Luca was pleased by the amount of work he had done the evening before. At this rate, in a few days, the bed would be clear. He explained to the gardener—calm, purposeful gestures—that he was making room for new, rarer flowers; soon they would plant them in that rose-infested earth. The man's amazement gradually gave way to an expression of suspicion, as if he had realized something that had escaped Luca himself. He stared at him shaking his head, almost as if he pitied him, or perhaps it was disgust. Then he went off dragging his feet. He seemed to have aged.

Later on, the branches had disappeared. Luca noticed that the stubborn gardener had taken some cuttings and planted them in front of his lodge. For the sake of peace, Luca said nothing. From that day, both Mohammed and his wife and children changed. The man, who in the past, as soon as he saw Luca emerge from the upper pavilion, still in his underwear, would dash up to him, take him by the hand and take him to admire the progress of the bush they had planted together, or the blossoming of the one that had been reinvigorated by their attentions, encouraged by their caresses, now avoided him. The women, usually chatty, had become silent. They would prepare his meals and serve him with eyes lowered. But Luca, far from being discouraged, continued to carry out his task. In the mornings he would go exploring, baptizing the new species, and sometimes, after lying down in a clearing, looking around furtively like a wolf obliged by hunger to come out of the woods, would hurriedly dig a little hole, unbutton his fly, pull out his prick, stretch out on his belly and unload, biting the grass as he did so. On returning home, he prepared the bed that would welcome his children, saving them from a world that wanted to make them disappear.

The time came to go to town, among the humans. It was late one April afternoon. The sea, which until moments before had been lapping at the hill, was frothing. The two rows of euca-lyptus trees that lined the road, after repeated rustling, began to shake their African wigs madly. On the roofs of the Moorish and modernist buildings that had been the pride of the White City, on the terraces and balconies of those turreted structures scoured by the salt spray, buildings that had once housed the consulates, embassies and legations of foreign powers, and were now condominiums divided up into poor apartments, sheets and patched sweaters—the banners of the new masters— flapped in the wind. The burnooses and djellabas and chadors of passers by, who were walking quickly, heads lowered, protecting their faces with one hand, swelled like sails. With one gust, the *shargui*, the east wind, had risen. Luca closed the windows of the car. His eyes were smarting. His lips dry.

The terraces of the pavement cafés had emptied. The street hawkers were wrapping up their junk in blankets. The steel shutters of the shops rattled as they were lowered. The sky was a metallic blue, but on the horizon the desert sand was gathering to form a black streak. Plastic bags and pages of newspapers fluttered, swirling, and rose flapping into the air. The only impassive ones were the policemen, far more numerous than Luca recalled. Stoical, hoods pulled down over their foreheads, they controlled every crossroads in groups of three or four. In the forecourt in front of the Great Mosque there stood a truck full of soldiers, sitting one next to the other, their rifles between their legs. Here as elsewhere, in the *madrassehs* of the outskirts, in the villages perched on the slopes of the mountains that the White City was swallowing as it grew, the imams were now openly attacking the Generals in power, maintaining that the causes of the country's wretchedness was their impiety, and the adoption, on the part of the rich and the powerful, of the habits and customs of the infidels. Some preachers had been arrested and taken to distant prisons. Since then, places of worship had been guarded, since they were considered to be hotbeds of insurrection. As Luca was parking in the little square before the Grand Socco, his suspicions were confirmed: there were soldiers there too, in front of the cemetery gates. He realized it for the first time: the city was on a war footing, in a state of siege. He studied the stone walls beyond which the cypresses, palms, and cedars flexed and rustled; on a parapet, rifle in hand, another soldier was seated. It would be impossible to get in. He felt a surge of defiance, a brief and ravishing happiness that made the blood rush to his heart. A door slammed. A branch of a pine tree broke off with a crack.

He moved off along calle de la Constitution. For a second he had the feeling that the wind, which was against him, was going to blow him over. He crossed place de la France and the boulevard. From the terrace where the cannons pointed out over the harbour—no idlers, itinerant photographers, sweet vendors, or shoeshine boys to be seen—the deserted city a prey to the storm was revealed to him as beautiful as it had seemed when he and Irene had discovered it together, years before. The barred shutters of the old Andalusian houses trembled, groaned, and struggled to protect their secrets. The wind whistled through the patios, trespassed in the hallways, slipped down the alleys that stank of piss and into the narrow passageways cluttered with fishing nets; lowing, it assailed the walls and the towers of the casbah. In the building sites near the customs-house, among devastated lean-tos made of cane and smashed-up corrugated iron shacks, sheep grazed below concrete flat blocks ten storeys high that still were, and perhaps always would be, devoid of window frames. The beach from which rose up gusts redolent of rotten wood and tar was a bed of smoking ashes, as if below the dunes there smouldered the same flame that burned in the sea: the reflection, on the field of waves, of the blaze in the sky. Beyond the Straits, clear, absurdly close, the European coast. The seagulls allowed themselves to be carried along by the current. Suddenly, everything was faded. The air, slime. The first drops of rain, sparse, freezing cold, were followed by a downpour. Luca ran up rue du Mexique, the water overwhelmed the accumulated filth on the pavements, gurgled down the steps leading to the basements; at every whiplash of wind, the branches of the orange trees streamed with water. He took shelter under a doorway. Two men were waiting, their sopping burnooses stinking of the cattleshed. One was smoking. The other, a plastic bag on his head, was humming. Running zigzag down the middle of the road as if avoiding bullets, a third man arrived. As soon as he reached shelter, a gleaming raindrop on the end of his nose, he held out his hand: "Sidi Mohammed, *salaam aleikum*," he said. Luca shook it automatically, but kept silent. No, he was not alluding to his gardener. He was a stranger. They looked at each other for along moment, astonished, then the newcomer said something to the other two, who burst out laughing. All Luca understood was the word '*nazrani*'. Holding his breath, he threw himself back out into the road, unpleasantly aware of the gaze of the three men upon him; he passed the Immeuble Beethoven, turned at the corner of calle de Hollanda, running full pelt, already he could see the plaque that announced the Casino Judío, he leaped: he had almost tripped over a figure huddled up on the ground, under a sheet of plastic. He was in the entrance hall. It was warmer. Only then, as he took the stairs, and as he was running his fingers through his hair and across his face in an attempt to dry himself, did he realize that he had not shaved for goodness knows how long. He was wearing dirty, torn clothes. The man who had spoken to him must have mistaken him for a local. Mohammed is the name of three quarters of the inhabitants of the White City. This gave him an idea.

Señora Martinez made the same mistake. Perched on a stool in the first room, in the well of light from the solitary lamp hanging from the ceiling, her arms like amputated winglets because her elbows were leaning on the bar, she was complaining about the wind, one of the principal obsessions of the inhabitants of the White City. She was squawking something about not being able to stand it. Slipping one hand into the neck of the house-coat she was wearing over a sweater and skirt, she said: "I can't breathe, Hassan, this time I'm going to die". The waiter restricted himself to nodding, and to filling up the umpteenth glass of sherry. When the stranger appeared in the doorway, soaking wet, panting, the customer decided to ignore him. With the straw between her lips, she bent over the glass, and sucked up the contents in one go. He was still there. He was looking at her, there was no doubt. He was staring at her with a glue sniffer's smile. Who the devil could he be, this drugged-up son of a bitch?

The lady did not have a clear conscience. Moreover, anyone who had had to steer a course through life for sixty-odd years in a seaport like the White City would have almost inevitably done something deemed worthy—by the injured party—of a knifing. The best defence, in certain cases, is attack. Regal, she straightened up, and, drawing together the skirts of her house-coat as if it were an ermine stole, she asked the waiter—in scornful tones loud enough to be heard even from the stairway—since when had the Casino been opening its doors to natives. The man glanced towards the doorway: he had no intention of getting himself into trouble on account of that old lush. The stranger, with a smile that would have frightened a dead man, was heading for the bar. Jaima stiffened, numbed, half closing her eyelids. Apparently innocuous because mum-mified, the iguana was ready to sink her teeth into the first strip of flesh that might come within range. "Señora Martinez! How lucky I am to have found you! ... Do you remember? Ritts-Twice's friend, the iris collector ... "

She got him in focus, then she closed her eyes altogether. She cursed him, blessed him, cursed him. As a result of the instan-taneous relaxation, her snout was reduced to a lump of flaccid meat. She drew a sigh that was a bellow. Reopened her eyes. Yet again, faced with her gaze, ferocious and caressing as that of a wild beast, Luca felt helpless, a little boy abandoned in the savannah. "*El niño!*" she was exclaiming, "what a surprise!" Her tone held a festive familiarity, as if they had known each other for a lifetime. Of course she had not forgotten his project! Finally someone who had some idea of how a garden was supposed to be! It seemed like yesterday! The irises! And, observing him from head to toe—the unkempt beard, the tic in his cheek, the scarecrow clothes—she was delighted to find him looking so well, she added, unable to suppress a smile whose perfidy was fully justified by the nasty moment he had just given her. Had his wife recovered from that horrid illness? She caressed her hair, in a strenuous attempt to spruce up the vestiges of curls reduced to greasy locks streaked with white. Come on, he was to tell her. She was anxious to hear the latest news of his studies.

It wasn't just the relief at knowing that things were not going to go the way she had feared (the last time, following the impetuous reaction of a young man to whom she had offered to sell the negatives of some photographs taken without his knowledge, the nuns of the Portuguese Hospital had had to keep her in for two weeks): Jaima was bubbling with joy, because all of a sudden certain spanking new armchairs, and a couch, and a television with a parabolic antenna had reappeared before her, surroundings as comfortable and clean as the little drawing room next to the director's office in the orphanage, where, centuries before, she had been able to sleep and thus avoid the dormitory, but only if she reacted like a good girl to the Father's punches and kicks, and obeyed his orders without a cheep. The advance payment Ritts had given her had flown away—or rather, it had dissolved in a few bottles. During the months spent brooding in her shack, the lady had ended up thinking that such a complex plan had been the fruit of the novelist's illness. In the good old days, he would have been capable of having himself invited to tea and then setting fire to Luca—or, through one of his connections, he would have had the house expropriated (but it was true that these days the authorities were less complaisant). In any event, it would have been easier to get straight down to brass tacks, to speak plainly to *el niño*: wifiekins with the cancer was the rich one, and so, no matter what Gordon said, it would have sufficed to offer Luca a fat backhander. But now, now that she could see him in front of her in that state, looking like someone who had just met a jinn, she felt that things would turn out exactly as foreseen by that vulture of an old friend of hers, may the Lord protect him.

While the little imbecile, who had sat down beside her, ordering a double whisky for himself and another sherry for her, dismissing the matter of his wife's health with a couple of words, was enthusiastically explaining his plans regarding the cemetery, Jaima had to make an effort to control herself. She could have kissed the little blond boy on the brow, on the mouth, she could have stuck her tongue between his lips. Not even in her rosiest dreams, had she hoped things would take this turn. He had gone *loco*. She didn't waste any time with objections. He had made a good deal of progress, was her comment. He had grasped the sense of her allusion, the other time, to fertilizer: "That's what it's all about, my little piglet!" And, smiling, she had nudged him with her elbow. Becoming earnest again because she was afraid that she had gone a little too far, she observed that irises were not flowers for just anyone, no indeed: cultivating and collecting them required a certain capacity to grasp the connections. The police, the soldiers? All play-acting to allay the fears of the tourists, now that they knew each other better she could speak openly. That the fundamentalist wave frightened the *maricones* who considered the White City their own private bordello, was right, normal. But *el niño*, *el niño* who was a respectable person, who wanted only to work, to get in a little botanical study, could consider it an element of local colour, like mint tea, the call of the *muezzin*, or belly dancing. Luca hung from her lips, his eyes clouded with fatigue and the sense of peace. It was marvellous finally to find oneself in the company of a human being able to understand him, to help him.

However, while reiterating that his was an excellent choice— and Jaima's voice took on a suggestive tone, as if instead of preparing to hint at a danger she wished to recommend her proselyte a secret source of delights—the old cemetery was the refuge of all the delinquents and the derelicts of the city. Horrendous crimes (a new smile, laden with promise) were perpetrated there. *El niño* knew this; he did know this, didn't he, the rascal? There was no question of his venturing there alone, even if he wore a burnoose that would have made him look exactly like a native. He needed a guide. Were they or weren't they good friends, by now? Contributing to the realization of his dream filled her with pride. She would see to it that he was found a trustworthy person who would guide him through that expanse of undergrowth and brambles that in some places was a dense as a forest, to the clearings in which, nourished for centuries by the corpses that decomposed under the ground— "under the ground, *niño*"—where the ... how had he called them? *Iris florentina*, of course, that was exactly what she had meant to say, where the *Iris florentina* grew. There was a flash of lightning. A thunderclap. The lights went out.

Luca stretched out his legs. Listening to her talking of blood, of decomposing bodies, of flowers, breathing in the smell of her, more acid than he remembered—the dwarf was sweating, and now, in the providential darkness, it seemed to him that he could feel on his arm the pressure of her breasts constricted by the housecoat as they rose and fell to the rhythm of her breathing—he got excited the way, of late, he had done on penetrating the earth of the fields. There was a rustling. He felt the witch's fingertips, ever so lightly, charitably, brushing against his hard cock. Jaima was rummaging in her bag. A phallic object gleamed whitely in the gloom. A strange fantasy flashed through Luca's mind. Before the dwarf had time to light the candle stub, the lights came back on. Jaima was smiling at him. Luca had to lower his eyes. Hassan reappeared at the kitchen door to announce that they were closing. Luca made to put his hand in his pocket, but Jaima stopped him. The drinks were on her. No, she would not go home: there was a bedroom for regular customers, in case of emergency, on the floor above. And she gave the waiter a withering glance. Would *el niño* write his telephone number on the back of an envelope? She would call him just as soon as she had come to an agreement with a guide, to give him the instructions he needed. In the meantime, he was to promise her that he would not move on his own account, otherwise … picking up the cylinder of wax and stearine from the bar, she waved it under his nose. They took their leave of each other with a handshake.

It had stopped raining, and the wind had abated. The night was cool. In front of the main door of the house, searching for his keys, the future saviour of endangered species realized that the banknotes he usually kept in his jacket pocket were no longer there. Taken as he was by his plan, and by the happiness that his accomplice had given him by confirming his hunches, he attached no importance to the disappearance. Perhaps he had forgotten to take some money before going out. In truth, there were no banknotes on the bedside table, nor in the tray where he usually tossed his coins. When, later on that same evening, the telephone rang—he was lying naked on the bed, his closed fist moving up and down his prick—he snatched up the receiver with his free hand, convinced that it was her, his little candle-holder, his little saint: he would carry on touching himself as he listened to her speaking, he would splash her with hot droplets before going to dry himself in his white terry towel mantle. But it was Irene. Irene who told him—but, if the Great Widower were to call for her, he was to say he knew nothing about her movements—that she was going off for a bit to play Irene in Saint Irene's: Istanbul and then Cappadocia, on a motor bike with Alfredino. Did he mind? It was decidedly the evening of the saints. He felt like replying that as those Byzantine saints were the protectresses of an Empress compared to the Virgin Mary, she ought to keep her little baby in her arms, not seated on her face, out of respect for a thousand year-old iconography. Mothers usually suckle their little ones, not suck their arses, cancer or no cancer, not even after the evening bath. But she was already asking him what he was doing. "Jerking off" he replied, quickening the rhythm. He hoped she would have fun. Irene said goodbye—there was bewilderment, in her voice—and hung up, without even asking how their garden, his garden, was progressing.

Progress that had not yet been made. The *shargui* dropped in the evenings, but it sprang up again at sunrise. The days passed, and Jaima did not show up. The empty flower bed was a constant reminder. In order to dull his senses, Luca began drinking whisky right after his morning coffee, and he carried on drinking until he collapsed. He was too weak to go out in the evenings. A strange phenomenon began to occur with growing frequency.

The first times, when it seemed to him that the living room windows, behind the eyelids of the two large curtains that cast a turquoise shadow, were eyes—the eyes of a tired man—or when the cement steps, dotted with crushed sea shells, which led down to the bottom of the garden had revealed themselves to him as slimy and alive as a big moist tongue bristling with taste buds (he had slipped and grazed his knee), he thought he was drunk. He was not seeing things, unfortunately. The two pavilions, the tower, the trees shaken by the wind, the garden walls made of stones like piles of livers shrouded by the veins of the ivy, by the tendons and the sheaths of muscle of the podranea, were parts of a body. These things concealed, badly, and only so that the discovery of reality would be painful every time, the limbs of a giant—dismembered but alive, disgustingly alive. All you had to do was look, touch, smell. The cracks next to the dining room door were wrinkles in his skin, the bushes on the verge of the lawn were hairy cysts, swellings of the dermis, while certain masses covered with lichen were teeth, decaying molars and canines. The roofs of the houses reflected, in the dazzling sunshine, a gleaming of fingernails. The wind blew in gusts hot and foetid as farts emitted by an anus puckered by wrinkles and fissures radiating out in the violet gorge, which snaked through the eastern hills as it made its way up the intestine of the world, until it reached the massifs of a gallbladder, of a pancreas, which frothed on the horizon. On contemplating the disaster of the landscape, or when, sunk in his armchair, he would stare at the telephone praying for it to ring (tonsils saturated with the tar of continuous cigarettes), he thought he could perceive who that shapeless being was, that being whose limbs, whose organs, would from time to time take on the aspect of the thing within which they lurked, pulsating. The flaccid orphan, the monster who sweated in the walls, the giant buried in the rocks and the cement who continued to breathe, were none other than himself. He who had once been able to fly. Dropping the bottle, Luca got to his feet and ran to the bathroom. On hands and knees he vomited into a bucket. He had given orders that the bucket was not to be emptied. After a few days—the level of the watery gruel that gushed up from his stomach had risen, its smell stank out the living room and the guest room—he determined to take it outside. He set it down on the grass, at the bottom of the garden, at the feet of an *Olea fragrans*, near the pink hibiscus.

Since then, instead of leaving the leftovers in the tray for the servants to finish, he had taken to grabbing handfuls of them, even sticking them avidly into his pockets, greedily, especially meat, preferably that of mammals rather than fish or chicken. On leaving the table, he would go out into the garden. He would throw into his cauldron whole lamb cutlets, minced beef, and handfuls of thick sauce in which gleamed gobs of fat, ripe fruit, grilled sardines, eggs, the bones of soles from which hung scraps of flesh and strips of skin, slices of cheese, then he would add the insects that, attracted by the smell, he caught in the mornings as they tried to scale the sides of the bucket, as well as those he found grubbing around, among the hair of the grass, among the inflamed pimples and boils of certain flowering shrubs, as well as those that came to him as if to a thaumaturge, buzzing and fluttering around sauce-impregnated pockets: wasps, ant-lions, psocids, slugs, spiders, millipedes, a mole cricket whose crunchy carapace was found to be full of yellow pap when broken in two, and worms, reduced to pieces. The gruel got richer, the giant breathed on the bottom: the surface was covered by a film within which bubbles of air surfaced, floated and burst like blisters. Even though the bucket was a certain distance from the lodge occupied by Mohammed and his family, the gardener, who had been ignoring Luca for some time, yet, undaunted, continued watering the plants and sweeping the paths without suspecting the great transformation that was being prepared, assailed him one morning. He complained about the stink. He wanted to know what that revolting muck was. Freeing his shoulder from the vice of the gardener's hand, the master of the house touched his breast to say food: it was fertilizer for the flowers he was going to plant in the new bed. Mohammed, after the brief delay required to understand, tapped his temple with his index finger. He was no longer afraid to let Luca know that he thought he was mad.

The two pavilions, in the silence of those nights, breathed. The groaning, the hissing, the gasping, would waken Luca, who could not get back to sleep again. The whisky would calm him. He guzzled down a couple of mouthfuls from the bottle he kept on the bedside table, stretched out again, made his plans. He was going to renege on his promise to Jaima. He was going to pay a call on Lady Weathergood. He knew that, in her capacity as the doyenne of the English colony, that old lady who was obsessed by famous women also assigned the places for the faithful at the Sunday service in the Anglican church, and that she possessed the keys of the land around it, in which lay buried many foreigners who had been leading figures in the social life of the White City. The cemetery of the *nazrani* was adjacent to the old Muslim cemetery. Climbing over the wall that separated them, at night, was one possibility. But what pretext could he use to convince that harpy, who was very fond of Irene, but deemed Luca barely worthy of a greeting if they were together, and pretended not to see him when he was alone? By flattering her? How? After the murder of the Germans? Jaima's phone call came early in the morning. A technical communication, a summit. No warmth, nor familiarity or emphasis, no declaration of affection: not even a little of the encouragement that Luca had expected. He listened to her orders, forcing himself to concentrate. He was having difficulty grasping the sense of her words, but the impatient, even peremptory tone with which, on his request, the lady had repeated the address of the café where his guide was waiting for him, caused him to refrain from asking for any explanations from her. Jaima wished him good luck. He was not to take any money with him, she would pay the boy, when the mission was accomplished. Luca could reimburse her later.

The docile executor of the plot hatched by his protectress, that same afternoon Luca scanned the terrace of one of the cafés on the Grand Socco, and with a tremor of joy, even at that distance, he spotted in the crowd of loafers who were celebrating the cessation of the wind a young man whose torso was swathed in a close-fitting jersey in the red shade that Jaima had defined as "geranium", while the colour was that of a pelargonium. He was one of the waiters. Having recognized in his turn the *nazrani* who was staring at him (the old woman had been clear: "He looks like a beggar, darling, he is one who is *loco* in the head, not one who is *loco* for arse") the boy gestured to Luca to take a seat at a free table. A pock-marked face and a great mass of black curls worn down to his shoulders, Kacem spoke in a low voice, continually shaking that species of wig and flexing his pectorals, encouraged by the hope that the business of the cemetery might have been one of the pretexts with which foreigners, especially the married kind, attempted to conceal their desires. What with the stink he gave off, of rancid food, this one was going to be a tough proposition. But twenty minutes in a boarding house room, even though less profitable than the amount the *vieja* had promised him, would have been a cakewalk, compared to that surprise ending. Nothing was of any use, not even when he said that he preferred men to women, insistently tugging at the crotch of his blue jeans. Resignedly, he told Luca the time and the place for their rendezvous, then he disappeared inside the café, re-emerging almost immediately holding a tray laden with glasses of tea. Luca got up, crossed the square, went through the gateway into the *souk*, and walked a part of the way up rue des Chrétiens. He went into a clothes shop. Pulling the hood of his woollen cloak down over his forehead, standing in front of the fly-specked mirror, he felt his anxiety vanish. That native was he, resurrected. Smiling with satisfaction at his alter ego—who returned his bemused smile—he baptized him Haroun al-Rashid, certainly not Mohammed, because finally he was making a hero's entrance in his own Arabian Nights. Without haggling, he placed the sum of money the seller asked into the man's palm. Sitting in the doorway, the shopkeeper watched Luca as he went off. You learn something new every day. Right from the moment he had seen that drug addict he would have sworn by Allah, glory be to his name, that he slept rough in the streets, and that his pocket did not hold even the few coins required to go to some dive to buy himself a bowl of the soup that the folk of the White City call the "lucky dip", because, depending on the customer's luck, in the one ladleful drawn from the cauldron there might be a piece of fish, a lump of meat, or merely some dirty water, a bit of broth.

III

THE CART drawn by the mule took the slope that leads down to the Phoenician quarter. The clatter of hoofs reverberated in the night making the tree-lined avenues seem broader. The boy looked at his watch. Eleven o'clock sharp. Punctually, the one who was *loco* in the head emerged from the alleyway, transformed into a picturesque figure by the burnoose. Before the other man caught up with him, Kacem walked off down the sharia Prince of Wales, wedged between the walls of the cemetery and the facades of dilapidated houses. At regular intervals the street lights projected cones of light onto swarms of gnats: thank to an accurate shot with his catapult that afternoon, one of the lights was out. A soldier was sitting on the edge of the wall. He watched the two pass by. Under his cloak, the khalif in incognito clutched the satchel containing the tools. In disobedience to his adviser, he had slipped his wallet into his pocket. If his memory served him well, even his namesake, in the course of those celebrated nocturnal forays in mufti through the streets of Baghdad, had also occasionally got out of trouble thanks to a bit of cash. Where the area of darkness began, the pavement was obstructed by a pile of branches. The wall had tilted over towards the street to form a spur, the outlines of which revealed a crevice that had opened up in its thickness, full of earth and refuse. Kacem, his belly and thighs hugging the landslip, toiled his way up from one handhold to the next like a beetle until he was almost at the top. Luca glanced behind him. He grasped a root and hoisted himself up, grabbing at a stone that promptly shot out of its lodging, but he managed to keep his balance by flattening himself against the edge of the crevice. While the stone landed on the street with a thud, he groped around until he found a resistant clump of weeds. Then he came up as if he were being pushed out by something that was expelling him, he too an insect climbing up the side of the cauldron, attracted by the effluvium of food that rose up from its mouth. He was on the top, stretched out on his belly. A hand, two hands, took hold of his, dragging him. He found himself squeezed up against Kacem, behind a bush. The soldier was a few metres away. The carbine pointed at them. In the end the man bent down to look at the street. Relieved, he walked off slowly, putting the cause of the sound down to a rat.

With Kacem's sticky hair against his cheek, soaked in sweat, Luca had the impression that he was a deserted circuit within which the blood was roaring along at an inhuman rate. Yet he could sense the smell of brilliantine and sebum on the head next to his, and the stench of shit and refuse on the ground, and the breathing of the body that was crushing him. They waited for an interminable time, trying to make themselves more comfortable with tiny movements. Then, given that not even that enforced intimacy had had the hoped-for effect, Kacem slipped out. Luca did the same. They advanced by a series of bounds, flattening themselves against the tree trunks, diving through the elderberry bushes and the ferns until they came to the edge of a clear area strewn with grave stones. Voices. Down again. Two figures arm in arm came out of the darkness, swaying: two boys on the verge of falling down held each other up before disappearing into the undergrowth. Kacem cursed, got to his feet, shook his great wig of hair. He vanished into the brambles on the other side of the clearing. Luca gradually opened up a breach in the screen of thorns. The darkness, deeper there, was scented with sap. He moved forward, hunched over the way he did while exploring, paying no heed to the scratches or the tickling of the cobwebs on his face. Another clearing. The vision was so celestial he didn't notice the music. Among the graves the sword-shaped leaves were fanned out, waving: the hilt fixed, the blades out-thrust. He fell on the flowers. He ran his fingers lightly over one: the petals as soft as a swallow's breast among the splayed winglets of the sepals, the cartilage suffused, in the centre, with a down covered with slightly bitter droplets. Only as he was sucking his thumb, did he become aware of the song. Someone was clapping his hands. There was a shout. Laughter.

Luca plunged into the undergrowth once more. He needed to know how far away the people were. The brambles tore off his hood, he grabbed it again, keeping it pulled low over his forehead. He crept along trying to hold his breath, hindered by the satchel over his shoulder, dragging himself along on his forearms, starting when a twig broke with a snap. The sound of the transistor-radio was clearer, there was a smell of burning, something slipped down the back of his neck, it was walking down his back, the vendetta of a spider or a millipede, the itch was driving him crazy, but he couldn't scratch himself through the burnoose. A fire was burning, framed in the leaves. All around it, in front of a ruined mosque, about a score of people were sitting. Among those whose faces he could see in the light of the darting flames, there were a couple of soldiers and some boys. They were watching a big fat woman who, bare-chested, was wiggling her hips to the rhythm of the music, her hair hidden by a turban. She was barefoot. The big white body was covered with wrinkles that, as they followed her swaying, became deeper at certain points while others vanished owing to the pressure of the fat. The men grinned, passing something from hand to hand, a box or a little bottle, taking turns at sniffing it. She, on foot in the middle of them, caressed the hollow of an armpit that was gleaming with sweat like a horse's rump. One hand lingered on a bag-like breast. Her fingers traced little concentric circles around the oh-so-easy target of the nipple, then they slid down, onto the belly that was bloated as that of a drowned donkey. Luca shut his eyes, trying to drive off the hallucination, then opened them again. Hanging from the butcher's hook, was her, the skinned gazelle exposed to the desire and the hunger of those men. Irene's legs were kicking in the emptiness … all around was flesh that stank of flesh, saturated with the sadness of flesh. From the audience of drug addicts a howl rose up, the woman slipped out of her trousers to reveal her panties; from behind, the outstretched buttocks trembled like tripe in a basin as the panties were lowered, offered, and the anus pulled wide open by the fingers that flattened out the puckered skin around its rim. A leap. She was face on once more. Irene's body flopped onto the zinc counter, she was immediately on her feet, unhurt, dressed, and, smiling, she said that the carcinoma was only a joke. Between the monster's heavy legs there dangled a chopper the size of a donkey's, the turban had come unwound to reveal the sweaty cranium. The spectators applauded. The big bald man went out of the circle. He came towards Luca. Completely naked, he stopped in front of the brambles, a few metres from his hiding place. Holding his prick between two fingers he pissed, then shook off the drops. When he returned to the scene neither the soldiers nor the youths paid any more attention to him, stupefied as they were by the glue.

The worm retreated backwards, struggling to make his way through the branches, using his weight to bend the runners, extricating himself from the thorns. He popped out. Blind with rage, careless of the satanic assembly that had congregated on the branches—his wife, the English novelist, and Señora Martinez, who having transformed herself into a hoopoe was staring at him with malevolent yellow eyes, asking what their spider was preparing to do in the dark—he took the little spade out of the satchel, lifted it high, above his shoulder, to smash her to the ground and to kill her once and for all, to make her intestines come squirting out. He couldn't. Someone, from behind, had gripped the spade. Kacem, gesticulating at him not to make a sound, had slipped the scarf off his neck and wrapped it around the blade. When the spade sank into the ground, the sound was muffled. The assistant retired to the edge of the clearing, leaving the surgeon to operate on his mother, operate on his wife. Under the cutting of the tool the leaves bent over, the rhizomes ready for transplanting emerged from the soil, the flowers rested their cheeks on the ground, little angels made drowsy by the anaesthetic. He gathered the clumps into a single bunch, they emanated an odour that was not of violets but human, of sweaty groins. Together with the spade, he carefully laid them inside the satchel. He started to run, trying to reduce the swaying to a minimum in order to avoid damaging vital organs. Kacem was already at the bottom.

The pavement was deserted. Luca began to climb down the wall. At the half-way mark he turned to look down. He saw Kacem get to his feet, take a bundle out from under his burnoose, and get rid of it. Their eyes met, then the beetle quickly scuttled off along the road, from one lamp-post to the next, hugging the wall. Luca let himself fall. He landed unharmed on the pile of rubbish. A spasm of pain in his back, between the shoulder blades, below the satchel. He tried to get up, but the pressure grew stronger. Someone was shouting. He held up his hands. Slowly, he pulled himself up. A soldier was pointing his rifle at him. Another soldier, with a slap, lifted up his hood. Luca stammered something about flowers, the only result being that the two soldiers simultaneously exclaimed "*Nazrani!*" and burst out laughing. But when, with the intention of showing them the irises and thus dispelling the misunderstanding, he brought his hand up to the satchel, the barrel of the rifle was pressed against his chest. Get moving, *vite, vite*. The rifle barrel shoved him forward. He walked ahead of one of the two until he came to a truck parked behind the protruding part of the wall. Thinking that, once in the cabin, it would have been the right moment to take out his wallet, he climbed into the front seat. The soldier sat down beside him, leaning heavily on him. The driver was bringing up the rear. He said something in Arabic to his companion, tossed a plastic bag onto the back seat, and took his place behind the wheel. As the man was turning the key in the ignition, Luca, trying to control his racing heart, declared that he was a tourist: they were wrong to treat him like this, he had money on him. And when the vehicle lurched off, he added in a tremulous voice that he demanded to know where they were headed. "Silence!" grunted the soldier on his right, giving Luca a dig in the stomach with his elbow that took his breath away. Then the driver gave him an amused look: "To the Grand Hotel, *nazrani* dog. Police headquarters".

He was naked, standing, with arms and legs spread-eagled. He had to keep his hands up because otherwise, as the little man sitting behind the desk had explained to him in impeccable French, he too would have lost patience—they were all tired and irritable on account of the continual provocations of you foreigners—and instead of doing things as they should be done, respecting hygiene—he stressed the word with a yellowish little smile, like a rodent's—he would see to it that Luca was subjected to the rectal search by his lads, out there. Wasn't it comfortable, the position their prophet had chosen to die in? Four kilos wasn't much, but it wasn't a little either. Had he been thinking of leaving by sea, or by air?

By this time Luca knew that it was pointless trying to reply. His appearance at police headquarters had been greeted with merriment, to the sound of the exclamation *"Arbà kilò!"* which resounded like a refrain from room to room. Some young men in uniform had gathered around the scales. They congratulated the two men who had brought him in with vigorous hand-shakes, while favouring him with looks that seemed full of sympathy. Taking advantage of this situation, he tried to explain. They were making a mistake, didn't they see that? That bag had been left there by some son of a bitch ... silence fell. A boy a bit younger than the others came up to him. He wore a contrite expression. The blow came suddenly. Luca staggered. His eyes were watering as if someone were holding a piece of cloth impregnated in ether over his nose. The boy was caressing his fist, nodding gravely and staring at him, as if to say now look what's happened to you, how sad, my friend, while someone behind him was yelling at him to strip off immediately, *maricón*, dirty infidel, and gave him a kick in the arse. He bowed his head. The blood dripped on to the floor. He slipped off his burnoose.

They were observing him, some with arms folded, others dragging fiercely on cigarettes. They were almost motionless, apart from a fat man who was idly drumming his truncheon against the wall, the back of his chair, and against the wall again. Luca gave his jacket to a policeman, who went through the pockets and laid his wallet and documents on the table. Fatso was using one hand to make his balls more comfortable inside the tight uniform breeches while brandishing the truncheon in the other: "*Vite! Hashishi de mierda!*"

Fear had Luca's intestines in its chilly grip. He bent over to unlace his shoes, took off his socks, unbuttoned his shirt, slipped off his trousers. He was in his underpants, his hands clasped over his sex. He struggled to avoid wetting himself. Laughing, one man pulled down his underpants, in front, behind. There was more laughter, comments about the size of his genitals, about his white arse. "You like to suck, *cabrón*?" Fatso gave Luca a gentle, but accurate, knock on his split upper lip—a flush of cold, then heat. Silence fell again. As if in a ballet, the semicircle of policemen broke up. Their backs to him, almost all of them were looking at the bag on the scales. One was leafing through Luca's passport, another was picking his clothes up off the floor. The little man who had entered the room went to sit down behind the desk. He unholstered his pistol and ordered the others to leave. Toying with the weapon, he gave Luca a watery gaze—he had protuberant eyes. He hoped, he said, that his lads had not made a nuisance of themselves. But now Luca was to open his arms and raise his hands, higher. He pointed the gun at him and exclaimed boom boom! but tiredly, as if rather unconvinced by his game. He was a pretty fair hunter, he explained, partridge, pheasant, the odd wild boar. Did Luca go hunting too, hunting for youths and little boys like all the foreign perverts in the White City? No? Was he married? That didn't mean much. From whom had he bought the drugs?

He asked that question several times. But as soon as Luca tried to explain what had happened—and by now even he realized how absurd the reason for his nocturnal visit to the cemetery must have sounded, even though the irises in the bag were the proof of this—the inspector interrupted him: it was time the *nazrani* cut it out, time they stopped enriching themselves at the expense of the inhabitants of the White City, time they stopped exploiting them with their trafficking. An intelligent and educated person like Monsieur could not but agree with this. He did agree, did he not? Luca begged him to open the bag with the flowers. He was a botanist, a collector of irises. The little man nodded. He reminded Luca to keep his hands up, otherwise ... why didn't he have himself circumcised? Did he not know that that little piece of skin trapped the dirt? In the look with which the man was appraising him there was something that reminded Luca of the blend of covetousness and disdain with which the locals observed Irene. He wanted to speak with the Consul of his country, he blurted out. It was his right.

The other man picked up his pistol again, and pointed it at him with his weasel smile. Was it still not clear who asked the questions, in there? Had he bought the drugs from a Spanish dealer, an American? Was he in league with the French? Monsieur was to understand that his reputation was irrelevant as far as the inhabitants of the White City were concerned. Smuggling was the work of foreigners, accustomed to thinking they could do whatever they wished by virtue of old privileges, vice-ridden scum that would soon be expelled.

Luca concentrated on a sole thought: how to get in touch with Irene, the Great Widower, Jaima. He felt a wave of energy running through him that, as it receded, left him empty. The tingling in his arms was diminishing. His lip throbbed. And the inspector's piping voice came to him from afar: for what organization was he working, did he have a contact in the customs service?

The little man got up. He looked like a tired father who wanted to get his business over with as quickly as possible so he could go back home and slip into bed beside his wife. He must have suffered from hyperthyroidism. Why had he changed his tone? Why was he yelling, telling Luca to bend over, to get down on his knees? The inspector grabbed his earlobe, and even this gesture would have seemed paternal, had he not tugged it with unheard-of violence. He gave Luca a kick in the shin with his regulation boot. Luca doubled up. He looked at the policeman's hand, convinced that it must hold his severed ear. Something struck him in the back, above the kidneys. Things went dark. His belly smacked into the edge of the desk. The inspector grabbed him by the hair and pushed his face against the wooden desk top, the pistol pressed to his temple. He told him to open his arse, bastard pusher.

A stabbing pain. His knees buckled, he felt the fingers force him open, moving inside him until they touched a point that unleashed a pain that was like a trumpet blast in his eardrums. "You like it, bastard?" In the neon-lit bathroom the woman leaned over him in the bath tub, her thin, goat-like head enormous: "My little spider" she bleated "my clean little spider, just so, inside too". With her soapy index finger Marta went in and out of his flesh, with the other hand she touched the stalk on his glabrous belly that was as easy to break as the stem of a flower ... "Mummy is ill." (Water lapping, a madness in the voice, a threat.) "Do you want to make mummy better? Do you want to help mummy, Luca?" A big bald man squatted down and voided himself in a bucket, tripe, bowels, scraps of bloody matter. "Sure you like it, bastard." He ejaculated. The inspector was adjusting his braces after having put the pistol back in its holster. He straightened the collar of his uniform jacket. Daddy preparing to return to his children. "A formality, dear Monsieur. Tomorrow you will feel more like co-operating. Otherwise, snip snip." And making a snipping gesture with his fingers he cast a languid glance at his dripping sex. Luca was huddled up on the floor. A man threw some pyjamas over him. Having donned the jacket and trousers, he let himself be led along a corridor. The policeman stopped in front of a door, opened it, pushed him inside the cell and closed the door again. A dark little room, devoid of any furnishings. Luca stretched out on the cement. He waited to die.

Then the Pekinese came—floppy jowls, disgusted mouth, and a tuft of silvery hair. The consular official, wearing a blue jacket, avoided looking Luca in the face, where the marks left by the blows were evident. He looked at his finger nails, or at his glossy slip-ons, and although he had invited Luca to give his version of the facts, he reacted to his recriminations with a bored gesture: the inspector had been joking, none of this was relevant from a juridical point of view. He needed concrete elements, to be transmitted to the court-appointed lawyer.

He didn't give a hoot for their laws, they were a bunch of sadists, cried Luca. His voice alarmed the man, who glanced at the door of the little room in which the conversation was taking place. The official was not to worry, he had never hurt a fly, Luca continued, even though, to tell the truth, he used flies and insects as fertilizer. And since there was no way that the other man could understand, Luca told him everything, right from the beginning, without paying any heed to the signs of embarrassment betrayed by the official, who was trying vainly to interrupt him, sensing, if anything, a growing sense of pride, of legitimacy, as his tumultuous account continued and took form, feelings that culminated in the intuition that he was free, entirely free. Irene, his wife, had been operated for a breast cancer; milk was food, food fertilizer, fertilizer gruel; after months of reflection he had come to the conclusion that within the vegetable kingdom there occurred mutations the study of which would enable man to escape from the genetic trap in whose grip he lay. He had broken no law in going to the old cemetery, because his sole purpose had been to find exemplars of *Iris florentina*, one of the endangered native species that he had determined to save, just like the *battandieri*, the *forrestieri*, the *filifolia*, and the extremely rare *Juncea numidica*. Men were destroying the iris because they envied its power to transform inert matter, decomposed matter, into sap. Human flesh—he pinched one cheek, pulling it and thus causing a stab of pain in his lip— was subject to a process of continuous death, perpetual death agonies. Wild flowers are born and born again without any need of mothers, by virtue of a power that was the secret of life itself, transmutation. He fell silent. The official was also silent. Finally, in a more prudent tone than before, he observed that, as far as he could gather, it would not have been very advisable to inform the lady. "She's in Turkey," Luca said. The man gave a grave nod, as if Irene's and Alfredino's destination were of enormous importance. He asked Luca for some more details, avoiding making any comment. Since Luca had no criminal record, he concluded, he could hold out some hope, even though the concept of personal consumption was not contemplated by the legislation of the country. They were in the hands of the judge. His advice was to co-operate, by revealing the name of his supplier. He got to his feet, ran a hand through his quiff, sucked in his belly and stuck out his chest. Why, he asked, of all the possible hiding places had he chosen a place guarded by the army—or had it been a delivery?

Luca understood that it was impossible to make him see reason. He couldn't understand why that boy, Kacem, had had him fall into a trap. Luca said he had never seen that bag full of hashish before the two soldiers picked it up. He swore to that. He suspected that his guide had been bribed by someone in the police force. The consular official restricted himself to replying—but in a whisper—that the arrest of a foreigner, who owned a house in the White City, amounted to an opportunity for the authorities to make an example. Unfortunately—and the volume of his voice went back to normal—the evidence against him was irrefutable. But they would get to work on the problem. Luca ought to show that he was willing to co-operate. The inspector was a good person. Did Luca wish to contact anyone?

Yes. He begged the man to go the Casino Judío that very evening. He would have recognized Señora Martinez, Señora Jaima Martinez, thanks to her unmistakable appearance. She was small, she had a big face, dyed red hair, she wore a lot of make-up . . . would he tell her what had happened and explain to her that money was not a problem? Irene was rich, the bank account in the White City was in both of their names . . . Message received, the official had cut him short with a nod in the direction of the door. They would speak again in the prison parlatory after Luca had seen the investigating magistrate in charge of the case. It would be better if he co-operated with the authorities and helped them in their investigation, and he was not to worry. The official would go to see that lady before the cocktail party at the Berber cultural centre, or immediately afterwards.

What glued him to the table around which bustled the warlocks, the witches with iguana eyelids, the exorcists, the specialists in surgery, in alchemy, was that word, analyses. The prison guard murmured it when placing a bowl and a bottle on the floor before grabbing Luca's hand and pressing it to the board-like hardness beneath the cloth of his trousers. Monsieur was lucky, he said bending over him, they were carrying out analyses. Why didn't they have a little fun: "Fuck-fuck *bueno, bueeeeno*". And when Luca freed his hand with a jerk: "*Hijo de puta!*". His face very close to Luca's, the man spat. "Son of a bitch, you will be everybody's cunt, inside." He went back to the door and locked it.

As he dried his forehead on his pyjama sleeve, Luca had already begun to repeat the magic formula to himself, analyses, analyses. He fell headlong through the funnel of the letter "y", plunging down tunnels and meanders along which the word echoed, until he found himself in the middle of the miasma-saturated laboratory in which alembics and phials bubbled. He was bound. There was a tube up his arse and someone was forcing his mouth open, splitting his lip, to insert the length of connecting pipe—the subject of a properly conducted analysis is first reduced to the condition of a chicken on the spit. The purpose of the high priestess Jaima Martinez and of Irene, the purpose of the alchemist Gordon Ritts-Twice and of the phoney beggar woman with the skinned plastic doll hanging from her breast even now as she was engrossed in inserting the tip of the catheter into a little ampoule, was to transform him. The little boy, pardoned for his sin—but what sin, who had held him still, who had stopped him from slipping out, slipping out from where? who?—had been chosen. It was he, it was really he. On account of his name. Having crossed the darkness of the first syllable (*lu*na moth in the mud), it finally emerged in the fresh, limpid Egyptian dawn, of a *ka* of rocks in the sun. Mummy's little spider had mutated. His muscles, his tissues, his matter, had become a chlorophyll-green philosopher's stone, capable of photosynthesis, the vegetable rock on which he would build his church.

Shaken by shivers, he was feverish. He urinated in the bucket and swallowed long draughts from the bottle. The water tasted of chlorine. He felt better. Jaima would testify in his favour, exonerate him. The boy would be arrested. They had no proof that that bag belonged to Luca. The cemetery was teeming with criminals. The Great Widower would step in. They were carrying out analyses. It was like a circle closing. They were all around him, their faces changed into severe masks, the servant Maria, *Alfredinus salvificus*, Kacem in his wig, an Atlantic whale, fatso with the truncheon, the inspector, a black sphinx, a girl skinned alive … they were crooning the lullaby that was none other than the endless repetition of his name, even Lady Weathergood was among them, and all the other characters of a distant nightmare, a cardinal held up by a little boy at whose feet crouched a monkey, a painter who moved his head in jerks, making the golden crest of his hair vibrate, a moustachioed retired colonel: "Luca! Luca!" Let them open him, let them search him, let them take out what was pulsing inside him, what was throbbing inside him, he felt pain no more despite the blows that were falling on his head, his shoulders, his back … Marta was shaking him. A man in uniform. A whole day and a whole might must have passed since his meeting with the consular official. It was morning once more. Hesitant, he was standing in the weighing room. The marine light coming in from the window obliged him to keep his eyes half shut. The bag was on the floor. His clothes on a chair. Behind the desk sat a small hyperthyroidal man in uniform who was telling him to get dressed, if he preferred he would leave him alone, even though by then their acquaintanceship was … and his watery eyes gleamed. He must have felt like a nice shower. Hygiene was the most important thing, was it not? They were all sorry about the misunderstanding, the lads too, but anyone would have made the same mistake. Each package was wrapped in plastic, sealed, in packets of exactly fifty grams … who could have imagined that it was one of their most common spices, cumin, one of the basic ingredients of the local cuisine, which had the colour and the consistency of *kif*? Monsieur should have been more careful. Someone had pulled a fast one on him. They, the army, and the police, were duty bound to protect foreigners, who were welcome in the White City providing that they behaved well … Luca slipped off his pyjamas and threw them on the ground. He put on his clothes. He couldn't wait to be out of that room. The leaves hung limply from his bag, pallid. The rhizomes would have to be replanted as soon as possible.

Unfortunately, the inspector added, one small problem remained. The analyses cost money, and the scant funds earmarked by the ministry ... So saying, he took Luca's wallet from the table. Luca nodded: let him help himself. He felt a curious sensation, the effect of the contraction of the abdominal muscles followed by their relaxation; he observed the man's fingers, the square finger tips that had entered his arse, as they caressed the edges of the bank notes, take out a few, linger in mid-air, then slip out another and another again. Thanks to the absurdity of the pretext—analyses to distinguish between a spice and a drug—everything had been cleared up. No trap, no frame-up. They had frightened him in order to extort money from him. Fortunately he had taken the wallet with him, without listening to Jaima. What would that money be transformed into? A little jewel for the policeman's wife? A fat tup? Toys for the children?

Monsieur, the inspector resumed, was not to bear a grudge against his lads. Little incidents of this kind happened everywhere. Luca was to avoid making a scandal, or talking to the press. It was important for him to be able to continue coming freely to the White City, if he had understood aright he had a garden, and what finer thing than the flowers, the animals, the birds, boom! boom! hunting too was an excuse to take a walk and breathe in some pure air ... he shook Luca's hand and smiled, revealing his yellow incisors—a rat surprised in the flour sack. It had been a pleasure meeting him. If Luca should need anything, he could count on him: it was the simplest of operations, snip, snip. Among educated persons it was possible to joke. He asked Luca to accept his apologies.

Once he got home, Luca realized just how exhausted he was. The light hurt his eyes. The whistling of the birds drove him crazy. He put his bag at the foot of the bed and drew the curtains. Disconnected the telephone. He rummaged through the medicine cabinet in the bathroom, avoiding looking at his face in the mirror. When he found Irene's sleeping pills, he swallowed one, two, and washed them down with a glass of whisky. He fell asleep immediately.

At the sight of these creatures in need of love, Mohammed made a face. Luca pointed out the bed ready to receive the irises. The gardener shook his head. By gestures—and he couldn't have been clearer—why not plant them somewhere else? he suggested, in a secluded place from where, when the heads had revived, and if they were presentable, they could transfer them to a place in full view? But since the master was gesturing at him to keep his ideas to himself, he stiffened. With a tilt of his chin, Mohammed indicated the wall that separated their garden from that of the neighbours. Paying no further heed to him, or to what he was trying to say, Luca went into the flower bed. Moved to pity by his aspect, by his gait, Mohammed wrenched the bag from his hands and took out the little spade.

The operation lasted a few minutes. The sedulous gestures that the man usually reserved for plants were cursory. He dug unwillingly, as if instead of these precious irises the holes were intended for potatoes. He laid the rhizomes in the bottom of the holes without breaking up the soil and without taking the trouble to open out the roots. He tamped down the earth over the neck of the leaves without having cleared the heads of the withered ones, and without bothering if any living ones were left imprisoned beneath the soil. He went away. The appearance of Alima, one of his two daughters, gave Luca a certain pleasure. Standing still on the edge of the lawn, the girl was looking at the irises. They were rare, he explained to her, very rare, and he had to repress the temptation to tell her about just what kind of adventure they were the result. To tell the truth, the way they looked in the late afternoon light, the limp leaves with sticks protruding from them on which the withered flowers looked like waste paper, induced him to justify himself. The girl ran away.

After long contemplation of his *florentinas*, which would soon reacquire vigour and would be joined by exemplars of other spontaneous species, thus transforming that little plot of land into a corner of paradise with a background painted in soft and scintillating colours; the nucleus, the model, of the new garden, Luca collapsed into a wickerwork armchair, and set to leafing through a magazine on the genus *Gynandriris* and correlated families. His arms and legs were aching, and his swollen lip was throbbing. He would see to the fertilizing the following day. A shout came from the porter's lodge, followed by a brief but heated argument. The gardener was coming back up the path. He was carrying a rubbish bag at arm's length, holding it away from his body as if it contained something repugnant. He loomed over Luca. Since he, uncomfortable, was feigning to be so absorbed in his reading that he had not noticed his presence, Mohammed took the book from his hand. No trace of rage remained on his face. Yet the gestures with which, having deposited the bag at Luca's feet, he was intimating that he open it, expressed an authority and a determination that the young man could not resist.

Swollen with sap, the flesh shot through with pale blue veins, the beard on the sepals, packed close to one another, emerging from the luxuriance of the ensiform leaves: the bag was full of them. Mohammed was repeating the gesture he had made before, indicating the neighbouring garden, and smiling at him the way a father would smile at a child after having imparted a lesson he feared might have been too severe, in order to say to him: "Have you understood, finally?" while asking him at the same time: "Will you forgive me?" They grew in the properties of all the *nazrani*, he explained, pointing to the Vieille Montagne. Before the American had had him eliminate the irises, these beds had also been full of them. The neighbour's gardener had been happy to rid himself of them. Was it for this that he had uprooted all those magnificent roses that had bloomed again after years of neglect and at the cost of all that work? Luca bent over the sack and, taking out a bloom, he examined it. A *florentina*—the smell of a sweaty groin. Down below, the houses of the White City were beginning to turn pink.

The giant went into the flower bed. He stooped over the clumps that had just been planted. He tore them up, ripped away the leaves, breaking and shredding the stems, savaging the flowers and mashing the buds. Blindly, on his knees, he sought the rhizomes in the earth and then he put the pieces in his mouth. Careless of his smarting lip and of the bitter taste, he chewed them fiercely, spitting them out when they were reduced to pulp. The gardener moved away, horrified. The slaughter over, staggering with fatigue, the giant got to his feet. His head was spinning and his ears were buzzing. A cry rose up on the still air. There was the whirr of a blackbird's wings. Luca was weeping. Living names resounded in his ears, wild irises blazed in the glittering of a hypnotic iris, but once they ended up in his spider's web, absorbed by his aching tongue, they were reduced to mere flowers, to dead words. He made up his mind. He would go upstairs to pack a suitcase and he would leave. He would go to the airport and he would force a pilot to take off and carry him far away from this accursed city. He parked his car near the Casino Judío.

He was walking quickly, and he bumped into someone, a man who opened and closed his arms around him and held him prisoner. The man stank of sweat and gin and wore a djellaba with wide sleeves like a kimono. He released Luca, he wasn't the fat guy from the cemetery, he wasn't bald, he had a mop of white hair and a face baked brick red by the sun. Careless of the scarlet pelargonium that was budding from one of his nostrils, he told Luca that it was a pleasure to see him, dear boy, he had meant to phone, but what had happened to him? He looked awful! Had he been rolling about in a pigsty? Was Irene with him? Had she recovered?

Luca felt as if he were dreaming. The togaed Roman, who with a fluttering movement of his little hand took a handkerchief out of his pocket and held it to his nose, was telling him that on hearing the news of poor Hans Peter's death he had rushed to the White City: the funeral would be held with the pomp worthy of a cardinal, one could rely on Isidro's sense of choreography, it was going to be a lark, they were burying him on the day after tomorrow in that enchanting cemetery ... and almost as if this word had triggered an inevitable association of ideas in him, kindling a gleam in his colourless eyes, was Luca proceeding with the garden, or had he given up his plans? Luca stammered something. Bending over Luca—his face, from so close, seemed more macerated and cured than baked, a leathern mask that concealed a little boy with a terrified look—Ritts-Twice said that he understood his passion for the White City. He understood it because he shared it, despite the political situation. They were made of the same stuff, the two of them. He swallowed, the blood in his throat had caused a coughing fit. And, clearing his throat: Luca was the first to know that his years of patience had been rewarded. The news was not to go any farther, but the house that he had found was marvellous. The deal, interminable because the owner had been unwilling to sell at first, was almost concluded. Luca said that it was late, he had to go.

The other man, staring at him, was prattling on about how lucky he was to be young, what could be more pleasant than passing *l'heure bleu* in the arms of a dusky beauty? The funeral cortège was to leave from Dar Sultàn. They would see each other there. He kissed him on the cheek. He hoped Luca would have fun with the pretty he had a date with, but he ought to be careful. Going around in that state—he brushed the blood-stained upper lip with his index finger—was tantamount to flaunting habits that demand discretion. Had he still not learned that the most exquisite blows are the ones that leave no marks? All the best to Irene.

Once he had passed the beggar woman, Luca turned. Having ascertained that the whore from the Late Empire had disappeared, he turned back. Inside the hall. Up the stairs. The bar. Naval rooms. Old men, sunk in their armchairs on the last cruise, stared into space as the sky faded into twilight on the other side of the windows. At a table four women were playing cards. As he had expected, she, the traitor, the procuress who promoted irises fit for amateurs, the Señora who deserved to sit at the cash desk of a nursery-concentration camp, was in the room at the back, the same one as before, on the gilt settee, between the two vases of *Monstera deliciosa*. Eyes goggling, she leaped to her feet, dropping her handbag. For a moment, they faced each other. Her jowls were trembling; toad, reptile, wretched iguana. She was not a dwarf. The torso was normal. It was her legs. The giant made to speak, but with one bound she was upon him, soft, warm, sticky. To anyone who had chanced to look into the room, the scene—the salamander clinging to the young man, her muzzle pressed against his stomach, her little paws locked around his hips while from her lips came that whimper, that slobbery gurgling, *niño, niño querido*, thank God he was safe and sound—would have seemed like the union between a cannibal beast and a human. Luca, now, felt that this creature covered with warts, panting, smelling of old age, of camphor, of cologne, of feet, of garlic, of poverty, was the incarnation and distillate of an ancient femininity, of a perennial femininity, the spongy mystery alluded to by the circle drawn on the walls of the caves at Lascaux and Altamira, the retractile sea anemone, the girl who masturbated thinking of her salty seaman, her crusader: the bitch, the nanny goat, the mother, the death underlying every fairy tale with a happy ending. He had to say something, but his head, his mouth, was full of cotton. The iguana detached herself from him. In her eyes that African ferocity glittered once more. They were bastards, she said, damned bastards, when she got her hands on that traitor ... The only important thing was that *el niño* was out, that she had managed to have him freed. She would never have forgiven herself had she been too late ... five, seven years in that sewer of a prison ... the remorse, the anguish, imagining the torments they would have subjected him to, the tortures ... she would have gone mad: "*Loca, mi niño*". She had understood how much she cared for him.

Gradually, listening to her, Luca entered a new world, a reality that had been revealed to him slowly, predictably, since it developed in accordance with a sole drive, in line with a sole logic: money. In order to continue their trafficking undisturbed, the generals in power, the drug lords, needed to toss the odd titbit to the hungry masses, furious about rampant corruption.

Jaima realized that she had been silly to tell him that Islamic integralism was an element of local colour. Even that delinquent, that Kacem, whom she had known since he was a little boy ... the country was no longer what it used to be. The climate was a sinister one. Clouds on the horizon. A foreigner, an infidel, caught red-handed in a holy place, in their cemetery ... if she hadn't realized the kind of risk involved in the enterprise, it was because she had known the White City in its heyday, she had, the White City of the free port, the happy years in which foreigners were permitted to do anything they wished, in the grand hotels they used to dance until dawn, and in the brothels there was no creature, regardless of speciality or age, who cost more than a head of lettuce or a bag of olives.

She went on, telling him that just as soon as the consular official had put her in the picture she had dashed home, and had unpicked the mattress—she had never trusted the banks— before dashing off to the police station. As luck would have it the inspector was an old acquaintance. It had proved impossible to get him to admit that the boy had been bribed by them. After an endless argument she had laid her nest egg on the desk. It had been the decisive move. Replacing the four kilos of black mountain hashish with four kilos of common and garden spice would be child's play for M'sieu le commissaire, would it not? A ploy that, unfortunately, had cost a lot. And here, after a sigh, staring at him hesitantly ... since good accounts are reckoned by good friends ... Luca was stunned. The sum he would have had to return to her corresponded roughly to half the amount Irene had sent to the White City bank for the work on the house and the cost of living there for the first year.

Hashish or cumin or whatever, he observed—his voice betrayed an enormous fatigue—he had been abandoned there by the guide that she had found for him. If he had gone to the cemetery alone ... and before Jaima could reply, he added that those irises, those oh so costly irises, grew in all the gardens. He did not understand how an expert in flora could have been enthusiastic about the idea that a such a common, such a vulgar species could constitute the beginning of a collection. He silenced her, for his mind was made up. He was quitting, he was going to leave.

The iguana was numbed, under formaldehyde once more, inside the jar: woman no longer, but a little monster fit for a *Wunderkammer*. If this was his gratitude for her having got him out of that mess, she hissed, five years, seven, the inspector couldn't have been clearer ... let him do without repaying her. He was right. The responsibility was hers. It was her mistake. She had thought that *el niño* had balls—a gesture of the paw in the preserving fluid, a floundering to conjure up something rounded—she had thought that he clearly understood the importance of the food with which a plant nourishes itself ... here the professional laid one paw on her breast; she caressed it slowly, voluptuously, through the soft angora sweater. Given that the young gentleman was frightened, she murmured— gazelles chased one another in her eyes—given that now of all times, at the crucial moment, he had decided to back out ...

Luca got to his feet. But the maelstrom of his metamorphosis was enveloping him, overwhelming him, inevitably finishing up by depositing him in the middle of the barren plain in which, stretched out on his belly, he was sucking, nibbling at her nipples: and he was her blissfully happy pup. Slipping one hand into his pocket he feigned an erection. He said that he would bring her the money the following day. Sitting on the sofa, Jaima watched him as he went off. She had won the game, but she regretted not having had enough fun. Something, in *el niño*, had awakened an appetite in her. She saw the armchairs, the television, the lace; she was nude in the mirror of the buffet, the torso the little legs the thighs trembling under the running fingers of that madman who ordered her to lie down, to be ready, and before spanking her would pinch her little bum hard, tell her to be a good girl, and not to whine, slutty little girl, smutty little girl ... she was getting sentimental as she grew older: "Hassan! Hassan!" With a shout she summoned the waiter. A little damp, the she-dog sat there, waiting for her sherry with ice.

Kacem was not in the café. The proprietor denied knowing

him. Then, faced with the insistence with which the *nazrani* with bloodshot eyes and muddy clothes described that mass of curls over and over again, he admitted it: Kacem worked there occasionally, he had vanished, perhaps he had left, he didn't know for where nor did he know when he would return. Back home, Luca rushed into Irene's changing room. He took the suitcase out of the wardrobe. The telephone in the bedroom was ringing. When they had made the bed they had reconnected it. He looked at his wife's clothes. The orange caftan, the velvet tunics designed by a friend of hers, all the same but in different colours, still impregnated with her smell of mushrooms, of beaver. An old skirt with a floral pattern. Cursing the telephone that continued to ring, he ran into the bedroom and grabbed the receiver.

From the other end, an explosion of abuse. Were they all deaf? stupid? wasn't there a single servant? what with the nightmare it was to get a line to that place? and the telephone forever occupied? What kind of organization was this?

Luca had never heard the Great Widower so furious. His words tripped over one another as he talked, in a voice that the satellite echo made metallic. He was in the United States. The boy, that boy, had fallen sick: in Salonika. To Turkey on a motorbike! They were made for each other, those two, he in that city in the middle of nowhere, the operator didn't even know the dialling code, hours before he got hold of the information service, but that damned house was going to be sold, so help me God he was going to put an end to her whims ... he had had them flown home in a hospital plane, sooner or later the time always comes when daddies come in handy, now they were in first class hands, he was the best, the one who had operated on the President ... she and her ideas about letting any old quack lay hands on her ...

There would have been a logical gap if, in the meantime, the Great Widower had not added something. Something that left Luca indifferent, Luca who was beginning to realize that he knew it already, that he had always known it. He had said "nodules" in a disgusted voice, then "lymphocytes", then "metastasis", then some initials, then other words. He had told Luca not to go, that there was no point in crying over spilt milk. He corrected himself, mumbling poor boy, that he loved him (it was the first time and it wasn't true), that he would keep him in the picture, and that Maria was there and would see to everything. No, he couldn't speak to her. The hospitals there were not like the hospitals in the White City: "half board for the half-assed". Luca was struck by the speed with which things were happening. They were off, said the Great Widower, this time they were both going to come off: "Total mastectomy, could have been worse. Buck up, son". Luca saw two spheres rising, pink like the cranium of a doll, half way through the sky the moon was a raw hamburger. A mare skinned alive was neighing; down below, the lights were coming on in the manger-scene that was the White City. He wasn't listening any more, the matter was of no importance. He was outside. In the darkness. Digging. When the hole was wide and deep enough, he huddled down inside it, as far inside it as he could get. As if awakening from a sleep on the beach, he felt an ancient sense of protection. Smothered. Emerging from its lethargy, an enormous chlorophyll-green spider ran in the night, attracted by the smell of milk emanated by the bodies of human beings.

PART THREE

IRIS JUNCEA NUMIDICA

I

THE BLOOD of all the peoples who had followed one another to this land and these mountainous cliffs, Phoenician merchants and Roman colonists, Berbers and Vandals, Fatimid fanatics from Sudan and Spanish Jews, Balkan Turks, ran in the veins of Jaima Dolores de la Concepción Martinez y Martinez, native of the White City and descendant of a race that worshipped gods greedy for children, gluttons for foreskins: the lady was an aristocrat, the last scion of an ancient and cosmopolitan family. This at least was what the iguana kept telling Luca, taking advantage of the pigeon's ignorance of the laws that governed the social life of the city—strict as those of any provincial township—in the belief that such magniloquence would ease the smart of the humiliations that her status as short-legged orphan bastard had always caused her. By then, the botanist did not even notice when in her tales she chanced to confuse Venus and Astarte, the khalif with the sultan, or to get a date wrong by a few centuries. Besides, any child of this city overlooking two seas, even if illiterate, had been fed since infancy, as well as on bread and beans, on a common legend, familiar as the chirping of the cicadas on summer afternoons or the roiling of the waves in the Straits when the wind was in the east, and was therefore able, especially if induced to by need—and perhaps with the aid of a few pipes of hashish—to make foreigners believe whatever he wanted. The daughter of One-eyed Pepa, an Andalusian skivvy who died bringing her into world, a woman so ugly that she could not go out of the house without becoming the target of mockery and rotten vegetables, and of her master, the pious Sidi Alì, who one evening and one evening only, out of gallantry, drunk on date liquor, had raped her in the kitchen and then abandoned the fruit of his old semen near the Dominican monastery, Jaima Martinez, the little girl with the big, square face who grew up in an orphanage on the strength of novenas said while kneeling on dried beans, and of ginger cakes if, when she was beaten by the director, she would admit that she had not washed properly, and who would unhesitatingly use her tongue to trace slavery crosses on his hands and chest, on his shaggy belly, on his legs and feet, on the floor, Señora Martinez, this outcast of White City society, this pariah officially avoided by *Oncles* and Aunties and Grand Duchesses, who frequented her only when their desperate winter solitude had touched rock bottom, this bawd accustomed to satisfying the whims of the tourists drawn there by the reputation of the place, only to blackmail them thanks to the complicity of the prostitutes of both sexes among whom she cultivated her only friendships, this expert in botany who would have been prepared to pretend to be an expert in zoology or in astronomy as long as she could buy a walk-in wardrobe, took pleasure in inventing fabulous, muddled genealogies especially for an insane young man: without realizing that she was prompted to ennoble her own past solely by the desire to shine in his eyes.

Like any ordinary old woman, Jaima—old Jaima who many years before, to survive, had learned to dissimulate her feelings so well that she convinced herself that she no longer had any— conjured up for the aspiring iris collector, who sat there listening to her befuddled with barbiturates and whisky, the splendours of the lion hunts organized by an ancestor of hers of English origin who had married a Kabil *sharif*. She did not fear even the commonest cock and bull story, nor did she retreat before the most hackneyed of stereotypes, and so, in her hoarse voice, she boldly told him of one of her Spanish great-aunts, the aristocratic abbess of a convent, who, after falling madly in love with a bull-fighter for whom she hung up her wimple, wound up organizing *tableaux vivants* for the Anglo-Egyptian troops stationed in Port Said.

They no longer met in the Casino Judío. During that spring, which was plunging into summer like a driverless cart into a precipice, every afternoon, towards dusk, they would meet in some bar, in some café in the *medina*. At first, having learned of the latest operation Irene had undergone in the United States,

Jaima had exhorted Luca to run to her side, without paying any attention to the Great Widower. The White City, accursed swamp, was not a fit place for two kids like them, married, in love. Although it was a critical moment, in the name of their friendship, she would help him find a buyer for the house.

The obstinacy expressed by the little boy in declaring that he would never abandon that garden, because it was his sole reason for living, had given the lady a pleasure as intense as it was unforeseen. Although she attributed the cause to the fact that, as was known, the hard nuts are the tastiest to crack, anyone who had had occasion to observe her as she pranced through the streets of the centre arm in arm with her foreigner, tricked out in spanking new suits, soaked in sweat with the effort of keeping up with him, would have put a different interpretation on her reaction to the news that *el niño*, unexpectedly, was staying on. In fact, the comments of the waiters in the restaurants where, more and more often, they would dine together—or better, where Jaima would devour gargantuan quantities of food, as the young man looked on, drinking whisky after whisky—would allude to the nature of the pleasure that that old woman must have got from the young *nazrani*—and was clearly able to give to him, judging by his wasted look. Sniggering, the youths in their white shirts and bow-ties would whisper all kinds of obscenities into one another's ears, should Jaima, a bit tipsy, stretch out a hand greasy with fries, to adjust the knot of the tie that her bemused escort had put on to make her happy. Luca's gaze, lost, fixed on the dwarf's breasts squeezed into a polka dot blouse, tickled those bastards pink. When words whose meaning was unequivocal came to her ears, and despite the fact that she had inherited from her mother the habit of being called far worse things—the insult is still an art among the inhabitants of the White City—the lady would get cross. In a voice that was a little too loud, running her fingertips through her freshly-dyed curls and obtaining the twofold result of sprucing up the latter while wiping the grease off the former, she would tell *el niño*, for the twentieth time, about her Martinez y Martinez forebears, a horde of cosmopolitan young men originally scattered throughout the most picturesque parts of the Mediterranean: "Seville, Marseilles, Ventimiglia, the Versilia" (the volume of her voice would rise to cover the sniggers and calls of "old woman", "madwoman", "witch", which came like lashes from the back of the room) "Antioch, Alexandria, Tunis, Algiers" (she was almost shouting, the warts on her big face seemed like carnations on the verge of budding) " . . . all of them wound up in this shithouse the White City, the homeland of *maricones*, a haunt for good for nothings . . . " After shooting a fiery glance all around, and, having verified that all the waiters had beaten a prudent retreat to the kitchen, Jaima, calmer, would pick up her tale again, in which Pablo the shoeshine boy became the pallid fop who had taken refuge on these shores in order to flee the attentions of a necrophiliac Spanish grandee, a peddler who sold fritters in the street was transformed into the celebrated womanizer summoned by the Sultan in person to reorganize his harem, and Carlito, a stable lad with a circus, rose to the rank of the black sheep of the family, the one who had abandoned wives and children, and lost a prime position, to follow the pirouettes of a Slavic acrobat of legendary beauty . . . Jaima was panting. She knocked back a glass of wine. She used a napkin to mop her brow. Another sip. A gargling. And, coquettish, she gave a sideways look at the boy who, apart from the director of the orphanage, had proved the best audience she had ever had, she concluded that men like her forebears weren't born any more, all with perfect teeth, slim hips, masters of the tango and the dance—the reptile wiggled her hips causing the chair to groan—" . . . in dancing the dance that we women prefer, think of your wife, *niño*, do you make her cry out? old Jaima is well aware that the little ones like you are the dirtiest ones, when they get stuck in . . . "

The revelation of this sensuality disturbed Luca. His guide was no longer the omniscient monster, the wild beast to be venerated. Outside the jar of formaldehyde, removed from the setting of the Casino Judío, intrepidly plodding along the pavements of the White City gilded by the light of the setting sun, Jaima had mutated from iguana into woman. There was something heroic in the way she managed to bolt down steamed fish and red wine and at the same time call up, puffing and spluttering, the splendours of her family: her voracity touched him, her eloquence distracted him from the desperate thoughts he had brooded over during the day, and the gruff sweetness with which she demonstrated her affection for him allayed his suffering. The cheap eau-de-Cologne with which she perfumed herself sharpened her smell of garlic, feet, and sardines instead of covering it. Framed by those arrogant little hats (her own creations, or so she said) her face oozed appetites and whims. Beneath those jackets, lent refinement with showy satin flowers pinned to the lapels, the celestially pendulous breasts rose and fell in a gush of festive consent. She was alive and ready to give herself, this prodigious female! While Luca was proud to hang around at her side to the point that he took for admiration the amused cruelty that at their passing glittered in the eyes of the men sitting on the terraces of the cafés, and especially of the women, he now yearned to find himself alone with his sweetheart, and one of those evenings, he would overcome his shyness and persuade her to let him take her home (on this point, until then, Jaima had been irremovable, they always said goodbye on the boulevard, and *el niño* did not know where she lived), and then he would beg her to let him come in to drink one for the road: but the basically natural course of their idyll was blocked, and re-routed, by an incident.

Having arrived first at the bar where they were to meet, Jaima, in pastel pink, her lids black with bistre framing the watery cornea like the open valves of a mussel, greeted him with a little cry of joy, followed by one of those smiles that struck Luca as being laden with a boundless, African promise, and probably they really were, since they were enough to silence the other customers. But on observing the cautious way *el niño* was coming up, the awkward way he pushed back the chair, and the stiffness of his posture once seated—he was paler than usual, the circles under his eyes deeper, the eyes lighter, while his face seemed even thinner—the lady's face grew dark. Had someone just given him a kick in the balls? she asked him point blank. Had some whore squeezed his nuts too hard? Vain were his attempts to justify his indisposition by attributing it to an influenza. His upper lip, still swollen, was beaded with sweat. Jaima punched him in the abdomen with her fist. Without giving him time to get his breath back—Luca, on the verge of falling off the chair, betrayed himself with a shout, giving her a cadaverous stare—and oblivious to the silence that had fallen on the room, she began to unbutton his shirt. While two tables away a Belgian widow put down her dry martini and summoned the waiter to order him to invite that duo to leave the premises, otherwise neither she nor her friends would ever set foot in the place again, from the lips of Jaima Martinez y Martinez—and she was once more the supreme iguana, a prehistoric saurian nailed to a meteorite by all the suffering in the universe—there came a moan. On Luca's stomach there was what she feared.

Had he done it to himself? she demanded. And the speed with which she regained control by assuming the colourless tone was worthy of a great actress. Why in that place, exactly? she continued, running a fingertip over the wound, as if opening up one's stomach above the navel, albeit superficially, were the most normal pastime in the world. Didn't he know that by cutting a couple of fingertips he would have had much more *sangre* at his disposal?

El niño gave in. In a sing-song voice, barely cracked by the stabbing pains that assailed him if he breathed deeply, he listed the ingredients that were fermenting in the bucket full of culture gruel, lizards included. And since she nodded, understanding, maternal, he continued, telling her that that same morning, after cutting himself with the nail scissors, bent over the recipient, pressing his belly, he had managed to milk himself on his own, and the milk that had poured out—blood, he corrected himself sketching a smile, and she was right, only a little had come out—had been enough to stain his magic philtre pink.

Jaima's expression changed. Her face became inscrutable, a rugged rock to which two mussels clung, the excrescences of warts and cysts forming a static picture between the harsh contours of the nose and the chin, around the mouth. Recently she had got into the habit of lying to Ritts. The job was done, she would tell him. When the bastard insisted, reminding her of their agreement, repeating that he was in a hurry, maintaining it was time to talk to Luca of Archìa, of the Countess of Andurain, of the end of Manolo's brothel—he could get hold of a quick-witted fellow, a butcher whose grandmother lived in the neighbour-hood, but she was not to worry, all they needed was a bit of strong stuff and that idiot would go right off his head—she would reassure him promising him that there would be no need to go as far as that. She knew him well enough to understand why he wanted to lure Luca to that deserted stony place that plunged down to the sea below, and then stuff him with drugs ... the poor fool that she was! At her age! To deceive herself with fantasies worthy of a girl with the hots! She had known since their first meeting that that gigolo was not her little pup! With an effort of will the lady drove out the memory of the last evenings, during which, instead of working, instead of talking about gardening, she had let herself get carried away, demented slut that she was, by the illusion that she had found a homunculus capable of appreciating her, and she had given herself over to the pleasure of being seen at his side, of being with him. Him, her boyfriend? Straightening up on the chair, as Luca was buttoning up his shirt, she observed that he had learned the lesson of the cemetery. He was an expert in fertilizer, now. He was ready. In the meantime she thought that she would teach him the difference between milk and blood, between woman and man: she would make him understand what a cauldron was, by stirring the infernal crucible of the leg-ends of the White City until she distilled from it the fatal potion that she would make him drink to the last drop, as true as she was what she was, they all said so, a witch. Why, she asked, didn't they go somewhere else? It was stuffy in there. Far from indiscreet ears, in a quiet place, she would explain to him where there grew an extremely rare iris, the rarest of the varieties that bloomed in the region ... "The *juncea numidica*?" Luca asked in a whisper. Jaima contemplated him with her ruthless gaze: the very one. The *juncea numidica* itself. Her desire to see the plan through, to get rid of this *maricón* who was incapable of dashing to his wife's side, was enhanced by the desire to revenge the wound that those nail scissors had inflicted, not only on the belly of the *nazrani* pigeon, but also on the amour propre of an ugly narcissist, inexhaustible like her, but faltering.

That chicken thought of the scalpel that was slicing up his better half and then huddled up like a foetus and cut his navel. He would appreciate the anecdote of the mangled legs, reduced to pulp: "My little legs, *niño*". Señora Martinez, who had begun her narrative from the climax, immediately realized that it was working. You just had to look at his face. Like a madwoman, the Countess, the Countess d'Andurain, had lashed out repeatedly with the iron bar, until Bébé de Mainville, who was holding the victim fast to the floor by pressing one foot down on her face ("He was so proud of his yellow buckskin boots, the poor shit!") had yelled enough, she should stop, calm down—before this one kicked the bucket too.

The young man and the woman were sitting beside each other on one of the cement benches of the belvedere behind the goldsmiths' mosque, above the Spanish Quarter. The breeze carried the odour of frying and laundry, blended with that of the rat poison with which the town authorities sprayed the pavements once a month. From an open window there came the music of a transistor radio. Despite the darkness, the lady had not failed to notice that, when she had pulled up her underskirt to show the scars on her legs, the boy had crossed his, swallowed, and he had slipped his hand into his pocket. The street lights came on in the avenue d'Espagne.

In a low voice, gazing fixedly ahead, Jaima told Luca the tale of the Countess: "It's time you knew the whole story. You mustn't be afraid, *niño*. At that time I cared for her, so very much ... " Her eyes were moist, and she smiled at him sadly. Then—the effect of the whisky and the tranquillizers or of the vastness of the night, moved by the token of friendship that this ill-used woman was giving him—Luca was overwhelmed by a wave of sentimentalism. They were alone, those two, two animals of the same threatened species, so tired of hiding that they had come out into the open on this terrace that jutted out over the sea like the prow of a ship run aground. As Jaima talked, her physical presence gradually faded, to give way to the swollen, sorrowful body of what now struck him as the history of the origins of their race. Only the voice of the dwarf remained, sketching in the outlines of a tragic and glorious tale: a tale that smacked of decay like her breath, and it was the mother and fountainhead of all tales, of all diseases. The bodies had been mangled. And this was why the limbs, the organs, writhed and quivered, prisoners of matter.

The old Levantine recalled Marga d'Andurain's arrival in the White City, fleeing from Paris after the Liberation, in order to escape a trial that would have concluded with a death sentence. A follower of the occultist Popov, a Russian mystic who had announced the advent of a new golden age, during the Nazi occupation of France, the Countess, a native of Bordeaux, had contributed to the ethnic cleansing that the world had need of. Even in exile here, during dinners with her intimate friends ("Bébé, Aqua Shawarbi, Marie-France de Chabrun, the archaeologist princess who studied the Isis legend, and Perla, Janie, Chichille, Jean-Loulou, your ancestors, *niño*, you should have seen what they were capable of in the garden"), Marga would repeat that she did not see what harm there was in amusing oneself with members of a race that was in any case destined to disappear, assessing their resistance to powerful sensations: contact with fire, the effect of electric shocks, and other stimuli, lack of sleep, force feeding ("they would use a rubber tube, handfuls of salt, and especially shit, they called it Jewish chocolate"), and apnoea in the bath tub: "Yes, *niño*. In the bath tub. How she would laugh, and how glamorous she was without being beautiful!"

But the events concerning flowers had taken place years afterwards. Was he tired? Cold? Did his tummy hurt? Let him get ready then. In the end all would be clear to him. The episode had begun with one of those moralization campaigns that periodically cause a shake-up in the habits of the people of the White City, precisely the way things were going now, and he knew something about that. Following the annexation of the free port to the state, a puritanical, bigoted state, which could not tolerate in its bosom the presence of that Sodom, of that Babylon, the Generals in power decided to close the brothels: "There was one for every three hundred inhabitants, more or less like the bureaux de change and the casinos. Half of the population, of those above twenty, lived thanks to the elasticity of the arseholes of the other half". Not even Manolo had managed to save his establishment, the most refined of all, despite the fact that his clientele numbered many well-known personalities. The militiamen, Muslims like all the riffraff that were now laying down the law, had attached seals to the main door giving onto calle Goya, now rebaptized sharia Omar Khayyàm. That was when Marga had put forward her proposal. Why not transfer the goods, all healthy, clean kids, subjected to medical check-ups—and if that sainted fellow Manolito had not taught them a trade they would have died of hunger or of fatigue in the fields—why not transport them to Archìa? *El niño* had probably never heard of Archìa. It was down there. Jaima pointed to the slopes of the promontory that closed off the bay to the west. Her hermetic profile struck him as like that of a chatelaine showing a subject the boundaries of her domains.

Then, having made her usual gesture to spruce up curls flattened by the humidity, she continued. Today Archìa was a pile of ruins smothered by vegetation. A large outcrop of rock screened the entrance. But in those days it had been a secluded residential area, ideal for those who wished to lead a quiet life. Manolo did not wait to be asked twice. One night, two carts drawn by oxen made their way up the old Portuguese drove road that followed the coast, thus leading the goods to safety. Marga saw to it that the kids kept quiet by pouring the contents of a couple of phials into the soup pot ... on observing Luca's earnest expression, Jaima felt satisfied. The moment was a solemn one.

Thanks to that woman's contacts, and she was a really sophisticated society lady—it was rumoured that even the secretary to the last Khedive of Egypt had fallen madly in love with her—business went full steam ahead at first. The coastguards received a large monthly sum. And so, although many foreign residents, following the annexation, had run for cover: some to Beirut, others to South America, and others again to some tropical island, every night the motor launches would cross the Straits showing no lights. On board there were lawyers, doctors, businessmen, even politicians and high-ranking churchmen who, overloaded with responsibilities and work commitments, appreciated the informal atmosphere of the Countess's place— also because the dictatorship of the old puppet-master on the far shore punished even the most innocent pastimes. Even a few Martinez y Martinez, not that they were *maricones*, would occasionally pop in at the villa, partly to say hello to their little cousin Jaima, Marga's *dame de compagnie*, and that's what she was, yes indeed, and partly because among Manolo's little suckling mice—this definition would fill the lady with a certain languorous pleasure similar to the one she got from piercing a blister with a needle—among those little trained animals there were some who were whiter of complexion and more expert than any female: "Smooth as butter, *niño*, and docile as pups, and when it came to discipline, she saw to that . . . " Those two old men, the one that had just died, the Cardinal, and the other, the gigolo from Barcelona, Isidro, also went to Archìa almost every day, as well as many other friends of theirs that Luca had probably met. He should try to question them, put them on the spot! He would have fun when he saw the looks on their faces!

The breeze brought a whiff of the stink of rat poison. Luca felt as if he were dreaming. He was entering the other White City, the capital of vice whose existence he had always sensed, even though it had vanished to give way to the summertime tourist destination of hairdressers who loved bodybuilders. It was as if the city of those days—at whose heart lay concealed a windswept village, the acropolis of adventurers and gangsters overhanging the sea, the vultures' nest surrounded by the remains of their meals scattered among the acacias and the eucalyptus trees in blossom—were embodied by the woman seated at his side. The wrinkled face of the last of the Martinez y Martinez, her mutilated body, her truncated legs, her sagging tits, were the living image, the sense, the essence, of the place as old as time in which he would cultivate his garden. "Listen, *niño*, listen ... " When in one of the rooms a client went over the score, and the bound boy screamed, Marga, down in the lounge, would put on a record and dance alone, embracing herself in her fox furs. It was consoling to think that human beings were the same all over, she used to say, in Paris the *danse électrique* was all the rage. And she would brandish her amber cigarette holder as if she wanted to insert the lit cigarette in some hole, in some cavity. She injected morphine without concealing the fact anymore, and she drank. She was drunk more and more often: "I'm sure you understand, *niño*."

Two men arm in arm were coming down the alley that led to the customs post. There was a burst of laughter, then the echo of their footsteps faded away. The moon was hidden by a cloud. Luca felt himself shrinking, his abdomen, his sternum, his retractile feelers, his ossified paws.

There came the first troubles with the police, the blackmail, the arrest of certain clients, then of Manolo. The problems grew greater and greater, income was derisory, and they were living on flour and beans. Marga sold her clothes and furs to the rag and bone men, the jewellery the German officers had given to her was worthless, trust those Jew bastards, all imitations. Even her friends had turned their backs on her, but instead of giving up she became more and more stubborn, determined to get by. Wrapped up in a sari, skeletally thin, she wandered smoking through the great empty villa, the kids were locked up in the cellar ... probably, at first at least, a woman like her, accustomed to reversals of fortune, would have thought that the situation would change. But the months went by, and not one visitor came anywhere near the villa. Even the police kept a wide berth. With hindsight, it could be said that the authorities, having got wind of what was going on, had preferred to ignore the matter to avoid a scandal of excessive proportions. By that time they were alone, she, Marga and Bébé. They ate once a day. Down in the cellar they handed out roots. But even though the kids were chained to the walls, it was frightening to go in with the buckets. The stink was indescribable.

Jaima sighed to conceal the pleasure she was feeling. The basic plot upon which she was embroidering with so much enjoyment had been supplied by Ritts. Nevertheless, however, among the hundred or more ways she had found to make ends meet, she really had been a servant in a brothel, and the madam really had put her though the mill. Much of this story, despite the English novelist's inspiration, was actually her own work. One day Marga decided to have the final experiments commence—brief pause. Ideas culled from her master, the great Popov. She was raving—the results of hunger and drugs. "The meat had a strange taste, cloying, but it was still meat, *niño*. You don't know what it means to starve for months on end." The boy had stayed alive all night, howling in his blood. In the morning he was dead. They had dragged him outside and buried him in the garden: "That's when the passion was born in me. You cannot imagine. After a few weeks the ground, still loose, was covered with wild flowers of all species."

The tiny arachnid, Marta's little spider, knew. The nexes of the chain of nature were inscribed in his genetic inheritance. The urgent pressure of the stream, the upwards thrust of the sap, the growth of the iris until the flourishing of its genital organs, were phases in a process that had its origin, its main-spring, in violence.

Who cares about innocuous transformations of matter! Who cares about the cadavers of old Muslims gradually decomposing in a cemetery! Mother Nature demanded freshly butchered meat, blood still hot, bones stuffed with warm marrow! Jaima was dwelling on the fact that after many years the extremely rare *juncea numidica* bloomed exclusively at Archìa, where it awaited the coming of its saviour, not only because the remains of Manolo's kids were buried there, but on account of the cir-cumstances of their torments, of their deaths: in chains for months in a cellar full of excrement, covered in sores, tormented by dysentery, reduced to beasts ... even two or three shepherds who chanced to pass by there "Berbers accustomed to doing it with goats, *niño*," went off cursing, spitting on the ground, without even asking for the loaves they had handed over in advance, and refusing to lay so much as a finger upon the little bundle of skin and shit that Bébé, after an inspection in the cellar to see who was in the best condition, had carried up in his arms and laid on one of the beds. And to think that in those rooms, until a short time before, bishops in incognito had plucked the wings of little angels, and wealthy married industrialists, married like him, had stretched out between the legs of the young boys to be used as toilets! They were dying like flies: "Like in your bucket of gruel, *niño*." The most terrible thing was the noise. One single moan, subdued but ceaseless, especially after Marga finished the injections. Although the walls were made of stone, she could no longer sleep. That racket was intolerable, she used to say. She had seen to shutting a few of them up in person; before going downstairs she put on a pair of waders, before smashing their skulls in with an iron. Bébé too had become strange. He talked to himself. Sitting on a rock, for hours and hours, he would look at the sea.

Señora Martinez's eyes were shining, shards of mica, obsidian. She would go for broke. She would be reborn, not just of average height, but also gifted with the most superficial of luxuries, a heart of gold, the last heir to an illustrious house! She cleared her throat. She had incurred the wrath of her mistress in order to save one of the boys. A couple of days after that, Marga had thrown herself into the sea and her body had never reappeared. But on the afternoon in question, having gone down to the cellar to see which of them was doing the most complaining, Marga had found Jaima bent over a blond boy: "A bit like you, *niño* . . . I was sorry for him. I was fiddling about with the padlock on his chain." In a calm voice the Countess asked her if she had decided to have them all finish up dangling on the end of a rope. Was she sure she was feeling all right? And she had kicked the blond boy in the face. From every corner, then, came the droning, terrible, inhuman, it seemed as if it were going to continue and grow in volume forever ... Marga snapped. Howling insults and abuse, she covered her ears, tearing her hair and banging her head against the wall before falling to the floor, in the shit, sobbing. Bébé appeared at the door. He was holding a pistol. Now they were upstairs, the three of them. Marga, wrapped in her sari soaked in piss, filthy with excrement, had detached a metal curtain rod. The traitor was already bound, a length of washing line. Bébé held her down. "She said good girl, you'll learn. Did I like to run? did I like to jump? Would I be happy to dance through the flowers with my little blond boy?" Jaima's voice was strident. She was cringing as if to resist an impact. She gnashed her teeth. Raised one arm. She was a fairy, waving her magic wand. Punctually, predictably, the spell was cast. A sunny room. Outside, the garden in bloom sloped down to the sea. A fluttering of butter-flies, a buzzing of bumble bees. Inside, in the silence of the hospital, the rod rose and fell, mangling the tibials and the extensors, shattering the kneecaps, flattening the soleus muscles, shattering the tibias and the fibulas, slashing the femorals, pulping the little white legs. The blood spattered all over, on the floor and walls. Bébé's boots, yellow like dogshit, yellow like the teeth of a little man in uniform sitting behind a desk, yellow like the *Iris juncea numidica*, were bedaubed with it: for this reason, only for this reason, he began to yell, entreating the Countess to stop. Luca's sight was blurred, his heart was racing. Jaima was giving off the heat of the stables. The cry came again. It was the siren of a ship coming into port, still hidden by the mist. The sea was a field of irises in bloom. There was no helping it. The spider drew its prey to itself. It clutched it close. Two tor-mented little children, both on the point of orgasm.

II

L ITTLE TITS—two eggs on a plate. Sterile little tits—a strand of albumen hanging from the finger. In the bark of the eucalyptus trees, in the carcass of the dog sleeping in the shade of a wall, in the wall itself, from which flakes of cement peeled off to powder his coat, in the patches of rust in the pail in which the countrywoman on her hunkers at the side of the road displayed her tomatoes, the agglomeration of corpuscles into clots that formed and broke up, amalgamating and separating in slow motion, was the proof that the primordial discharge of thromboses had occurred thousands of millennia before. Everything was dead. In the warm wind only fermentation, only putrefaction, was in progress.

Following Jaima's instructions, he parked the car where rue de la Vieille Montagne came to an end, at the top. Down below, Africa bathed its feet in the sea. But the palms, the eucalyptus trees and the acacias, even the pines, the cedars, in clumps, which until some time before would have seemed like coarse hairs on those phalanges steeping in the water, were now revealed to him as the barren simulacra of a phantom forest. The blocks of stone and boulders along the coast were not calluses or thickening caused by the running and play of the elephant-hide continent, but splinters of rock strewn about at random. Rather than baroque carcinomas on necrotic skin, the great abandoned villas, with their façades calcined by the salt spray and with the first bougainvillaeas sprouting from the gashes in the roofs, were masses of tumbledown walls, mounds of bricks in which snakes lurked. On looking up, instead of the rotundity of the buttock and the hairy chasm of the big negress's vagina, the sky was a motionless sheet, the twin of the marine one below. The seagulls wailed, professional mourners thousands of years late for the funeral of a vanished cadaver. A man in shirt sleeves came out of a gate. He was holding a jute sack inside which something writhed, scratched, hissed. Once across the road, he threw his burden into the ditch—then Bébé de Mainville, or perhaps it wasn't he, retraced his steps shuffling his feet. The light was radiant. It was one of those May mornings to which the White City owes its fame as an earthly paradise.

Luca, carrying the satchel containing his tools, slightly unsteady on his feet, began to make his way up the Portuguese track. Every one of the stones that paved it was a stone, with its sharp edges, fissures, fungi, moss and procession of ants, even though the path itself, were its coils to be contemplated from above, was a serpent rolling about in the warmth. Rock roses and lavender as far as the eye could see, snapdragon, *moricandia*, squill among the bryony, milk-vetch, mignonette, spurge—all the bushes, on that first windswept Atlantic spur that plunged down into the Straits, had short, contorted branches and hard leaves, wrinkled as rind, which when rubbed emanate the scents of a medieval pharmacopoeia. Then he crossed a stream, a gush of water from a pool covered with lesser celandine, among cushions of sage and campion. As the coast gradually sloped down towards the south to form a dark fjord, the trees grew thicker. He made his way forward into the shade of an oak forest that dipped down right to the water's edge. Stuffed birds posed, festoons of wild clematis hung from the branches, hartshorn plantain, gargoyles of cork, fans of ferns, maidenhair, myrtle, snails attacking fungi sticky with blight. In a clearing, the splendour of the fading blooms of an acacia. On the boulders, lichens like smears of fig jam dried and flaked off in the breath of the sea. Devilberries, Snow White-red, and others, hung from leafless bushes. He had been walking for more than an hour feeling like the worm in an apple. From the top of the mound on which the promontory ended, you could see another bay. He flopped down on the grass. There was a rustling. From behind the branches came some Sumerian goats, grazing, surrounded by horseflies that buzzed around glittering like precious stones: the goats stared at him with bistred eyes; bleating, they stretched out priestly beards before moving off swishing their flyswatter tails. Then came the goat-herd, a decrepit Berber quick to lift up his burnoose every time one of the animals presented him their hindquarters encrusted with faeces. He was leaning on a stick: "*Salaam aleikum*". "*Aleikum salaama*". To the far right, the eastern periphery of the White City was foam whipped up by the waves slapping against the feet of the dead mountains; to the left, where he had always thought there was the Cape after which began the stretches of Atlantic beach, a large rock protruded. Once more he heard the voice of his mistress, the chatelaine of those places. Down there the ruins of Archìa lay hidden.

The youth emerged from the same path. He was wearing a blue denim jacket, tight trousers and American trainers whose diffusion among the young local people was limited only by the price. On observing the boy coming up, big and gangling in that moon-landing footwear, Luca noted that his face held something oriental, Indian, which depended, more than on the cut of the almond eyes with which he was staring at him as if he had never come across a foreigner in all his life, on the fleshy alae of the nose, which the sweat had made glossy as two cowrie shells. Luca had the impression that he had seen the boy before, perhaps one summer, on some beach. Stressing the effort of his climb with much exaggerated puffing and blowing in order to conceal his embarrassment at the intrusion, the boy dropped down at Luca's side, and, panting, he said *hola amigo*, everything okay? in the tone with which a mountaineer would greet one of his climbing party on catching up with him on a ledge after hours of climbing. The contrast between all that effort and the body, which at a guess was a strong one because of the thick neck and the muscular forearms protruding from the sleeves of the denim jacket, dispelled Luca's impression of things Indian and aroused his suspicion. The listlessness of the boy's movements, his smell of eau-de-Cologne, the coquettish-ness with which, having taken a comb out of his pocket, now that his breathing was back to normal, he was titivating his hair, struck Luca as indicative of his intentions. He was one of those young bucks who cannot believe their luck when they bump into a tourist in a secluded spot, given that foreigners always have their pockets full of money, desirous as they are of purchasing one of the local goods that can be consumed only far from witnesses. As Luca had foreseen, the boy—and he was caressing his thigh in the excessively tight trousers—asked him once more if his *amigo* was well, really well, even though Luca had already replied. Faced with his silence, changing tactic, he came out with a trivial consideration about the fact that life was hard for those who were poor and were obliged to work. Then, as if suddenly remembering something of great importance, with an affected formality that was intended to be reassuring— and in a certain sense it was, since it betrayed his ingenuous and passive familiarity with the local bureaucracy—he proffered Luca his identity card. In the meantime, in that incongruous, effeminate voice, he introduced himself, surname Glaoumi, name Rashid, profession butcher's boy. And as Luca was noting that, as well as the boy's personal details, the document also gave his blood group, Rashid asked him what he was doing, all alone, on that track. Where were his friend, his family? Did he not know that going off the beaten track could be dangerous, the way things were going? Did he have children? Was he looking for something? He winked, and gave Luca a smile of complicity.

Señora Martinez's disciple replied that he had been admiring the countryside. And he went back to looking at the sea. But Rashid Glaoumi, far from being discouraged by this rather unsociable attitude, said that Luca—so he knew his name— was not obliged to justify himself since everyone in the White City knew who he was. He was the *nazrani el' nouar*, the *nazrani* of the flowers, who was always in the fields looking for flowers, and even spoke to them, lying down on his belly, as if they were people … there was no need to worry (distracted from his con- templation, Luca looked at him uneasily): he did not think that there was anything strange about that habit, all the *nazrani* had their manias, they called them hobbies (he pronounced it *Obis*, like the Japanese belts). In proof of his statement, Rashid began to list the manias of some residents, the passion for farts of an old army man who used a special soup to give his guests colic, the passion for punches of the American from Boubana, who gave you lots of money, but you had to work hard for it, thumping him for hours on end; there was the Swiss who wanted to cover you with forbidden foods, slices of pig meat, *jamón*, all over, and then he used you as if you were a plate, and there was the old man from the big house in the casbah, Dar Sultàn, for whom farting was not enough, and who ordered copies made of the clothes of the imam of the *nazrani*, the Pope of Rome, but small ones for the little boys, with a special hole … Rashid shook his head. Luca was beginning to realize that he ought to be careful. In that drawling tone, the boy continued: his grandmother—she was old, an old mountain woman, they were all poor, they were—also had the Obi of plants, she had been a gardener once; he had just had a row with that son of a dog his boss, and had decided to go to visit her to forget his problems … talk about coincidences. Grandmère lived down there, at Archìa. Had Luca ever heard of Archìa?

Luca thought that if he were to get up, say goodbye and go on his way, the other would have stopped pestering him, even when he realized that they had the same destination, in obedience to the rules that safeguard and render sacred the privacy of the stranger on those mountains, infested with bandits until a few decades before. But Rashid, perhaps sensing Luca's intentions, was quicker off the mark. You didn't mess about with Señor Gordon Tiburón Mariposa: all the *chicos* who had had dealings with him knew that. He knew the government people, and was as rich as a Saudi. This was Rashid's passport for England, this was his escape from the shipwreck of the patera. With a ceremonious gesture he handed Luca a plastic bag, offering him the contents, insisting that he help himself, trapping the foreigner in the role of guest, obliged to submit to the attentions bestowed upon him in obedience to the law of Allah. The stuff had been prepared by a devout man, an old *hadj* from the neighbourhood who cured diseases. Luca was to take a nice piece. He would feel on form, *hombre*, the flowers would seem more colourful.

The sight of the *majoun*, the sweet cake made of hashish, honey and belladonna seeds that can be fatal (they had tried it once a few summers before, in bed, Irene had babbled on for hours about electric cats, she couldn't handle it any longer, she was going crazy, until Luca had put down the book that contained a secret text written in the spaces between the words and had called a doctor who had given both of them an injection of tranquillizers) aroused the memory of her with the violence of a whirlwind, a violence that blended into the spicy taste of the cake, into its acidic caress in the pit of the stomach. Irene still in the United States, Irene with whom he had not talked for over a month, was together with him on the stage of a little theatre, the one of their happy years, of the dinners in the new house furnished with carpets and the lanterns acquired from among the junk of a flea market in the suburbs. Mentally, he formed the words "I love you", hedged about with lots of inverted commas, an open curtain on the stage, into a director's megaphone the Great Widower announced in a stationmaster's voice their imminent return to Europe, "But I don't know", "We'll see", names of the next stops of the toy train that raced and rattled on but was imprisoned within a closed circuit . . .

"No. Don't vomit, *amigo*." The boy was slapping him on the back. Tiburón Mariposa, the butterfly shark, had been clear. Luca's stomach had to be full. The *nazrani* were operated on by doctors even when they were dead, an autopsy it was called, while they went to Allah because they had no money for medicines. He told Luca to breathe deeply, that it was good stuff, *muy bueno*, and he insisted that he took some more. Luca obeyed. Rashid broke off a piece in his turn, and popped it into his mouth. It would help him screw up his courage. Only then did Luca notice the expensive watch on his wrist. The boy smiled, the sky-blue white of the cornea, a hint of two wrinkles of dissipation at the corners of his mouth, still commas but engraved in the flesh. With his index finger he traced spirals in the air to let Luca know that now it was showtime, then he walked off, leading the way along the path running along the sheer drop down to the sea. Luca was trying to set his feet exactly where his guide had set his, so that when the other suddenly stopped he bumped into him: "Careful *amigo*. The pool. Down there".

He pointed out, at the bottom of the cliff, the rocks. It was impossible to reach, unless one were a falcon, or a seagull. They both ate another piece of *majoun*. As he was swallowing it, Luca had a hallucination. The one who was pretending to be Rashid Glaoumi grabbed him by the shoulders. He pushed him towards the precipice. His hairy muzzle was that of one of the goats he had seen before. His eyes, Sumerian wellsprings. The intensity of his gaze, Semitic. He bleated. As a result of the regurgitation of the bolus of resinous seeds he had been gorging on, his herbivore's breath—emerging from the flaring nostrils in little clouds that floated and dispersed in the crisp, Himalayan, air—stank of sulphur. That's where he had seen him: "Do you want to make mummy better? Do you want to help mummy, Luca?" He clung to his neck, but Marta twisted his hand and gave him a kick. The murmuring of the herd came again. Rashid leaped backwards. Luca managed to keep his balance. Everything was back in its place (the darting of a lizard, ants around the carapace of a dead cricket, here, while the stagehand carried on shaking the faded periwinkle-blue tarpaulin that served, in the middle of Tibet, as a marine background). Preceded by his goats, the old goatherd was coming up to them. They both leaped, they were balanced on a rock, Rashid reached out and slipped off Luca's satchel, putting it on his shoulders. A leap and another leap again, clearing abysses, hurling themselves over ravines whose walls were pierced by roots, above black shafts, farther and farther down. The flow of the rocks the boulders the lapilli was the visual counterpoint to Luca's dizzying burst of tachycardia, step-stone-step-stone-step-stone faster and faster, until the loss of arms and legs. He was flying the way he used to, from foothold to foothold, with the ease with which a petal breaks off and glides away, in his eyes the reflection of the sun on the sea, thousands of golden pots, Irene's golden sarcophagus lowered into the sea, the cupola cast in gold, the petal in the sea. They were at the bottom. Luca glanced upwards. Climbing back up would be impossible. For the first time in months, in years, he was bubbling with a wild happiness. Rashid, vanished. He was alone, in a cove at the foot of a precipitous mountain covered for kilometres and kilometres with a black forest. The dawn of history. A Neanderthal man. A Neolithic fisherman looking out over the sea. He kicked at a mound of dry seaweed, smelling of iodine. He picked up a clump of it, swarming with sand-hopper larvae: the tiny bodies aggregated and dispersed rapidly, seething with life. A fresh burst of tachycardia. He had to move, reach the sea from which he was separated by a rocky reef, conquer it, colonize it. He climbed onto a rock. On this side there was a shallow pool about twenty metres long, in its turn protected from the ocean waves by other rocks arranged to form a barrier. The water flowed in and out the way blood flows in and out of a lung. The level of the sea was higher: held back by the bastion, it roiled martially, a leaden threat to the oasis of *homo sapiens*, to his nursery of shrimps to be devoured raw before holing up for the night in the back of a cave. An islet of bone-white pebbles emerged from the pool. Rashid Glaoumi was standing on that *kythera*. Splay-legged, his pelvis thrust forward, naked apart from his socks, he was making the only move possible in order to gain an advantage from that situation, made even more delicate, now that his departure had gone up in smoke, by the fact that that old bastard, up there, was spying on every move they made, and if he had seen anything odd he would have dashed into town to tell everybody. Rashid was doing the most pre-dictable thing a *chico* could do in the presence of a foreigner. As the old goatherd had had to do many times, in the days of his youth, the way all the sons of the White City do and have always done when they find themselves alone with a *nazrani* convinced he was safe from the gaze of others, he was displaying his wares. With commitment, methodically, he was masturbating.

Luca thought that although the colour of his body, city-pale, was a discordant note, his bulk, the vigour of his movements and his grimace, were Neolithic. The great beast invited Luca to join him, smiling at him. But, instead of complying, the collector, still balanced on the rock, pointed to the socks. Rashid, docile, slipped them off. He threw them onto the pile of his clothes with the affected nonchalance of a stripper ridding herself of that last lacy triangle. His two hoofs appeared broad, gleaming.

The centaur laughed and, still milking himself, he beckoned Luca with his free arm. This wriggling on his part, this thrusting forward of the hips while pawing the pebbles with his large nails and shaking the bait (and several sharks, in the course of his career, had bitten)—this show, in short, was the fruit of rigorous professionalism, and it was having the desired effect. To the eyes of the spectator, that mass of flesh gave off no sorrow. If anything, Luca was realizing (analogously to many clients before him, even though opening his eyes to a vision that was only his) that that body was not the cellar in which the condemned children suffered, but the grotto, the Atlantic grotto in which the festive horde danced around the reclining boy child. Luca joined him without even realizing that he had gone into and come out of the water, his shoes and socks were drenched. He caressed the boy's chest, squeezed his nipples, palpated the rippling muscles that were craniums of new-born babies under the taut skin. Rashid ran his tongue over his lips and murmured a few words of encouragement, then, confidently applying the pressure of one hand on the nape of Luca's neck, he tried to push him down. He said that the milk was good, that all the *nazrani* liked to taste the milk of the White City. Luca thought of Irene. He was on his knees. Once he overcame the first olfactory barrier—boiling tripe—the smell given off by the centaur's sex was familiar, peaty. In mental comparison with his own, pink and with a glans that revealed irritated flesh as the foreskin was drawn back, this one seemed even longer, more massive. The same colour from the root to the tip, without secrets, it stood there erect like a worker awaiting the boss's orders, or like a soldier accustomed to jumping to those of his commander. It was few centimetres from his face. The goat was a goatfish, there. On opening and closing the urethral meatus—wide and with fleshy lips—by pressing it with his fingertips, it looked like the mouth of a fish. Rashid enquired if it was big enough. It would grow more if sucked upon. Would he not like to take him to Europe and have him all to himself? Luca squatted down on his heels in order to grip it and bring it to his lips without having to pull it downwards. He opened his own mouth wide, and after a quick lick at that mute, salty, fishy one, proud of the rapidity with which he made his tongue flicker, his living tongue, his tongue that swooped, struck and lapped with precision, he swallowed it and got to work the way he would have liked an iguana to get to work on him.

It was logical that, after a climb back up during which the ants were themselves (the collector still had that slightly bitter gelatine in his throat, under the pretext of helping to hoist him up the centaur caressed his buttocks and asked why it was that he didn't want to take it up the arse, the *nazrani* usually couldn't get enough of it), it was logical that after having penetrated a seemingly endless tunnel of boughs and branches and twigs and withies—a little stream dotted with fresh cow pats meandered through the muddy earth, and at certain points the ceiling was so low that in order to avoid getting clawed by the harpies they had to flatten themselves onto the ground and make their way, on all fours, with undulatory movements of their hips—it was logical that, after the harbinger of a mineral phosphorescence followed by the slash of a blade of light, they should find themselves, a tourist and his native guide out walking, a *nazrani* and his autochthonous stud goat, the Neolithic fisherman and his goatfish grilled or salted, the breathless nymphet beside the faun, the boy Achilles with Chiron, on a country road. A country lane or path or track that began at the edge of the forest, and lazily made its way down between walls overgrown with roses run wild and honeysuckle and convolvulus and aristolochia, as well as quince trees, date palms, figs, mulberry, olives, Judas trees, alpinias, banana trees, a few cedars, cypresses, and vines, set out in rows and in clusters, which, despite the proliferation of *oxalidacea* and nasturtiums, proved that that neglected land had once been divided up into gardens, orchards, and holdings.

"Archìa" said Rashid, in the tones of a host who, having opened the last door before a guest who is convinced that the visit is over, suddenly shows him an eighteenth-century parlour on whose walls lined with multicoloured porcelain the sunbeams kindle the reflections of a celestial harmony. The dogs were barking. He picked up a stone. Convinced that an invitation to meet the family would show the *nazrani* that he was an honest lad, as well as one equipped with the biggest chopper in the White City and district, he mentally gave thanks to Allah that he really did have a grandmother who lived in those parts. He told Luca that now they were going to visit Grandmère. She would be glad to meet him, and to talk of flowers with him.

After his guide had pushed open the gate and the house appeared at the other end of a field of flowers, Luca found himself faced with a spectacle that made the parlour of before look like a broom closet. Before him lay his dream, but made more resplendent by the fact it was there, within reach, tangible proof of the results of the fertilizer. The cottage disappeared under Mermaid roses, the pale yellow siren that climbed up one side of the front door, wound its way along the façade and from there to the roof, where it exploded in the concert of a million canaries in season against the blue leaves of the aloe growing in the shade behind the roses, which was why it was blooming so late, orange-coloured pine cones, erect, as if made of lacquer, which swayed when a breath from the sea silvered the olive trees, made the petals rain down from the apricot and peach trees, and brought the scent of eucalyptus, juniper, and lavender. Rashid, smiling, asked Luca if he liked the garden. With difficulty, he tried to tell him that he had never seen anything so beautiful in all his life (crimson honeysuckle peeping out of the ivy; chalice vine with flowers soft as chamois leather clinging to the wisteria on the garden wall; green tea flowers, jalap, fritillary, butterflies and ladybirds). They went on down a gentle slope, among acanthus leaves billowing like the sails of felucas; birds' tongues emerged from the buttery lips of the arum lilies, the crests of the strelitzias nodded, the moraeas hid their heads behind cowlings of leaves. The grandmother appeared in the doorway. At the mere sight of her, Luca was dumbstruck. He had immediately recognized the skeletally thin old woman who was waiting for him.

Disguised as a peasant from the White City region, a kerchief knotted at the back of her neck and a synthetic djellaba hanging down to her bare feet, she managed to resemble an associate of

Mahatma Gandhi, one of his followers who was forever fasting and ready to lie down on the tracks in front of any train. In one sense this masquerade confirmed the Indian impression that the so-called grandson had created on his emergence from the forest. But it sufficed for Luca to see her open her arms to clasp to her bosom her emissary, who for a moment, big as he was, vanished between those excessively wide, melodramatic sleeves, to realize that the Indian mannerisms were a part of her technique of dissemblance. There was no point in racking his brains, there was no Calcutta connection, the old actress was wearing peasant clothing out of a ribald taste for things pastoral, with the same aplomb with which, at a cocktail party at the Gestapo High Command, she would have worn a sari, maybe the same one that a few years later, at the door of a cellar, would be soiled with faeces and soaked in piss. She greeted him without smiling, feigning embarrassment when he kissed her hand, even withdrawing it as if his were on fire. She pretended to speak only a few words of stilted French. She invited them in for a glass of tea. Of course they weren't in India! She and the minotaur or centaur—Luca's ideas were no longer clear on the matter—had worked with Teutonic precision and synchrony. They had spirited away not only the pictures, drawings and the tables laden with treasures plundered from the homes of deportees, but even the floor—in marble or parquet, or perhaps it had been tiled—leaving a beaten earth surface and an empty room. Irene would have come in handy. Thanks to her knowledge of furnishings, she would have understood at a glance how the room would have looked before the removal that had left it bare as a cell. Luca glanced at Rashid, unsurprised by the two horns that had sprouted from his forehead. He had arrived. No longer Achilles, but Theseus, in the heart of the labyrinth that he had entered while still a child, and in which he had lost himself on following the call of the unnameable enemy who had stolen his body.

Stooped over the kettle, the old woman prattled on in the dialect of the White City, which she mispronounced however, about foolish things such as how difficult it was to transport the bottles of gas there by donkey (she pronounced the final "s" of gas with a revealing sibilance, pregnant with obvious and sinister memories). Then she scolded her grandson, at least as far as Luca could manage to understand: it was shameful of him to make a visit to his poor old grandmother without thinking to bring her a present of some necessity, a packet of sugar, some biscuits, I don't know, a good job his friend was there ... who, with a shiver, noticed only then that the two criminals had left a shelf up. On it, in full view, owing to an oversight or more probably to a perverse pleasure in sowing clues, there was an amber cigarette holder, which heaven knows how many times had served to stub out cigarettes in orifices of sizzling flesh ... the botanist swallowed. In impeccable French, he complimented her on the elegance of that object.

They were drinking tea sitting on the floor, on the mat, as required by the mistress of the house's masquerade. This last, putting down her glass, limited herself to looking at Rashid, who, after having spoken to her in agitated tones—the only intelligible word was "*majoun*"—turned to Luca, and told him that the cigarette holder was a memento of a lady for whom his grandmother had worked many years before. Luca nodded, trying to show that he was convinced by this explanation. His stomach was contracting with cramps. Drops of sweat beaded his forehead. Jaima's lie, that the Countess had committed suicide by throwing herself into the sea, could have had one reason alone, one purpose alone: the *dame de compagnie*, down in the city, was still working for her mistress, procuring her the living bodies required to fertilize the garden. The iguana had told him that story of cannibalism and massacres at whose conclusion, by way of a happy ending, there was the golden gleam of *Iris juncea numidica*, only to lure him there, into the clutches of the great gardener. This explained Rashid's apparently fortuitous appearance from the forest. Luca pulled the satchel, lying abandoned on the floor, to him. He would defend himself with the little pick. He wanted to leave the room. "*Chère madame* ... " he began. "*Ma chère madame* ... "

His voice, unnaturally shrill, broke. He realized that he was talking like her old accomplice Bébé de Mainville, but he had nothing to lose, might as well go for broke. He told her he was searching for the *Iris juncea numidica*, which must have grown in her spectacular garden thanks to fertilizing methods that were perhaps rather unorthodox, but of undoubted efficacy. Addressing her with a smile, he added that he was acquainted with her discoveries in the field of botany, of her final experiments. Although the hag was looking at him impassively, he continued, pleased by the ease with which he was finding the words, savouring the precision of the adjectives, with the growing awareness that he, the lapper of goats and goatfish, had finally come into the possession of the living tongue concealed behind taxonomies. He declared that the results achieved by the lady were amazing: the exemplary balance between order and randomness, the outcome of a plan to which the climbing plants and the annuals, pruned with such magisterial skill, contributed their dazzling coloration ... the old woman's self control was remarkable: she looked away. She was staring incredulously at her grandson. After a preamble—the *juncea numidica* was a *xiphium* whose bulb, covered by a wrinkly tunic, had around its apex some small rough edges whose function was to anchor it to the ground, given that it preferred crumbling, sunny slopes—Luca got deeper into a detailed description of the blooms, the flower-laden stem, anthers, crests, dwelling on the nuances of yellow of the sepals, similar to the colour of the spectacular display of mermaid roses outside, but more full-bodied, Neapolitan, a warm shade that seemed to allude to a past coldness, to its ... Rashid told his grandmother that the *nazrani* was looking for a yellow flower.

The old woman got up and beckoned him to follow her. She walked along shaking her head. The fact that the garden, now, struck Luca as neglected brush in which only the strongest plants barely managed to flower, ought to have aroused his suspicion: but he put this impression down to habit. In the back garden, beyond the aloe, evidently obsessed by the details of her choreography, the Countess had hung out the clothes to dry: and what clothes! A patched djellaba, a few rags, the chequered kerchiefs that the peasant women use to cover their heads, identical to the one she was wearing. In the muddy farmyard hens were scratching about. She pointed out to him, among the weeds that grew around the rill of water that drained away from the washtub, a cluster of yellowish flowers. Luca inhaled, exhaled. The air smelled of manure. They were freesias. The temptation to wade into her, to batter her with punches and kicks, was a strong one. Who did she think she was dealing with? Summoning up all his capacity for self control, he managed to say that, despite the fact that freesias are of the iris family, *chère madame*, they had very little in common with the extremely rare *Iris juncea numidica* . . . the same sneer with which he had slaughtered the *florentina* deformed his face. Laying one hand firmly on his shoulder, Rashid pushed him back inside the house.

Standing in a corner, the pair had confabulated for an eternity, or better, the centaur was providing the Countess with explanations while she played the part of the honest woman who had been offended, and she limited herself to countering in brief peevish bursts, tilting up her chin every time to indicate the *nazrani* as if he were a dog. The botanist managed to grasp that the old lady absolutely did not want him, this *loco*, to take Rashid to Europe—but who had ever thought of doing that? After a final explanation from the grandson, the hag concluded that all the *nazrani* were the same—all they could do was hope in the mercy of Allah. Finally the boy got up, and ordered Luca to come with him. When, once they had retraced their steps under the old wild rose among the half-blown arum lilies, in the middle of the bushes festooned with the plastic bags that the east wind carried everywhere, they found themselves at the bottom of the garden once more, Rashid stopped, and in a resentful tone he told Luca that his Grandmère had not liked him, she had found him strange. Why had he behaved so badly? But Luca merely asked him for some more *majoun*. He chewed on a piece. It calmed him.

They went down along the ridge of the peninsula at the end of which, among the garigue, there emerged the ruins of a building. His guide told him that his grandmother had once worked there, in Madame's villa. The legend had it that Madame had been wicked, that she had been a trafficker, but that she had always been kind to Grandmère ... Luca wasn't listening to him anymore. In the air there was a vibration. The seagulls fell silent. The stones of the tumbledown walls, the lumps of cement, the rotten beams that had held up the roof, were arranged in a semi-circle. In the centre, the earth was calcareous, white at certain points because of the shards of seashells and bone fragments that had come to the surface. The tufts of little leaves that sprouted here and there, some straight like little swords and others coiled around themselves, were dense and fleshy, of a dull green. The flowers, held up by stems so short that they seemed to have been laid on the ground, although they were delicate as butterflies, conveyed an impression of vigour precisely because of that implacable fragility in contact with the parched earth, inconsistent as prisms of light, but clinging tenaciously as octopi to the rocks. They were the colour of pus; the gleam of jaguar's eyes: like the cubs of some wild beast, they basked sated in the warmth. The boy looked behind him, to see if his grandmother was spying on them. His eyes fixed on the irises, Luca pulled down the zip of Rashid's trousers and felt around in his underwear. Grandmère was not to be seen. Encouraged by his client's lunacy, but wary of his testiness, Rashid was saying that he was tired of this *vida*, that he wanted to leave the White City, to have the *dinero*, the ticket and the visa he was prepared to do anything ... *todo lo que quieres* ... he wanted to try ... like a little vase ... to insert ... to insert a flower in his chopper? The botanist grasped his prick, absently caressing the glans and in the meantime sensing the nexus that existed between the epithelium over which his fingertips were running and the petals that gleamed in the sun. The *Iris juncea numidica* was his.

Having uprooted the clumps that seemed most vigorous to him, every time taking away a large clod in order to avoid cutting the roots, and having lovingly laid them inside the satchel, Luca insisted on going back to the old woman to bid her goodbye. When he opened the satchel with a grimace of triumph asking her in a loud voice, a really loud voice, if she had finally recognized them, she, prepared to play any part as long as she gave him no satisfaction, had stared at the flowers, first dumb-founded, then, faced with his insistence (oblivious to any need for caution he was shaking the bag under her nose), horrified. Why did the effects of her fertilizing technique have this effect on her? In vain Luca tried to take her hand to kiss it again. The old hag moved out of his way. With a ridiculous little run she took refuge behind Rashid, who called Luca, telling him to calm down, *amigo*, that it was time to go. But he bounded right up to the criminal and yelled in her face that she had been for-given nothing, harpy, mangler of legs, the day was going to come in which Jaima Martinez would have her revenge. The shove that that goat of a grandson gave him very nearly made him fall. Luca had the time to see that the Countess had covered her eyes with one hand as she muttered an exorcism.

On the way back, the boy was taciturn. He seemed sad. In monosyllables, he communicated that he would accompany Luca back to the car. He insisted on carrying the satchel con-taining the flowers and the tools. Once they got there, he refused to get in alongside Luca, under the pretext that he wanted to visit some friends who lived in those parts. But the iris collector knew that the reason was so that he could go back to the old lady and decide with her what steps to take, now that she had been discovered. Rashid asked Luca if he had nothing for him: "For the sex, for the flowers, *amigo*." Luca gave him some money and the boy pocketed it without thanking him. Then, taken by a sudden inspiration, he handed over all the *majoun* he had left. Were the *nazrani* to eat it all at once, what he thought was a fair supply would have been enough to satisfy the desires of Señor Gordon: perhaps, Rashid thought, this prospect would have kept the butterfly shark sweet for a few days, provided he got plentiful amounts of his favourite fish (admiring it before guzzling it down, in the room in the boarding house, he would tell Rashid that it was the eternal part of him, the most ancient part, and he called it my Greek goatfish). At home Mohammed had taken the flowers with his customary condescension. Although dusk was falling, Luca ordered him to plant them right away. He went into the tool shed. He picked up the saw and took it into the bathroom. Instead of having dinner he drank several cups of tea and ate a little *majoun*. A couple of whiskies and he went out. Thanks to a stroke of luck, he came across the electric cat, the dead cat, at the first attempt. He had parked in the exact spot in which, that morning, the pseudo Bébé de Mainville had thrown the sack into the ditch. Back in the bathroom, he bent over the tub. There was the smell of raw chicken. For a moment, he thought it would have been simpler to buy some fresh meat, steaks from a butcher, why not from Rashid, a piece of liver, a round of beef? The saw lacked some teeth, and it made especially heavy weather of the part around the spinal column and the point where the rear legs were attached, where the cartilaginous ligaments were tougher and the muscles heavier. But the abdomen, softish, yielded easily, even though a rib snapped and injured his finger. He managed to get eight pieces out of it. The head, the paws, the trunk split in two, the stub of the tail. The fur, matted with blood, was blackish, sticky down on the cranium of a new-born baby. He would have to get better tools. He wrapped up the pieces in a newspaper. With a sponge, meticulously, he cleaned the tiles of all traces of organic material. Then he used the shower head to wash away the rest. He went out leaving the door of the upper pavilion wide open. He buried the pieces in the flower bed, near the clumps of irises, digging with his nails, delicately, heedless of the smarting of his finger, being careful not to damage the root apparatus, the umbilical cord of the hungry jaguar cubs. The next day he would have a layer of fresh earth added. The east wind had risen, bringing the stink of human beings from the White City. The boughs of the old cypress and of the Brazilian pepper tree groaned, the bushes moaned, the flowers waved. The moon dangled in the sky, full but concave, a colander hanging from a nail.

III

THERE WAS A PAUSE and then silence. Matter had closed
in on itself, rotating around a hub. Intact, intangible, it
was on the other side of a glass. Luca saw, but differently. The
garden, the two pavilions, the little tower, the bare flower bed
from which the flowers emerged like the heads of people buried
alive, the leaves that were hands stretching out from the blanket
of earth to beg food, even the city, down there, yawning in the
mists of the *shargui* as if it were moving away, looking like a
piece of cotton wool left there to fill the gap between the horizon
and the sky, all was on the other side of the pane. The evidence
appeared deformed, secretly deformed, in a way that was perhaps
imperceptible to the others, to Mohammed, to his wife, to the
two daughters, but crystal clear to him. When Irene telephoned
him pretending to be the Great Widower, to tell him that a boy
named Alfredino, genus Alfredinus, rhizomous, species salvificus,
had not made it, was dead, and that he was to call his daughter,
to try to be close to her, to be ashamed of his behaviour, not
only did he recognize her right away, but he understood that
she was alluding to his plans. What was the use of boys, if not
to die and rot in order to fertilize lands and their histories? He
hurled down the receiver. As he had predicted, this call was
followed by another. Now Irene was brazenly pretending to be
herself. Like a peacock fanning out its tail, she expertly mar-
shalled all her arts, pauses, the husky voice, golden reflections,
treasure, I don't understand, what's going on? only to betray
herself with a shudder, a stiffening: "I'm ill Luca. I need to talk
to you. I'm worried … " He was unable to restrain himself: he
gave a savage laugh, while she was saying that Ritts-Twice and
other residents of the White City had told her of his arrest, that
he wandered around like a sleepwalker, that he was painfully
thin, that he looked ill … still laughing, he told her not to
worry, he had never felt better in all his life. They ought to
leave him in peace, he had no time to waste, he was busy.

"Please, spider. Things are so hard as it is … why don't you come back? Let's sell that house!" Again, he hung up. He smashed the bedroom telephone against the wall until it broke, and he battered the one in the lower pavilion to pieces with a hammer. He told the servants that he had dropped them. Given that everyone was dissembling, he too had the right to play his part.

It was no longer the time to fool around with infantile pastimes. He kicked at the bucket of gruel, emptying it where it stood, beneath the *Olea fragrans*. With the hose he washed away the residue of that mush, good perhaps for the nourishment of ordinary plants, but certainly not suited to the demanding palates of his children. When Rashid dropped in to see him, and standing in the main entrance had insisted on entering his domain (with one hand in his pocket he was caressing the goat-fish, making it swell, in the meantime saying that he felt like making love, five minutes and no more, come on *amigo … todo lo que quieres …*) Luca bade him a curt farewell, without even answering when the other asked him if he needed any more *majoun*, and he felt a slight regret only when, on making his way towards the upper pavilion, he was struck by a doubt as to how much, of that body, was muscle, how much flesh, nerve, bone. Perhaps he should have asked Rashid, he was a butcher after all, but his intuition suggested that the boy would have inter- preted such a question in a negative light. He locked himself up in his room to think—he had been reflecting a great deal, of late—and he came to the conclusion that he had done well to drop the idea. Rashid was part of a trashy India, a little centaur idol from a souvenir shop. He needed much more than that, by then. He needed substance.

He felt fine, or rather, he would have felt fine thanks to the decision he had taken, had it not been for the insomnia, for the pain in his belly, and for the swollen finger. He had found several packets of sleeping pills in the back of Irene's drawer of creams. But even though he was taking two, even three pills at a time, he could not manage to sleep. He would doze for a few moments, then the calling, the murmuring would begin. It was those damned souls who were still moaning in the cellar, and there was no way of silencing them. On opening his eyes, he found himself sitting on the bed, his back against the wall, his arms hugging his knees. He knew the insomnia was caused by the *majoun*, but he had to keep eating it regularly, since it conferred upon his vision the lucidity that was indispensable for a saviour of wild irises of his rank, the *juncea numidica* and all the others. He met Jaima on the boulevard, and he spoke to her about the matter. Concealing the relief that his appearance had given her, the dwarf hastened to agree, but he was to be prudent with the dosage, to be careful. The Countess d'Andurain had committed suicide almost thirty years before, that old woman must have been a peasant from Archìa, clearly the *muchacho* was a *cabrón*, a stud *maricón* on the look out for single *nazrani*, the important thing was that *el niño* had found his flowers. But the collector was detached, objective. The trauma that Jaima had suffered had blunted her sensibilities, clouded her intelligence. By convincing herself that her torturer was dead, she was protecting herself from a reality that she could not face. The scars on her legs had still not healed, probably they never would. And to think he had suspected this poor hurt woman! He looked at her with sadness, the little iguana, sitting on a café terrace, as if appraising a change that had come over her face, trying to interpret it. Luca decided that his plan would remain a secret even to her. The risk was too great. For the first time since they had met, Jaima invited him—only if he wanted to, if he had no other commitments—to dine at her house, an intimate little dinner, the two of them: "You and I alone, *niño*." He hastened to agree. There was something virginal, then, about the lady's smile as she blushed, dropped her gaze, and, offering him her best profile, she set to staring at the landscape wearing an expression intended to be romantic and dreamy, whereas it accentuated her resemblance to a chameleon scanning empty space as it waits for a little fly to pass by. Later that same day, Luca fertilized himself, tasting his own shit on the tip of his index finger. Irene's skirt, the old one with the flower pattern, fitted him perfectly.

He had expected a modest house. It was a hovel. The corrugated iron roof from which jutted a parabolic antenna backed on to a lumber yard. The quarter, behind the casbah, was veined with paths and stairways that led down towards dark lands, in which drunks pissed and tramps slept. Under a lamppost, down there, some boys were torturing a cat. The hecatomb of the inferior domestic breeds in favour of the wild ones had begun. The number, marked in oil paint on the wooden door, was the right one. He knocked. The incredible apparition of her big hydrocephalous head crowned by a rigid mass of carrot-coloured curls. Beneath the open sweater, Jaima was wearing a housecoat with a plunging neckline. After a shrill cry of welcome, she kissed him in a regurgitation of warm onions, and holding him by the hand she took him from the hall stinking of squid on whose back wall hung an image of the Virgen de Pilar, and led him to the living room. As if there were any need to do so, she told him what she had been cooking. She left him to wrestle with the wine and the corkscrew and vanished behind the curtain that gave onto the kitchen.

The room was lopsided, the floorboards separated by fissures through which you could see the naked earth. Here, in her lair, in the secret laboratory in which so many strategies had been forged, hybridization programmes perfected, grafts conceived, there was a sofa and two spanking new armchairs upholstered in lead-coloured synthetic material: the armrests and headrests were covered by lace antimacassars. Two lamps hung from the ceiling. The table was set. On a wheeled trolley with glass shelves stood the television; the lower shelf housed bottles and glasses. On coming back in holding a pan, Jaima garrulously asked him if he liked her little house. And she nodded at him to take a seat.

Luca was wondering why it was that she too, like the Countess d'Andurain, had transformed her hiding place for the occasion of his visit. It was incredible that a scholar of her rank, a connoisseur of the rarest bulbous and rhizomous plants, lived in a house that looked like the inside of a caravan, with a little parlour like that of Mohammed and his family, where the only sheet of printed paper was a Spanish glossy magazine lying open on the floor, from whose cover some starlet gazed into space. He murmured something about everything being so clean, so new … her smile, triumphing over all false modesty, was radiant. Caressing the arm rest of one of those armchairs, glossy as the bodywork of a car after a chrome job, she confessed that she had been unable to resist the temptation—a bargain, sequestered goods from the customs post.

The squid with peppers were delicious. The wine too. They toasted, to *las flores*, to the garden, to their friendship, to the *juncea numidica*, even to the White City … Jaima served him another portion, Luca had not eaten so much and so willingly for months. And since there was no more: "Dig in, *hombre*." She used her fork to shovel what was left in the pan onto his plate. They opened the second bottle, the third. There were no windows. The curtain that gave onto the kitchen was a cotton affair in a light blue and white check (Vichy, he remembered, was what Irene used to call that material). He had become so used to the room that on his noting, in a corner, a fern in a vase, he attached no importance to the fact that it was a plastic one. Intercepting his gaze, his host hastened to justify herself. It had been a present from a neighbour for whom she had done a favour, she had forgotten to throw it away. Would he like a coffee, a sherry with ice, or would he prefer to carry on with the wine?

Luca became aware of the downpour only when, sitting beside her on the sofa, he finished his third or fourth sherry with ice. It was not a hallucination. It was stuffy, yet outside it seemed as if it were raining. He recalled that their first meetings had always been accompanied by torrential rain. By then, rather than disappear into the overall pattern, the warp and weft of which reality was woven stood out clearly to his eyes: there was a bond, between their friendship and the running of water. Probably the free flow of the preserving fluid out of the jar in which, imprisoned for years, Jaima had been waiting for him to come and free her. He looked at her. Sweating as usual, she was sucking on her straw. She seemed ill at ease. No, it was not one of those downpours initially accompanied by an increase in the temperature that herald the end of the *shargui*. The sound was coming from the door next to the kitchen curtain. Either someone was in there, or it had been her. She had turned on a tap when she had gone to get more ice.

At table the lady observed him as she waited for the right moment. It must have come, judging by the brusque tone with which, putting her glass down on the table and making herself more comfortable against the back of the chair, she began by saying that she hoped with all her heart that *el niño* had enough wits left to accept the proposal she was about to make him. It was time to stop playing with fire.

Wary, his nerves on edge because of the water pouring down, Luca immediately sensed what the iguana wanted to get at. She hastened to say that the person interested in the purchase was reliable, solvent, and above all dangerous. No, he was not to interrupt her. The client was in a hurry. The sum he was prepared to disburse would be enough to buy a bigger house, surrounded by a far bigger garden.

Luca declared that he would not give up his house for all the gold in the world. In the meantime he congratulated himself for having said nothing to her about his purchases of that afternoon, the bandages in the chemist's, the rubber gloves, the new saw, the imported shears, the plastic sheet, all safe inside Irene's wardrobe. He touched the key in his pocket and blessed this premonition.

But the dwarf, stubborn and grotesque under the bloated wig that made her seem even smaller, carried on, and there was no way to make her shut up, and there was no way of stopping that damned downpour: it would be idiotic not to accept an opportunity that would never present itself again . . . the payment could be made without his wife coming to know the entire sum. Once he was rich, he would be free to create a garden, never mind a garden, a park, anywhere he wished . . . and amid the intensifying noise, amid the gurgling of the liquid that continued to flow in the adjacent room, the dwarf weighed him up with the eyes of a sow preparing to devour one of her offspring. Was he not curious to know who this madman was, the one who was prepared to spend an astronomical sum for a house in a country from which all westerners were very soon going to be kicked out?

Luca leaped to his feet. He shouted that he knew already. He was through there. The full bathtub. The client ready. They would drown him. The walls had begun to move, they were closing in on him, expanding and contracting like membranes. Luckily, in the middle, in the middle of the scene, there was Jaima, who smiled at him and told him he was a silly little boy, there was no need to get angry, whatever was he thinking? if the noise was bothering him she would go to turn off the tap, she always had a bath before retiring ... but Jaima Dolores de la Concepción Martinez y Martinez was no longer herself, thanks to one of her metamorphoses her pale face highlighted by her flaming locks was that of a young girl who consented, and who gave herself to him—Irene, in the days of their love. *El niño* was to sit down again, she was proud of his reaction. When Luca, calmer even though sullen, flopped back down onto the sofa, she came close to him, and whispering sweet nothings in his ear she tried to coax him out of it. She reached out a hand and caressed his stomach. Did his little tummy still hurt? Why didn't he make himself comfortable? Why didn't he relax? And while her fingers began to unbutton his shirt, in cheery tones, as if this idea had only just come to her: why didn't he take a bath? he would feel better. By that time the bath, no matter how long it took to fill, must be ready.

Misinterpreting Luca's silence, Jaima insinuated that, if he didn't feel like it, she would be the one to go for a quick rinse: she felt as if she were on fire. And slipping one hand down her neckline, she moved it to and fro over her breasts. The boy, faced with this spectacle and the simultaneous dissolution of the possibility that had flashed through his head, admitted, with some hesitation at first, that the idea of a bath was not a bad one. More purposefully, he allowed that he wanted one, even needed one, going so far as to confess that he hadn't washed himself for days. Repressing a surge of happiness, the lady feigned surprise. In that case, she observed, he must be dirty—she used the adjective *sucio*. Men, especially if they work in the open air, get pretty filthy, and not just with dirt and dust. Her face had wrinkled into a grimace that was the reflection, deformed by the mirror of time, of the smile with which a little girl had carried out the orders of the principal of the orphanage. The sebum in his hair, she murmured, stank, the spaces between his toes, the grease round his neck, the sweat in the armpits ... was *el niño* not ashamed to neglect himself like this?

The heart of the two officiants beat faster. United, even without knowing it, by the upbringing they had had regarding matters of bodily hygiene, they recited their ritual formulas. He, mummy's little spider, admitted that yes, he was a bit ashamed, but recently he had had other things to worry about. He was holding back tears of joy. Apparently impassive, the iguana told him that this was no excuse. She demanded to know why he did not wash more often. At which Luca, hesitant, replied that in order to wash all over, with that sore finger, he needed someone to give him a hand. Jaima nodded gravely. Screwing up his courage, in a whining, childish voice, the iris collector said that partly out of haste, and partly out of the stress that possession of the *juncea numidica* had caused him, he felt dirty in a strange way, dirty inside too. In what sense? inquired the iguana. And with a flash of loving light in her eyes: "Inside your botty?"

The little boy nodded energetically. A thread of saliva ran from his mouth. He needed to be rubbed all over, he mewed, outside and inside, the way his mummy used to do before she died. His heart was beating so fast he was on the verge of fainting.

Now it was clear. All their meetings had been a preamble to this, in this dump lined with white tiles, soaking with steam, with the mirror clouded over and the cast iron tub ready to serve as the venue for his consecration. Reflecting on the role played by a bathtub in his plan—he had imagined the scene in detail, and he had not forgotten to buy the sticky tape with which he would attach the plastic sheet to protect the wall above the tiling from splashes—on looking at this bathtub, Luca smiled. Present and future were reconnected with the years of his early childhood, the years of the nightly bath in a bitterly clean room. This fluid continuity, this uninterrupted flux of forms and meanings, was the world he was on the point of entering.

In fact Jaima Martinez y Martinez, a real person albeit one of fabulous ancestry, embraced him rapidly, almost as if she wished to conceal her sadness at the farewell that preceded her *niño*'s departure from the scene. This was the starting point of his journey. She held out her hand so that he could give her his clothes. She was calm, inscrutable under the liturgical wig. There would be no human sacrifices, not there, not then. The transformations would occur later, thanks to the artifice that had been chosen in advance.

Luca stripped off, strangely aware of his every gesture, even the slightest involuntary movement, the contraction of a muscle, the darting of a nerve, without feeling any embarrassment even when, on taking down his underwear, his erect cock, the glans already uncovered, had sprung out. Jaima limited herself to gesturing at the bathtub. And turning towards the sink, which very nearly came up to her chin, she rolled the sleeves of her sweater up over her skinned elbows. She lathered up a piece of sponge.

The little boy, taken by the solemnity of the moment, put first one foot then the other into the water. Then he sat down, letting out a groan and stretching out, filled with a sensation of well-being that would have been total were it not for the burning in his finger. Jaima stood over him. He was hers, in her power. She gestured at him to sit up. Thanks to her stature she had no need to kneel in order to soap him the way Marta had had to do. Standing, all she had to do was stretch out her arms to rub his stomach, back, groin, arse. And then he too had grown, over the years. He was no longer a little baby lost in three fingers of water. Luca noticed that, as the massage grew gradually more energetic, the more parlous became the oscillations of the tower of hair. The dwarf's breathing was coming faster, the sweat making her throat shine. Her sweater had slipped down to reveal one shoulder. Finally the tottering construction collapsed.

The curls slumped back, unravelling to form a dark orange mass, a curtain of fringes from which her face emerged like that of an old doll tormented by generations of little girls. Giving way to a playful impulse, Luca withdrew his pelvis from her fingers, bending forward and stretching out his torso towards her. Jaima, resigned, ran the sponge over his pectorals and his nipples while the foam, running down his stomach, rather than slip into the water as it should have, went to collect among the pubic hair that had sprouted goodness knows when. Mischievous, the little boy arched his back and pushed out his chest. Marta laughed. Laughing, she grabbed his stalk. Luca wriggled his thin hips, arching his back the way a cat does when it wants to be fondled, all unknowing of what was going to happen to him. Patiently, the woman dropped the sponge. With one hand she gripped his cock, which pulsed; with the other, she caressed his buttocks, down and up and down again, every time lingering a little longer around the anus. The little boy opened his legs. Once more he felt the initial pain of the policeman's inspection, instantly soothed by the gentleness with which Marta, absorbed in the task of cleansing, titillated the rim of his sphincter with her fingertip, tickling it so that the muscle would relax, going barely beyond the opening, probing, she lingered on the threshold, withdrew and almost immediately re-entered, gradually sinking into his rectum. He reached into her neckline and grabbed one of her breasts.

Contrary to his fears, contrary to what had always happened to him all his life, contact with that overripe flesh was not enough to loosen the knot that wrung his belly. The lily did not spit. It remained erect, curious, eager to explore. Jaima looked up. She wore a terrifying expression: it was as if within the priestess a monster still lay imprisoned, not the one of the *Wunderkammer*, but a being whose existence Luca had never suspected. This being, this entity, was pleading to be released from the body that was smothering it. Behind the big square mask with the sagging jowls, somewhere, behind the iguana, behind the sated wild beast, behind the skivvy with the broken legs, behind the lady of the irises, there was a woman: a woman who was clumsily struggling with herself to find the courage to ask him a question. He pulled down the shoulder straps of her apron, her breasts had broken cover, a mollusc extracted from the shell, the stomach of the tortoise ripped out of the carapace. The rhythm with which Luca caressed, palpated, tormented these continents of flesh, pinching and pulling the nipples, was in synchrony with that of the finger that was still going up and down in his insides, in and out, like a piston. The finger came out. Jaima withdrew. The question in her eyes was pitiless. He nodded, throwing his arms wide open to draw her to him, and he really was Christ—sin did not exist, had never existed.

The woman, her back turned, emerged from her dress. She slipped off her wig, revealing sparse hair stuck together by sweat. Beneath the fold of fat that surrounded her waist, the briefs of the gigantic, almost bald new-born baby seemed even more skimpy. Even after she pulled them down, the mark of the elastic still drew a bright pink band on her flesh. The buttocks were gibbous, two colanders of cellulite, two full moons. She turned round. With one arm, modestly, she concealed her breasts as best she could. Gallant, he helped her into the tub, contemplating the jiggling of her belly and thighs. He sat down, his back against the cast iron. And since Jaima made to do the same, he stopped her. He begged her to remain standing for a few minutes without covering herself. He wanted to look at her. Jaima smiled with a threadbare coquettishness, like a daughter of the White City. And like a good daughter of the White City, she consented.

The surface of that gelatinous, martyred, sainted body was criss-crossed by a network of veins and capillaries, some green, some blue, some violet, which like a complex hydrographic system debouched here and there in bluish-leaden lagoons. Warts and cysts like those on her face, but smaller, blossomed on her belly, brown berries furrowed by cracks from which sprouted white hairs. In certain zones—below the breasts, around the navel, between the hips and knees—the cellulite formed spongy reliefs like strata of sodden land. Even what in the darkness of the belvedere he had taken for scars, were folds in the skin, ranked closer towards the inside of her legs, where the adipose deposits were less conspicuous. Below the flaccid mass of the belly, the pubes could barely be seen, trimmed with dry hairs that, similar as they were to tufts of stubble emerging from a split, for a moment gave him the illusion that she was no more than a puppet stuffed with straw. As he looked at her, he was masturbating. The dwarf squatted down on top of him. She did so gingerly. Her expression was marked by the concentration of a trapeze artist about to grasp the hand of the companion who will save her from the void. The level of the water rose. Supporting her back with both hands, Luca helped her get settled, her little legs splayed, the deformed feet up, wedged between his armpits and the sides of the tub. The vagina swallowed the penis. Festive, a bubble of air rose to the surface to announce this.

They stayed still like this, welded to each other. Then, squashing him with all the weight of her pelvis, hanging on to his shoulder with one hand, the woman managed to heave her torso forward. Luca felt her other hand brush against his testicles under the water. Using the leverage of his arms, with an effort, he arched his back, penetrating her more deeply and permitting her fingers to insinuate themselves into the point where it was necessary to continue with the cleansing. The dwarf's swollen tongue lay motionless between her half-open lips. Her eyebrows arched. In her gaping, mad eyes gazelles chased one another no longer: they were like murky pools of mud in which hippopotami wallowed. She began to move her hips, up and down, making them rotate around the pivot of his penis as if she wanted to screw herself onto it, she who had always been broken in two; she filed it so that it would correspond to her shape, she bevelled it so that she could receive it, and be received, she planed it furiously while emitting groan after groan; Luca backed her up by raising and lowering his hips, sucked down into two sources of pleasure, which flowed into one mobile point within him, one moment filled, forced open, delved into by her fingers, then clutched by the muscular walls of her sex; the level of the water rose and fell, overflowed, the floor was flooded, the dwarf grunted, she threw her head back and rode him wildly, sweeping away the holy images accumulated in a lifetime of fears. There were no more chrysalides to capture, no more monkeys trained by dint of electric shocks, no more amputated breasts reduced to bleeding circles on which a suckling vainly stooped to get milk. There remained this African power, this long contact between pachyderms, this caress between dragons, this double conjoining of their bodies in an aquatic prehistory: a saurian cub exploring his mother's cavern, probing it, while her diligent tentacle filled, cleaned and emptied him. "Watch out *niño!*" Amid splashings and spurtings the she-elephant got up trumpeting, just as the sperm was gushing from his penis: "*Cabrón*, have you no shame?" And faced with his astonished expression: "I could be your mother, *maricón.* That's enough now, you're clean, I'm thirsty again."

PART FOUR

STILL LIFE

I

IN THE DAYS THAT FOLLOWED Luca realized that the transformation he had undergone with the baptism in the bathtub was necessary for the happiness of his jaguars and their foster brothers. Yet, during the panic attacks that assailed him despite the *majoun*, despite the sleeping pills and the whisky, he could not resign himself to the fact that he was no longer a botanist with a passion for nomenclatures. He reconstructed events wondering where and when his change had been revealed: on all fours licking the goatfish of a goat, on a *kythera*? or even before that, slitting a nipple that was a vagina beside his navel? on finding himself after years and years in his old garden in Archía? or recognizing in Martinez y Martinez not his mother, not Marta, but the traitorous and lascivious skivvy of those days? Even when the anxiety loosened its grip, permitting clumps of irises to expand freely among soapy hairs, it was still difficult to adapt to the personality of her who, having taken control of his body, was rattling on nineteen to the dozen inside his brain, obliging him to change his gestures and way of walking, even his voice, adapting them to hers, modelling them on hers until they were an identical replica of the original.

He was wearing Irene's skirt. Below that he had put on the usual pants. On his head one of her foulards. He was imagining the moment in which the boy, sitting beside him in the car, would reach out to fondle his breast: "No dear. I've had an operation. Total mastectomy."

It seemed to Luca that he could see him nod gravely. The natives liked technical terms whose meaning they did not understand. She was not going to take off her underskirt. She was the one who was paying, therefore she decided what was going to happen. In any event, he had wrapped a bandage around his chest, and even though a few hairs, above and especially below, near the scar, were still visible, on looking at himself in the mirror he was satisfied by the overall effect: a putrid mother, one of

THE AGE OF FLOWERS

those who graze on little boys. But what if instead of an Alfredino he were to bump into an adult man, one with bulbs, accustomed to women? Hazards of the Indian profession. As long as he was puny, that was the main thing. The Countess d'Audurain would be able to overcome him by brute force.

Until then all had gone smoothly. When, in the late afternoon, Mohammed had delivered Lady Weathergood's invitation—as usual Irene's name came before his—Luca had explained with gestures that he had prepared this famous fish soup. In fact he had spent the morning in the *souk* choosing the ingredients, and the afternoon cooking, arousing Alima's amazement. But for quite some time by then, since the elimination of the *Iris florentina* and especially since the destruction of the telephones, the deaf-mute gardener had harboured a diffidence towards Luca that had not diminished even when he had thrown away the gruel. Luca led him into the kitchen, showed him the big pot, the aroma was delicious, no, he had not used wine or other forms of alcohol, it was too much for him, he had already eaten, it would give him pleasure if they would accept it for their dinner. They went down to the lodge together, Luca leading, Mohammed following, carrying the pot. In front of the rose cuttings, Luca had the forethought to stop, bend down, and caress the little russet-coloured leaves that were sprouting from the branches, feigning amazement at the speed with which they had taken root. The moment the gardener's face broke into a touched smile, he knew he had won the first round of the game. The second was harder, not so much because of the two daughters, who looked up from their embroidery and limited themselves to thanking him, but because of the wife, who had seen Luca cook only once or twice in the space of a year. He guaranteed her—and Mohammed nodded—that there was no wine or pork in the soup. The woman decided to taste it, and with the wooden spoon still in mid air she said that it was good, *muchas gracias*, *mucho pescado*, lots of fish—and she put the pot down on the unlit stove. Luca could not resist asking her why she didn't heat it up right away, while it was still lukewarm, so that they could enjoy such a delicacy right away … looking him straight in the eye the woman replied that they ate later.

172

He went back up to the house, unworried. They wouldn't throw it away. The repugnance that poor folk have for waste was too strongly rooted in them. He locked the front door. Standing on the edge of the bath, he used adhesive tape to fix the plastic sheet to the plaster above the tiles. He removed the bath mat. The floor was made of cement, and so it would be easy to wash it. He put the stone, which was flat and pointed like a prehistoric weapon, on the ceramic shelf above the tap, beside the soap and a seashell Irene had found on the beach. The new gloves and secateurs, and the poultry shears—belonging to the house—ended up in the bottom of the laundry basket. He wondered if he should put the white bathrobe somewhere else. But it was hanging from a hook nailed to the door, too far from the bath for any splashes to reach it. At first, in preparation for the operation, he would have to use the nail scissors. If the boy were already shaven—and as far as he knew this was a widespread habit among Muslims—it would have been more difficult to lure him into the bathroom. But it was essential that he manage this, not so much because of any asinine fixation about bathing, but because in the bedroom, with the carpets and sheets and so on, the work to be done after the operation would have been too much even for a cleaning service. He would have to ask him straight out, reach out a hand to check. Were he shaven, she would tell him to get out of the car, what she liked, her passion, was cutting hairs, she was a shaver of pubes, a tonsurer expert in tonsures (certain Jews tied up in bathtubs knew her well, the *tondeuse de toisons*), an enthusiastic fondler of goatfish, of pike, of moray eels, of catfish—yes, catfish—with the palm of her hand slippy with soapsuds. Perhaps it would be a good idea to tell him she was married, it was her last night of freedom, it was madness, madness, her husband, *son époux*, would arrive the following day, she was terrified of insects, she was sure that he was not infested, you could see right away that he was a clean boy, but after months locked up in a cellar ... Luca ate all the *majoun* he had left. Guzzled some whisky. He went back down trying not to make any noise. The door of the lodge was open. The three women had flopped down on the benches that by day served as sofas and by night as beds for the girls. Mohammed, lying on the floor, was snoring. Luca tried calling one of the daughters, but they slept on. He clapped his hands. Still nothing. The empty bowls were on the table. He crossed the room. The pot was almost empty too. He was put in mind of the old proverb about the devil making the pots but forgetting the lids. The Countess hurled the lid into the air the way clay pigeon shooters do, and there it hung, a rusty moon on the verge of finishing up in a thousand pieces. It gave him a strange feeling, to be responsible for natural phenomena, planetary orbits included. To think that in an incautious moment he had toyed with the idea of liquidating the servants with rat poison. Listening to the regular breathing of the drifting sleepers, he was struck by the fear of having overdone it with the dosage. They weren't accustomed to medicines, only four pills were missing from the box of sleeping pills, that left sixteen therefore, which divided by four makes four ... but they were healthy, and Marga needed time, the task that awaited her was a lengthy one, it would be daytime before she finished, Mohammed was usually up at half past five. It was important to remember, every one or two hours, to come down and check that they were still snoring. The key was in the usual place, on the little shelf, behind the photo of the Kaaba. Out of prudence she locked them in. She would unlock the door in good time. Heaven only knew if on reawakening they would suspect anything.

Back at the house once more, she checked everything. The plastic bag was in Irene's wardrobe, beside the new saw. She went into the toolshed, took the spade and propped it up against the trunk of the cypress. The children were still awake, a wee bit tired. They were hungry, poor dears, only a cat, no wonder. The doubt crossed her mind that, instead of a stone, she should have procured a bar, a metal bar like the one with which she had smashed the legs of the traitor. The east wind had dropped. The moon was waning—the pot lid gradually immersed in a dark pool. Just for a change, the dogs were barking.

The Countess d'Andurain drove slowly, the night was made of ink, and she was aware that she was the cuttlefish that was producing it. This indispensable darkness was emitted by an atrophied gland of hers that had miraculously begun functioning again, to envelop her, to protect her, to conceal her from the eyes of her designated victim.

There were some passers-by, hurrying along with the mountaineer's gait of the locals accustomed to retiring early; at the corner between the boulevard and calle Sevilla, a cart was selling ... a flickering neon light, the leaden smile of a skull, between the heads of the three customers who were standing there ruminating you could read "sa-wich, sand-ich, sandwich", the toothless sand-witch grinned, Luca's throat filled with the taste of the whisky and the *majoun*, a Mercedes hearse overtook him and pulled up at the kerb in the place de France, where a little man wearing a tarbush and carrying a briefcase under his arm got in, the usual Ottoman bureaucrat who stamps documents until late at night, then goes home and gasses himself, or dines alone—a wave of memories overwhelmed him, the destination of a motorcycle trip, the glorious days of the Sublime Porte, the massacres of the Armenians on the radio, with the shrieking of the women as they miscarried live, and dancing the tango at night in Galata, passing from mouth to mouth the grapes of the Bosphorus, big and ripe like Alfredino glands, like carcinoma ... a pavement café still open, the eyes of the customers followed her, she slowed down, but she couldn't do it there, right in the centre, with the streetlights on, in front of the Byzantine court in session in St Irene's. The Countess d'Andurain, a squid rowing along with her tentacles, mighty enough to impale any snotnose, to disembowel him, slipped away. Headed for other histories, other geographies, she went down to the sea, a steep alley between buildings from the forties (she was born in Bordeaux, she spoke exquisite English), where the *gafir*, the Nile-shore nightwatchmen, lay stretched out in their burnooses; their cudgels in their laps, the glass of tea close to hand, they groaned as they dreamed of Colonel Lawrence's soft kiss on their erections. Then a building site, the corrugated iron shack where succulent working men slept and farted, goodness knows how many of them, seventy, eighty kilos apiece, the child labourers less, she just couldn't recall what the percentage of water was. She took the avenue d'Espagne that skirted first the harbour and then the city beach, with a raised walkway in the middle and on the other side the little summer restaurants and bars, all still closed, the Macumba, the Miami, the Roxy, the Eldorado, the Tortue qui Mord, the Monocle, the Mar y Playa, which were filing past in that very moment—reed canopies, Andalusian lanterns bobbing in the backwash—behind the eyelids of heaven knows how many Liverpudlian hairdressers, of heaven knows how many window dressers from Dusseldorf ... two soldiers sitting on a low wall were smoking and scratching and bollocks to the fundamentalists. Here, in the centre of the world, she had this memory of herself on the sand, shaken by fits of retching synchronized with the rhythm of the breathing of a nurseling child—a white monster came out of the sea and announced his future in one word, smothered, smothered—a roaring in the ears, she adjusted her foulard, changed gear. Past the roundabout, on a bench in the public gardens, bingo! but there were three of them, one dark two fair, obviously no good therefore. But she slowed down and opened the window, leaning out with a smile worthy of a Luxardo diva ... "*Maricón!*" shouted one of them making a vulgar gesture. The other two laughed, come here, come on beautiful, we'll show you a good time, come on ... his heart in his mouth, Luca accelerated and took the road that led inland. There were times when he realized he had gone mad.

At the fifth or sixth junction, finally, a boy was walking along the pavement. The octopus pulled over, in wait: "Do you want a lift? Want to take a tour?" The boy looked at her, inspected the cabin, and then got in beside her. No, no one had seen them, the submarine plunged into the depths once more, the prey got settled in his seat with those measured movements that are typical of those accustomed to discomfort, to taking up the least space possible. He was skinny. He kept his back straight, his open hands resting on his knees. It was heart-wrenching to

see his clothes, so threadbare and clean, and in his profile
chopped out with a hatchet the Countess was successfully identifying the product of the maternal genes and the chromosomes
of the thrifty, suspicious aunts, and how much he had inherited
from his father, from the young peasant who was his father.
She offered him a cigarette. He smoked greedily, without trou-
bling to conceal his joy at such a luxury. If anything, he leaned
against the seatback and looked ahead, boldly, determined to
enjoy the run in the car. She asked him if he felt like going to
her place, she was alone in the castle. He replied that it was no
problem. A pity that beneath the words there was a hiss, a
whistle of bronchial consumption. He must have been asth-
matic. But the bone structure, judging by the wrists, seemed
rather massive. That fruit of generations of bearers of sheaves,
of ploughmen, of muleteers, having shrivelled up in the city,
would have found renewed vigour in the earth. Taking the
road that led to the villa, the Countess asked him if he was
shaven. Since he gave no sign of having understood, she reached
out a hand and laid it on his sex. The boy said to wait: love at
the house. She insisted. Did he have hairs, or did he cut them?
Finally—and the movement wrung a smile from her—he
pulled down his zip and lowered his underpants. Grasping her
hand, he drew it from the wheel and guided it to his pubes.
Short, but they were there, Allah be praised. With a scissors
gesture of the fingers, she told him that once they got home she
wanted to cut them. The boy nodded, repeating that there was
no problem with a smile that was at once cunning and resigned
that, by sketching a cobweb of wrinkles round his eyes, made
him the image of his aunt—Farida or Amina? They had arrived.
The Countess—and by then even this ingenuous young boy
had sensed who he was dealing with—switched off the engine,
gestured at him to get out, got out in her turn, and locked up the
car. As she preceded him through the garden she realized that
she was a fabulous creature, a goat-chimaera worthy of the
White City and its legend. In the bathroom she ordered him to
strip off. The boy, working on what he had heard from his
older and better looking friends, had been expecting different

behaviour from a *nazrani*, ventured to say: "You too." But the Countess had the situation firmly in hand. Haughtily, she told him to hurry up, because she wanted to shave him, otherwise she would take him back down to the city. The boy gave in. He was standing in the poor little heap of his stuff, slender, with his pelvic bones sticking out and his Adam's apple bobbing up and down out of nervousness and embarrassment.

She had him sit down on the edge of the bath. It seemed that he hadn't even noticed the plastic sheet protecting the plaster. But how could he know what a bathroom was like, given that there wasn't one in his house? He had a scar on his chest. A motorbike accident, came the explanation. In Salonika? He pretended he did not understand. The Countess grasped the scissors and knelt down. She cut away the bulk of the hair, resisting the obvious temptation, and threw the tufts into the bathtub. Then she took the shaving foam and the Gillette razor, the little fool was sniggering, his penis was half erect, every time the hand had to push his penis and compress it on one side or the other to allow the blade to penetrate between the thigh and the scrotum, she felt him squirm, the little eel out of water. She would never have believed that shaving some-one's pubes was such a long job. Once she finished, she ordered him to turn around so that he could put his feet inside the tub, and she pointed to the flexible shower head with which he would wash away the blanket of foam and hairs that, flowing down from his groin, formed long johns reaching down to his ankles. She took the shower in her left hand and turned it on. The boy laughed with surprise and pleasure (his mother's reac-tion to a gift from his father, a shy iris pulled out of a deformed pocket) because the water was hot, he wasn't used to that. The Countess was embracing him from behind, her cheek against his little man's back. With her right tentacle she reached for the stone next to the soap, bumped into the seashell, and, after dealing a blow like a rabbit punch to the nape of his defenceless neck, she hauled herself upright, dropped the shower head, wielded the weapon for a second time with all the strength of her outstretched windmilling arm, striking with the pointed end. There was a sound like when you tread on a snail's shell. The boy turned round a fraction, looking at her from over his shoulder, a glance unexpectedly veiled with sleep, and now he was a grown man, he was his father coming home dead beat after a day's work in the fields, and that wasn't nice, he might have given her some attention, she was convinced she deserved it, it was too easy to fall asleep like that, he was trying to say something, about time too, she ground her teeth, are you waking up? what's that you say, my dear? He was saying: "Mo ... "

A third blow, like a slap but a wicked one, to the temple, that'll teach you. He was about to fall backwards, she pushed him inside the bath, he said: "Moham ... ", she brought down the stone with both hands, now you're talking, at last, now we're getting somewhere, the brow ridge burst, a precious whitish matter spilled out from the hole at the root of the nose. Another flat blow smashed his incisors, in a gush of blood and drool he gurgled: "Mohammed", then he arched, racked by a shudder, while she continued hitting him, perhaps it really would have been easier to go to a butcher, she would never know whether he had wanted to say his name or whether he had been calling on the Prophet, finally the cat stopped threshing about, it was all hers, to look at it like that it seemed ...

Down in the lodge they were still asleep, she had been to check. She slipped off her clothes and undid the bandage, but even though she was naked she was sweating. Her back was aching and the muscles in her arms hurt. She had been doing so much kneeling and bending over, she was tormented by cramps in the thighs. It wasn't much use telling herself over and over, in order to get her breath back and to brace herself up, that this was the most important experiment of her life, and she had the time required to bring it to a conclusion. Lifting him up every time, getting him into a suitable position, was extenuating. Her head was spinning. A monstrous task even for Marta.

Nor did the exactitude of this body—offered and therefore redeemed, delivered from the shadows within which dirt spreads like wildfire, and cells proliferate like mould—suffice to encourage her. She took off the gloves, her hand could fondle the top of the cranium where it was still intact, rounded, her finger could penetrate the crater from whose rim hung the flaps of the temporal and zygomatic muscle. Cautiously, in order not to hurt herself, she went beyond the gaping hole in the parietal bone, where her probing fingertip felt the ineffable softness of the cerebral membrane and followed its folds to run along the recess of the fissure of Sylvius, which separates the temporal from the frontal lobe. Here she lingered, her breathing heavy with emotion. But it was time to get to work. She got similar feelings of pleasure from exploring the anogenital area. She could open his legs, massage the scrotum, pinch it and pull it, stretching the wrinkled skin, crush the testicles as much as she wished, compress them, use her nail to torment the lips of the urethral meatus, squeeze the glans, fold the penis in two, slip a hand under the buttocks and force the anus with her thumb. Then, after having taken a little blood from the smashed mouth to lubricate her fingers, she managed to insert her index, middle and ring fingers into his arse, all the way to the join of the metacarpal bones, moving blindly inside him, swinging from the coccyx to the prostate, thrusting towards the bladder, where, beyond the soft and still warm mass of the large and small intestines, it even seemed to her that she touched—there was a tear—the beans of the kidneys in their crunchy pods, the tip of the calf's liver ... but she must not dally. It was wonderful having her son there, within reach, this had to be said, settled down in a luminous cradle and no longer subject to those con-tinuous changes that are the curse of matter. But she had to act. She put the gloves back on.

The skin was elastic. Before it yielded, it stretched surprisingly. For a fraction of a second the dermis was lily-white, then the severed capillaries flooded it, making it scarlet. But the sheaths of muscular tissue, especially the pectorals and the rectus muscles of the abdomen gave her terrible problems. To open them she used the shears, and it was like unpicking canvas sacks. In order to complete the task of separating them she turned to the poultry shears, more pointed. Then she operated with the saw. The saw was the ideal instrument for the cartilage and the small bones. But every time she came to the crunch, and a big bone—a tibia, a humerus—gleamed white in the flesh, she was obliged to mangle it without ceremony, pounding it with the stone until the marrow spurted out and it was smashed to pieces. She cut each leg into three pieces, merely detaching the femur from the sacrum and the coccyx cost her an hour's work, while it took just as long to reduce the iliac to three big shards befouled with fecal matter and the mushy pap that was all that was left of the organs after the battering. She couldn't take it any more, she was on the verge of fainting and she would have given anything for a mouthful of *majoun*, but it was finished. The loving thought of her hungry flowers came to her aid, she went into the dining room, drank a whisky, couldn't find the cigarette holder, smoked a cigarette without sitting down in order to avoid dirtying the sofa, stretched her legs, then got back to work, industrious as an ant. It was surprising how, the more she broke off and severed that matter devoid of subterfuges, the more she flayed and tore, the more she ripped and removed in order to open it, poke about in it, delve into it, the more it seemed closed: the inside was made of the same stuff as the outside, and so on, she could have gone on chopping it up *ad infinitum*. As she recalled the days when, wherever her glance had fallen, she would see that amalgamation and separation of clots, she came to the conclusion that she was the victim of a pro-longed hallucination. She was having a hallucination even then, from the glass door of the bathroom there came the glimmer of dawn, all that remained attached to the torso was the head, yet the naked boy lying in the bathtub was asking her with a senile little smile if she had liked it, if that was enough, to pass him his clothes, it wasn't much money for a whole night, more, please, sir: "*Estas loco? más dinero, hombre, más, más, amigo*". Instead of the Great Lady Surgeon she was a man, a man who for hours and hours, with savage tenacity, had fondled licked and sucked the body of an adolescent, after having shaved him in order to have the illusion that he was pre-pubescent, a little baby boy in his power, the babe in a bathtub that had been gently rubbed and penetrated by the finger of a mother obsessed with cleanliness

... the boy punched him. A yell rang out. Luca fell to the floor. A kick. Someone was rummaging about in the room, was taking something, was running out of the bathroom ... *It had not been in the bathroom.* The memory surfaced—a bullet fired all the way up the arteries to lodge in the brain.

"Mummy is ill, do you want to make mummy better, Luca?"

Marta dried him, led him naked into her room. The whole time, as she undressed, she contiaued fondling her little boy's stalk with her free hand. With an insane, innocent movement, she managed to guide him, to make him enter her ... the yell had come then. He had hurt mummy. He wanted to get out of that soft, unknown part of her, but her hand was pressing her buttocks and wouldn't let him. The nannygoat knew she was doomed. She wanted to enjoy her little boy. She moved her hips and shook her head to and fro on the pillow, uttering words with no sense, syllables that were all the same: "Mortim ... Mort ... mrt ... ", the lowing of a sea of magma at the bottom of which resounded a second, desperate yell. The hand had freed his buttocks, allowing him to slip out. His body was lost. He had forgotten for twenty years. But now, after the sacrifice, the divine response was the innocence of the mother and the child. All children of the seed of a lily.

He awoke. He was naked. He was alone. The bathrobe was no longer there. His satchel had vanished. The coins in the tray had vanished. He went down to the lodge. Mohammed and his family were still sleeping, stretched out in the same positions as the evening before. Their breathing was regular. The clock said noon. He put the key back behind the photo of the Kaaba. He went out, pulling the door to behind him. He would say that he too had slept like a log, suggesting that among those fish there had been one whose flesh was soporiferous, an opium popeye, the narcotic flounder. The pieces would already be buried among the flowers, but even though he knew he had dug the holes he couldn't remember when he had done so. He would order them to spread fresh soil on the flower bed, in a corner of the garden there was always a pile of it available. Having put back the spade, he folded the plastic sheet. He put it in the rubbish bag along with all the rest. Then he put the bag in the wardrobe, locked it, and slipped the key into the pocket of the trousers that he had thrown on the armchair when undressing. He was too exhausted to get rid of the bag now. He would do it the next day. Better to fill it with stones and toss it into the sea, because if he hid it in the forest the werewolves would find it and rip it open, scattering clues. Barely able to stand, he washed the tiles and the floor. The water ran away with difficulty, he had to use a finger to clear the drain, pulling out tufts of hair that he then threw down the toilet. He rinsed and wrung out the rags. After laying them on the edge of the laundry basket, he re-examined everything. He was forgetting the poultry shears. He ran into the kitchen and threw them into the drawer. All was in order. No traces remained. No one in the world could have ever imagined what kind of an operation he had managed to perform in that room. There was no stink, only the smell of shaving foam and sweat. He took a shower and washed himself at length, inside his arse too. He swallowed a couple of sleeping pills. After drinking another whisky, he threw himself onto the bed.

When he awoke he was shivering. It was dark, it must already be evening. He groped around for the *majoun* in the bedside table, but as he was opening the drawer he remembered that he had finished it. He listened to the beating of his heart. No help for it. It was a shock that from the middle of his chest, between the lungs, radiated out towards the periphery, as if from the inside of his body something, someone, was rebelling. Under the lash, his torso arched and crackled like that of a condemned man bound to the electric chair. His arms and legs writhed and went rigid. He dragged himself into the bathroom. He got down a sleeping pill, drinking from the tap. He looked at himself for a long time in the mirror, because he couldn't believe the image he had glimpsed on bending over the sink. It was he. His face. An old nannygoat, the thin skin clinging to the skull, the eyelids irritated, bluish circles under the eyes, the cheeks covered with down like a beard still growing on the face of a corpse. He shaved. He was transformed into a greyish little boy, locked up for months in a cellar. He showered again, washing with maniacal care. When, once he was dressed, he stood looking out over the garden, he realized that it wasn't as late as he had thought. In all, he must have slept a couple of hours. The wind had come up. The darkness depended on the mass of clouds chasing one another across the sky, herds tumbling down from the ridges of the hills. At the bottom of the terraces, Mohammed, bent over beneath an orange tree, was removing the dead leaves from the agapanthus. Avoiding looking at the iris bed, Luca went out keeping close to the wall, so that the women would not hear him, incapable as he was of dealing with a confrontation. In his pocket was the key to the wardrobe. There was a flash of lightning far off in the sky. After he had been driving for a bit, he had to yield before the evidence. He had forgotten again. He was terrified.

He took rue 26 Juillet, men in djellabas were standing in groups on the pavement near the great mosque, it must have been a religious holiday. In front of the walls of the old cemetery, on the corner of the sharia Prince of Wales, he took calle Azenmour, among abandoned thirties-style detached houses with their windows in smithereens and gates held closed by chains. He drove along an avenue lined with eucalyptus trees towards the Sallam district, built over the ruins of the Roman necropolis that overlooked the sea. He passed in front of the synagogue, in whose garden, beneath a *dombeya*, the carcass of a Rolls-Royce lay stranded. Sitting packed shoulder to shoulder in a truck, soldiers observed the passers by. Priestesses in multi-coloured clothes went in and out of the bakery. Barefoot children scampered about on the pavement pushing tin hoops with sticks. Cement buildings constructed after the war filed by. On the thresholds of these buildings groups of young shamans, in pyjamas, sat smoking and watching the veiled girls coming back hand in hand from the market, or whistling up a younger brother to run to the café for a glass of mint tea to be sipped, glowering, emaciated, on those steps cluttered with refuse. Past the stadium and the acacias black in the livid light, past the villas in the Norman style in which French and Belgian functionaries had lived in the days of the free port, the mercury sea glittered. Driving slowly, he wound down the window. He wound it up and then opened it again. But the smell was growing stronger. It was everywhere. It was in the air swollen with humidity, it saturated the land currents whose blending with the oceanic ones created the microclimate of this magical, accursed city. It was the smell that had tormented him during his childhood and during Irene's illness, the smell that impregnated their house, the smell that had obliged him to spend his days on the streets, repairing to bars in order to study the life of flowers: human, laden with frustration because concealed out of shame, fear, decorum; putrid breath always lying in wait despite attempts to defeat it with perfumes. He drew up at the kerb. He brought one hand up to his mouth, and, exhaling, he sniffed his own breath. This stink came from him. It was inside him, in his breath. In that same moment, matter opened up again. He had to find some *majoun*. Anything, as long as he didn't have to witness this.

   The people, the parked cars, the trunks of the trees, the walls of the tenements, the dogs, the children playing marbles in the dust of the alley, the women looking out from the window above an advertising sign, were crumbling into decay. There was a rotatory movement, an acceleration, a vortex at the bottom of which, ineluctable, the mass of worms seethed. Fat, white larvae, pupae in perpetual motion, millions of little blind creatures curling up and stretching out, creeping, dragging themselves along. As if from a cornucopia, the larvae came pouring out of the cracks in the walls and the fissures that split the faces, they invaded the ground, climbing back up the legs of the people from whom they had emerged. Luca got out of the car. He dragged himself towards the wall. An old woman with a hunch-back looked up at him—and she looked at him the way the waiters in the restaurants looked at Jaima, when, in the course of their soirées, she would lose control and shout out the genealogy of her family. Then the grubs emerged from her lachrymal sac, they began to fall from her eyeballs onto her breast, her belly, tumbling down to the ground, writhing. He vomited. Bent double, the old woman walked on up the hill, leaving a trail of larvae behind her ("*Nazrani afuera . . . Nazrani* go home . . . "). He vomited again. The smell was still there. He sniffed at his hands, his forearms, the hems of his jacket, the acid breath of gastric juices again. He had the simultaneous sensation of warmth and coolness. A rumble, a crash. He had killed a man.

"*Nazrani afuera!*"

It was raining.

It took him a few seconds to realize the implications of this. He was driving flat out towards home, but even with the wipers going at top speed he could barely see. It was like driving through a tunnel and trying to get to the other side before the level of the water stalled the engine. It wasn't one of the usual springtime showers. Lightning bolts rent the sky, pursuing one another like praying mantises with serrated forelegs of light until the thunder shattered them with a roar that shook the houses to their foundations. Rivers of mud inundated the streets, pouring down from all the slopes, the deserted pavements were strafed by windy blasts. Too late to add more soil. The bank would already be closed. He would take his passport and flee. Disappear. It was the only eventuality that he had not foreseen. The forgotten pot lid. The earth with the lid off, the barely tilled earth that would subside as it absorbed the water, its level shrinking to reveal . . . herds of bison from Lascaux and Altamira pissing and stamping their hoofs, reducing everything to mush: this was the significance of the rains that had accompanied his first encounters with the dwarf, this was the truth heralded by the downpour in the bathroom! A far cry from lavage of the arse! The mother was the mare squatting down to inundate the land with piss, the leader of the herd who drowned humans in the bath, and ensured that the pieces of their bodies came to the surface. Thanks to the unusable telephones, perhaps the caretakers had still not had the chance to inform the police. His only advantage was the weather. The weather. On passing through calle de Hollanda, which was flooded, the car raised a wave that washed over a figure huddled under a plastic sheet. In the farce the extras were always in the same place. Time did not exist in the White City. The beggarwoman disfigured by eczema was nursing the doll again, he was entering the dark hallway again, and again and again he was going up the stairs with fast-beating heart in search of the woman with whom he had fallen in love, little Jaima of the swollen feet, the supreme iguana under formaldehyde who had engineered his downfall, and again and again she appeared before him, the monster enthroned, between the two vases of *monstera deliciosa* . . . two, three jeeps full of soldiers. At the entrance to rue de la Vieille Montagne, absurd, a tank.

The road was blocked by the stones brought down by the force of the current. He took the main road to the Cape, before the barracks in front of which the soldiers were assembled he entered the lane that led to home. A flash of lightning, extremely close, and a roll of thunder. He was hanging on to the wheel. The water opened up around the car; it came up to the doors. The engine cut out. It wouldn't start again. Luca jumped out, he still had about a hundred metres to go; he started to run and was immediately drenched. He slipped the key into the lock, but the door—opened from the inside—gave way. He was inside, under the canopy booming with the drumming rain. Mohammed stood before him.

He was wearing a yellow oilskin. From beneath the hood he regarded Luca with eyes like burning coals. Luca repressed the impulse to throw himself at his feet, to cling to his knees and beg for mercy. The gardener raised one hand as if to strike him, he looked like a prophet, Moses, he was holding out a blackish thing. It was an object the size of a fist, covered with lumps of mud, bristling with hairs. The man was holding the white tri-angle of an ear pinched between two fingers—the cat's head. Luca's gaze shifted to his judge, who spat.

Luca took off. He ran under the rain as far as the old cypress. The flower bed was boundless, a lunar landscape scattered with mountains and peaks among which yawned abysses and precipices at the bottom of which roiled torrents, which, as they gradually descended, swelled until they debouched into complex estuaries. Piled up on the path beside the spade, beyond the apocalyptic scene, there were six or seven little bundles. In the centre of the flower bed, on a little mound, incongruous, a wishy-washy yellow in colour, there sprouted some freesias like the ones an old peasant woman had shown him behind her shack, but weaker and more stunted because they were wild. So these were the *Iris juncea numidica*, these were his jaguars!

Mohammed grasped him by the arm and, pointing to the remains of the cat, he asked for an explanation. Luca broke free and ran up to the house. In Irene's changing room. He opened the wardrobe. The sack. He took it and emptied it out. A pair of rubber gloves still sealed inside the packaging, a saw and a pair of shears, both brand new, and a folded plastic sheet with its edges held by adhesive tape all fell to the floor. No trace of blood. All fresh from the shop: a little carpenter's set or a little gardener's set to be given to a child. There had been no need for sacrifices. Silence fell, and in the window there appeared the outlines of the rainbow. The iris. It wasn't raining any more. In the sunbeams, droplets glittered on the blossoming branches of the plumbago, and on the scarlet pelargoniums. Luca had never seen this aurora borealis. Names and words dissolved, a boundless field of Dutch iris ruffled by the wind. He lay curled up on the floor. He was awakened by the sound of knocking, knocking at the main door. Late afternoon. He had slept on the floor all night and a good part of the day. Groping, he went out into the garden, his lids half closed to keep out the excessive light. Alima, who had already opened the door, greeted him with a smile. Behind her, some figures were emerging from the shadow of the canopy: "Magnificent, dear boy, your masterpiece!" exclaimed the oldest one, theatrically raising one arm to indicate the exuberance of the blossoms, so that the sleeve of his djellaba uncovered and laid bare the sagging flesh of his elbow, the overly clear skin. The two locals kept their eyes lowered: a cockroach in a wig and a goat, Kacem and Rashid.

II

BRINGING TO BEAR a self control that he would not have believed himself capable of, and as if in obedience to a pre-established rule, after having invited the two young men to take a seat on the armchairs already dried by the sun on the lawn scattered with leaves and petals, Luca preceded his enemy along the path that led to the last terrace. On passing in front of the bare flower bed, he gestured for Gordon to wait for him. He stooped over the freesias, flattened by the rain and clinging to the little mound of earth surrounded by tiny landslips. He was about to uproot them, when the memory of the ogre who had slaughtered the *Iris florentina* immobilized him. He looked up, and for a second, as if in a kaleidoscope, a scintillating image took shape: flowers hanging from the dry stone walls, festoons of flowers cascading from the cypresses and the pear trees, flowers on the arches, in the beds, a sea of flowers raising their heads below a freshly lacquered, lustrous sky. In the Atlantic light, the garden was an island, an intact world. The storm had opened no wounds. Fecundated by the rain, the earth had given birth, tranquilly. He retraced his steps delighting in the thousands of movements around him—wrens dancing minuets among the branches of the cherry tree, the aerial courtship of cabbage whites, bees at work, hornets on special missions, the solemn flight of a stork, the Egyptian one of a hawk, a tree frog climbing up the branches of the solanum . . . Ritts-Twice gave him an approving smile.

They were at the bottom of the garden. There was the chirping of a cricket, the first of the season. It was sufficient to make the sky bluer, the air warmer. Summer again. The cycle proceeded with no need for human intervention or fertilization. The chirping continued, and it was the siren warning the inhabitants of the White City, from Ciar Ben Dibbane to Djeliba, from the Cape to the casbah, of the imminent arrival of the pigeons among whose number, perhaps, there would be hidden the goose that laid the golden egg ... Luca was in a hurry. He wanted to go into town, to telephone Irene.

Exhausted, the Englishman flopped down on the wall, in the shade of the *olea fragrans*, in the exact point in which, for days and days, the cauldron of gruel had bubbled away.

"You have amazed me, dear boy. After a couple of nights in police headquarters I thought you would have packed your bags. Then I was convinced that you would have gone to your reward without making any fuss. Instead, you're one of the family. Don't think me cynical. No one would have suspected our stallion, given the quantity of hashish the pathologist would have found in your belly." Luca saw again the muzzle of the Sumerian goat coming up to him there on the top of the precipice—the eyelids like Marta's, the flaring nostrils, the pallor of the boy who released his grip on the arrival of the old goatherd, like a lover disturbed by a peeping Tom ... a murderer surprised by ... he punched Gordon in the snout. Black, dense as bramble juice, Ritts's blood spurted onto the djellaba and the grass. But despite the gurgling gush, the Gorgon was still smiling, a sneering stone gargoyle spouting rustily into a fountain: "Now is that a nice thing to do, giving a poor old man ill with leukaemia a haemorrhage? I could be your uncle, you know?"

With the tip of his tongue, Gordon licked the blood that had collected on his lip. He took a handkerchief out of his pocket and set to dabbing at his chin and neck. In the meantime, he was talking. He urged Luca to save his energy: he wouldn't have managed to excite him even if he carried on slapping him for hours. Then, crossing his legs—and the meticulousness with which he ran the piece of cloth over his dirty face conjured up for Luca the image of an ageing actress vainly attempting to powder over the ravages of time—he said that, finally, Luca could relax: he was obliged to give up on this garden, " ... my garden, dear boy."

Did Luca know that it was the most beautiful garden he had ever seen? He couldn't imagine just how much he had fallen in love with it, how many moments he had spent recalling that first visit at the end of the previous summer, when the setting sun lent the paths a fairy-tale look, and in the darkening walks, among the bushes, the creatures of the night began their dance ... he could not believe that the house he had been seeking for a lifetime had always been there, before his eyes, the home of a boring American whose invitations he had refused, now the property of ... "It's hard to define creatures like you two, treasure."

He thought again of the things he had waited for in his life: waiting for estates to be divided up in order to get hold of paintings, sculptures, objects whose beauty only he had recognized ... waiting for days, on desolate tropical islands, until the initiation ceremonies were over and he might buy from a village chief the masks that would have otherwise ended up on a bonfire ... and setting down the handkerchief-powder puff to show that the make-up was finished, the actress came on stage: all his life had been a succession of waits in order to rescue from the ignorance of others some object that had not been appreciated, that had not been loved ... a Sung monochrome bowl used as an ashtray by an ignoble dentist, a marble fragment of an archaic Kouros used as a door stop in a Venetian palazzo owned by vulgarians, certain Ottoman tiles adorned with wild roses and carnations embedded in the rear wall of a small villa by a criminal of an architect ... "And now I am waiting ... it's curious how some words are unpronounceable for a civilized person, isn't it?" He straightened up his torso: "Myeloid leukaemia. The first haemorrhages worried me. It was the spleen, they told me, which was acting up. Then, late one afternoon towards the end of summer, on arriving here, I found myself in the garden in which I knew I could have calmly received the most rapacious collector of all ... I already told you. It's as if we were family."

Finally Luca understood. In a small voice he asked Gordon why he had used that dwarf in order to get his hands on their house. "Don't you think you're exaggerating? My lady friend is merely a bit short in the leg!" And giving Luca's knee a squeeze, before he had time to move away: "The fact that you like mature ladies outside the canons of Greek beauty is no mystery to anyone! You don't know how many times we laughed about that, together with Irene. Did you realize that she knows nothing about botany? That she couldn't tell a convolvulus from a nigella?"

Silence fell. Luca let his gaze roam over the lawn, to the garden wall, until it fell on the city below. And the White City struck him as alien, an agglomeration of ugly constructions of different heights and styles that had nothing romantic or exotic about it, an ordinary seaside town ruined by property speculation. Was the story of the mangled legs, Luca asked, an invention? The end of the Countess d'Andurain? The massacre of Manolo's kids? The bag full of . . .

Ritts-Twice interrupted him. He had no desire to listen to another repetition of the idiocies produced by the mind of that Levantine woman. He had to prevent the blood from rising to his head. For his part, he had restricted himself to giving her a few suggestions, providing her with an idea or two . . . you could buy cumin by the hundredweight in the *souk*. He had come across a charming hecatomb of whores in a Mexican short story. As for stock characters like the Countess . . . there wasn't one action movie or one *noir* . . . in reality, she had been one of the many collaborationists tormented by remorse who had buried themselves alive in one of the suburbs of the White City . . . yes, it was called Archía . . . and she had wound up a suicide, throwing herself into the sea. Wasn't it touching that despite her age and experience of life, poor Senora Martinez was still sufficiently coquettish to attribute the cause of her stature to torture? It was risible, human nature.

"Gordon, did your brother write *The Road to Kabul*?"

For a second, Ritts was tempted to tell him the truth. But he couldn't. He didn't know what it was any more.

"I thought you had a certain experience of advertising campaigns, my boy! How could he have written it, since I was alone during the journey? A debatable stunt like the murder of a relative is sometimes enough to guarantee the success of a boring book . . . it was no accident that all, almost all of the people involved in this affair had survived, so far" . . . Ritts added that he was about to take Rashid to England even though he had

shown himself to be a coward incapable of giving many destinies
a hand with a single shove, but Luca was to refrain from foolish
considerations: he had no desire to realize Forsterian projects:
" ... together in the country, with the bare-chested toy boy
grooming a horse in the shadow of an oak, as, confined to my
wheelchair, I observe them from the window of the Japanese
drawing room ... "

He was taking Rashid back with him, nay, he was following
him, because he was in his hands: "Here, to be exact". And lifting up the sleeve of his djellaba, the old actress ran his fingertip along the inside of the forearm covered with bruises and
riddled with tiny black holes. "Two doses of fifty cubic centimetres keep me on my feet for the present, as long as you
don't get too insistent with your caresses. More than one hundred and fifty, in the long run, would be fatal to him. We have
a precise agreement. Can you imagine me, in one of those hospitals that stink of vegetable soup?" And after a pause: "Will it
last another two weeks, two months, two years? I would have
much preferred to continue my treatment in the White City, to
witness the end of the farce, which believe me, is nigh ... but
these boys are dying to go abroad, and as well as being well
hung they are also stubborn, like their mules ... it isn't so much
a question of compatible blood groups as the incredible capacity of his bone marrow to produce ... my big beefsteak!" Ritts-
Twice smiled: "It must be the hides and the offal that his
ex-boss fed him on for years! I detest syringes, and I know what
the youths of this place have nicknamed me, *Tiburón Mariposa*.
I assure you that I would have never attempted to transform
myself from a shark to a leech, from a butterfly to a mosquito,
if his identity card had not fallen out of his pocket, he told me
he had shown it to you ... but all we carnivores, if you think
about it, have a curious tendency to confuse semen with milk,
milk with food, food with blood ... perhaps even you, who I am
told give it a decent suck ... an inheritance from the cannibalism of the primordium?"

Again, he smiled at him. His eyes, glittered, light blue, almost
violet, and it was as if the boy trapped inside him had managed

to free himself: he was there, out in the open—a desperate boy. Luca was on the point of saying something, but Gordon beat him to it: "You can think what you wish. I am convinced that being a parody is the only greatness that destiny allows such as us." It was getting late. He and Rashid were expected at the consulate, the bureaucracy was hellish, he would never have believed that obtaining an emigration permit, especially when it was inopportune to reveal the real reason, was so difficult. Finally he understood why the locals would spend hours sitting contemplating the Strait, the European coast: they were in prison. And to think that in the past he had thought them to be contemplative romantics! He struggled to his feet: "Our perception of this place is so subjective that I sometimes wonder if the White City really exists. I have wasted your time. I wanted to say goodbye to my garden. Consider it the last flick of an old shark's tail. You are both lucky. Young, masters of an oasis you think is yours, and alive, at least for now". He moved off, preceding Luca up the path.

On their appearance, the two youths got to their feet. Luca headed for the entrance to the living room without looking at them, but Rashid called him back. Why, one of those days, did he not take a gift to his Grandmère of a little sugar or a few tins of tuna to apologize for his behaviour? If she realized that even the *nazrani* had manners, she would have been less worried about his going to England. Luca had shot back that his aggressiveness had depended on the *majoun*. "Only on that? Are you sure?" asked Ritts-Twice. Rashid nodded gravely: from now on, he would do without it, in any case in England there was heroin, there was cocaine, ecstasy, crack ... "You'll read about me in the papers!" was the Englishman's cheery comment. "Old, ill novelist murdered ... and don't you talk nonsense. The only people who use drugs today are bank clerks, my angel, and I am the only one who touches your veins ... "

Kacem, bewigged, had not opened his mouth. As he moved off, from behind, with raised arm, Gordon waved bye-bye with one hand. Between the two young natives in T-shirts, blue jeans and tennis shoes, with that djellaba fluttering around his thinner body, the old actress continued to invite the applause of the public until he left the scene ... and he looked like a madwoman in a night-gown who had been conveyed to a place of constriction by two nurses in civilian clothes, unaware of what awaited him, and therefore affable and worldly the way only certain monsters or innocents can be: what Senora Martinez, like a good daughter of the White City, would have defined as one who was *loca* for arse—when he was one who was *loca* for blood, an equally widespread type, in those parts, among the uncles and the aunties who lived here, as it was among the carnivorous summer pigeons.

After a few attempts, the car moved off. In the phone booth in the Central Post Office the heat was torrid, with the smell of stale tobacco smoke hanging in the air. On the plastic-lined walls there were names, figures, scribbles. As Luca was dialling the number his eyes returned to a biro drawing of a penis that ended in a fishtail, the two gills forming a glans that was an upside-down heart ... an allusion to the multiplication of the Nazarene, the symbol of a cult of Chinese lotus eaters—or was it just a shark-sucker, an April fool. The line went dead. He mopped the sweat from his brow. Dialled the number again. After a rumble and some static there came the ringing tone. A woman's voice answered. It was one of those voices you hear in the villages telling complicated stories of relatives and neigh-bours, frequently interrupting itself to invoke the aid of God. "The Lord be praised! The journey went well! Young master ... " Had she been at his side, Luca would have embraced the odious Maria. He told her he wanted to speak with Irene.

"Where are you calling from, for heaven's sake?"

From the White City, he replied. At the other end of the line a silence fell.

"Maria! Is she there? Where is my wife? What's happened? Maria!"

The woman then uttered a few incomprehensible words. He begged her to repeat them more slowly. Maria intoned her incantatory formula, and she was like Jaima, one night, on the belvedere behind the mosque of the goldsmiths. A prophetess on a mountain top. What she was saying was simple, and clear: to be careful, that the master, Miss Irene's father, was worried, Luca had to get the telephone repaired as soon as possible, avoid any incautious moves, health was the only thing that mattered, Miss Irene was well but tired, she was not to expose herself to the sun during the hottest part of the day, she was to continue with the vitamin injections ... the echo of distance grew louder and louder. Luca hung up the receiver. He was outside the cabin, on the road, in the car, already home. A canvas bag on the lawn. With a radiant smile, Mohammed, standing still at the foot of the steps, pointed to the upper pavilion, Luca was to hurry. In the entrance, in the half light, standing out against the background of a large deal sideboard bought from a second-hand dealer in the *medina* ("In France it would be *Henri Quatre*, in Italy *Coppedé*, here it's *Felipe Segundo*"), walking in that unmistakable way, her bust slightly tilted and her long arms dangling ever so slightly, a woman, this woman, was coming towards him. They were both in the light. "Luca! What a state you're in!" it was a pale girl, the yawn of the blouse open at the breast afforded a glimpse, alongside the sternum, of a scar in relief on the skin. She was in his arms, eyes closed, lips united. There was one of those sighs that herald a sob. But the mouths opened, the tongues brushed each other, left each other, and found each other again in that alternation of lingering and flight and contact that Irene defined as the "seminarist's kiss"—only a seminarist who practised abstinence, she used to say, could kiss like that: "A future priest or a soldier boy on leave, spider ... "

But the recomposition lasted only a few minutes. A young woman slipped out of his embrace and, sprucing up her hair, said that it was late, that it was time to get ready for Priscilla Weathergood's cocktail party: "You cannot refuse me this, it's the big pre-season wash. Goodbye to the white flux that will dry with swimming in the sea and the sun ... "

This was Irene, just as the parties and the receptions of the

White City were a grand finale every time. Of course they would go, he said. "Do you know that Gordon wanted to kill me? Do you know he's dying?"

The girl-bird giggled: "To think that I fooled myself into thinking that I had become monstrous enough for you to like me a little!" Her voice held a strident note, but then the tone became sophisticated again: "Poor Gordon, he's an old mermaid. He says he's ill but he is always the same. In reality you haven't changed either. Apart from the gardens, nothing changes, it's like dreaming the same dream all the time. I've never seen so many soldiers about. Who knows if one day we'll wake up."

III

FROM THE GROUP of elderly ladies that preceded them along the path illuminated by kerosene torches—the crunching of gravel, shawls and turbans adjusted with nervous gestures—there came a burst of sounds. Then, silence. In the silence, the telltale trumpet blared out again, until it faded away on a flat note amplified by the emptiness of the evening. The old ladies stopped as one. And almost immediately the breeze spread a stink far stronger than the whiff of mothballs that their voile dresses left behind them like a wake. Irene clutched Luca's arm. They stopped a few metres from the group, pretending to admire the landscape, the tops of the pine trees in Lady Weathergood's garden that sloped down like an avalanche of clouds towards the ink of the sea.

A sob arose. Bent forward, legs apart, brandishing her evening bag as if it were a shield, an old woman left the path and opened up a passage among the canes and the bushes. None of her friends accompanied her. On the contrary, as soon as she vanished into the thick of the vegetation, they were overwhelmed by a fit of hilarity. The relief at not being the victim of the catastrophe revealed on each one's part the awareness of just how imminent that threat was. Giggling, spluttering, they drove away the spectre of senile wretchedness, and became little girls again. In schoolgirlish tones, made grotesque by hoarseness, breathlessness and coughing fits, they made fun of their friend, who was not to get steamed up, it brought good luck, and they exhorted her to be careful not to let the rats bite her there, on her bum … one, long and lanky, dressed in silver, holding her nose, her eyes goggling, was repeating a rhyme containing all the words that children use for faeces. And as she did so she was spinning around in a circle and stamping her heels like a woman possessed.

The sound of the gravel announced the arrival of new guests. The witches had recovered their composure, one puffing up her hair with trembling hands, another checking for smeared make-up in the mirror of her compact case, another again blowing her nose in a lace handkerchief. They had turned back into respectable elderly ladies waiting for a friend who had gone off to satisfy one of those needs that become more frequent with age. The two young people passed between them with heads lowered. Voices drifted up from the pavilion in which the party was underway. "This place is unique in all the world", whispered Irene. "Are you excited?" Shivering, Luca quickened his step.

"Priscilla!" "Darling!" "Señora Calderón, the Consul." Standing beside the Moorish portal, between two enormous lanterns placed on the grass, her curls topped by a tiara and her body bundled any old how into a muslin dress, the lady of the house was greeting a group of friends. She drew them to herself twisting her neck to suck with her wizened lips the air from their cheeks, from their ears. "You know everyone, make yourself at home, come on" was the brief phrase that signified instant dismissal. When one woman, a bit more gaga than the rest, attempted to broach the subject closest to everyone's heart (not even the daily papers had come out that day) she reacted unceremoniously, pushing her inside by main force, into the arena, where the wild beasts were waiting: "Have fun, treasure." The salon behind her, illuminated by more lanterns and monumental candelabras, was thronged with a multitude of people. "Irene! My child! You're still alive!" Luca noted that she really did place her lips on his wife's cheeks. Then, staring brazenly at the level of her breasts: "You're in great form. Flat-chested women are always the most elegant."

"It's touching to hear you talking of elegance, Priscilla."

Lady Weathergood held out her beringed hand for Luca to kiss: "I shall be keeping an eye on you. You will meet a person who, judging by what I have been told, is very dear to you ... here you are! Always late! My adored ones! Come on!" And she turned to the new arrivals waiting in line to greet her: "I detest these circuses, I had to invite all this riffraff again."

"What say, Priscilla? A marvellous evening ... "

199

"You know everyone, in you go, come on."

Even as they were coming in the door, and making their way through the crowd to reach the buffet, Luca was struck by a familiar sensation. The walls, all the way up to the coffered ceiling, were hung with hunting trophies, especially deer-heads, mementoes of the epoch in which, in the forests around the White City, the local dignitaries, diplomats, and prominent members of the international community would organize hunting parties that went on for days and days. But perhaps because of the patches of damp and the cracks in the plaster, perhaps because of the threadbare hangings that screened the two doors at the far end, those moth-eaten animal muzzles betrayed the deterioration of the city rather than evoked its past splendours. The big room full of smoke, which had struck him at first as being like one of those bars in the mountains from whose walls, among calendars and cuckoo clocks, the inevitable stuffed grouse reminds customers of mine host's good aim, had been transformed into the recreation room of an old folks' home. All the faces were decrepit: *Oncles*, Uncles, Aunties, Grand Duchesses, in other words failed artists, old folks whose pensions were too miserable to allow them to survive elsewhere, retired shopkeepers, hairdressers to ancient divas, military men cashiered from the service who had become interior decorators.

"*Niño! Qué tal?*" Pushing aside a little man skinny as a rake inside his dinner jacket (and he had first turned round, then bent over to inspect her with a ferocious expression), tripping over the train of Perla Lytton's underskirt (a good part of the contents of her glass was absorbed by the peacock-colour silk, but the writer of bodice-rippers was too drunk and too busy looking down the décolleté of an Italian widow to notice), and managing, despite her stature and thanks solely to her determination, to elbow her way through the bodies, the person to whom Lady Weathergood had alluded was heading towards them.

"Who's this moth then, spider?"

Decked out in a dress with flounces down to the floor, puffed sleeves, and a little shawl over her shoulders, perhaps because of her hair gathered up in a chignon, or perhaps because of the unusually discreet make-up, Jaima Martinez y Martinez looked like an ordinary old lady. Her big face wore a cordial expression, and even though you could see that the legs below the barrel of her drinker's stomach were too short, of the supreme iguana, of the monster, no trace remained. Luca's initial amazement at seeing her in such a company, she, the pariah who lived in a shack and got by on swindling and blackmail, gradually gave way to a certainty, and this certainty was confirmed by the impression he had received on entering the room. Before the summer farce, before the attribution of the roles that would accompany the arrival of the pigeons, among the foreign residents there were no class distinctions. The iguana was standing in front of them. Yet again, despite himself, Luca was struck by the intelligence and vitality of her expression, by the beauty of her smile. He introduced them. He declared that Señora Jaima Martinez y Martinez was the greatest botanical expert in the White City, an expert on the iris family, and a connoisseur of the indigenous species ... he realized that he was behaving towards Irene in exactly the same way as any Uncle or Auntie would behave towards a pigeon. The local mythomania was contagious. He ought to have hated Jaima, but he felt sorry for her.

The Levantine woman was in her glory. For years and years she had given up on the idea of being accepted by others with kindness and had become an expert in the excessive, and risky art that consists in submerging them either in insults or gushing compliments. Having weighed up the young woman, she began by saying that she knew all about her. Her husband had talked to her for months about her illness, the poor dear. It was rare to see a husband suffer so much for his wife, *la compañera de su vida* ... but his prayers had been answered! She was cured! And who ever said that love was blind? Every word that Luca had told her, weeping, of Irene's beauty, *por Dios*, was true as the fact that from now on they would live together happily ever after ...

The strange thing was that this was really what Jaima thought. Irene struck her as stupendous. And as well as her pride at having seduced a young boy accustomed to so much— a little arse that was a melon, a face as fresh as the *cabeza* of a freshly netted tuna, and a pile of *dinero* in the bank—there was the additional pleasure of finding herself at the centre of attention, conversing with the youngest couple at the reception, she who on similar occasions was usually squashed up against the wall like a cockroach. As she was complimenting Irene on her recovery, as she was inundating her with compliments, partly out of self interest and partly because, like immoral people often do, she had a soft spot for stories with a happy ending, Señora Martinez was inspired by a desire for Irene to like her. Luca was listening to her with difficulty (his breath stinking of whisky, Sir Everest was stooping over his ear, and was rambling on in a disjointed way about a matter of enemas, and unavoidable slip-ups). But Luca was more and more nervous, persuaded as he was that from one moment to the next, Irene, exasperated by all that flattery, was going to seize him by the arm and oblige him to dump the iguana. Inexplicably, however, the young tuna had taken the bait. She was smiling. She was leaning over Jaima. Both of them looked furtively at Luca, then they burst out laughing. Heaven knows why, but the gazelle and the toad shared a common language and, as in one of Aesop's fables, they were chatting away like old friends, without his being able to hear what they were saying. The natterjack rummaged through her purse and, taking out a piece of paper, she handed it to the fawn: given that she needed injections ... Luca got rid of Sir Everest with a shove. He went to put his arm around his girl's shoulder, determined to put her on her guard against the scorpion that stings in the middle of the river ... but why on earth should she believe him? She was just an ordinary little old lady, a little old lady dressed up in her Sunday best and a little tipsy, this creature who was giving him a sugary smile, pretending to abandon herself to the flow of her memories as she repeated the standard line of patter about Medinablanca in its heyday. But it was an edulcorated version that called up the cleanliness of the streets and the fidelity of the servants instead of sighing over the elasticity of the arses of the boys on sale in its brothels ... interrupting her, he asked Irene to come and have a drink with him. She replied that for the present she wasn't thirsty. Her friend was telling her some amusing things. Jaima lowered her eyes, her cheeks flushed with pleasure. Was this the infuriated she-elephant, the story teller capable of all metamorphoses? With that face, and such ways? How could he have thought that she was free as a wild beast, this petty thief in search of an alibi? Nondescript, mawk-ish: she wasn't even his type physically, he concluded to him-self. He headed off to the bar, alone.

Someone embraced him from behind. A shroud stinking of vodka, in a floral print, was lowered over his face—irises as big as barbecued chickens. Then, thanks to the intervention of Hassan, her husband, Isabella regained her balance, and read-justing the drapes of her ample dress: "Still on the raft of the Medusa?" She placed her lips on his. And while with one hand she tried to tuck the lock of hair hanging down from her temple back under her turban: "Thank heavens Priscilla has rented the house for the summer. She's holed up in a dump in the casbah. Provided there will be a summer."

Isabella burped. Shaking Luca's hand, Hassan made polite noises enquiring about Irene's health. Before Luca could announce her arrival, the woman started talking again: had he heard the story about Isidro? No? on which planet was he living? This is what comes of cutting oneself off like a savage! It had emerged—she wore an avid expression—that Hans Peter had grandchildren: "They turfed him out on the street with a suitcase full of caftans by way of a payoff! After fifty years of daily masses!" And laughing, with her bosom jiggling: "The descendant of Montezuma! He'll end up working as a guide in the *medina*!" By that time she was shouting: "And dear Gordon? What do you have to say about the great novelist and his discovery? To arrive at death's door only to realize that you like a cock that is a public pump ... that there isn't a hairdresser who hasn't filled up there ... isn't it a denouement worthy of that old hen Perla?"

Hassan bent over his wife, he whispered something in her ear. Isabella shook her head. "I apologize, I apologize, I apologize. But if she's a lesbian and stinks because she doesn't wash there's no harm in saying so round town. We are certainly not here to judge." She cast a glance around. "Adieu Luca. Do you still go to the Casino Judío? If you hear from her again, say hello to Irene from me. We'll be seeing you in hell, it'll be more fun." and, leaning on her husband, she walked off swaying like a cow camel. At the bar, Luca asked for a whisky on the rocks.

The waiters were the usual ones, those who were exiled to the kitchens during the summer season, served for the rest of the year in the foreigners' houses, and were all hired for occasions like this one. Old like their masters, they knew their habits to perfection, and with knowing smiles and looks betrayed the familiarity that bound them to the relics whose beds in remote times they had almost all shared, before their transformation into accomplices able to inspect the cafés, the gambling rooms, the squares, to identify and hire the companion most likely to alleviate the boredom and sadness of the old *nazrani* during rainy afternoons:

"You're looking fit, señor".

"Is your leg any better, sir?"

"How are the roses doing this year, Monsieur?"

"Have you seen little Abdallah? Taste one of these, Zora made them, they're the ones you like … "

Luca glanced around, and smiled. A few weeks after this, with the arrival of the pigeons, similar talk and attitudes would be banned. Everyone would occupy his place on the stage. But now, now the French people beside him could talk freely of the stroke of luck enjoyed by Priscilla, who had rented the house to the Great Designer for an unheard of sum: " … she passed off this brushwood for a garden sloping down to the sea … not to mention the state of the mattresses, they wet the beds every night … "

Now Richard Springsummer could discuss the political situation with his new companion—no Sir, the soldiers were no longer prepared to present arms the way they used to, when all you had to do was smile at them and they would unbutton their uniforms—and could conclude that within a few months they would all come to the same end as those two German fairies caught red handed playing with a still-fresh corpse: " … that is, still warm, my boy."

Now Dolores, the proprietrix of the boarding house downtown, could ask all over the shop if anyone knew the details of the new tariff about to be applied that summer by George, the aristocratic Englishman exiled here for half a century following a very Victorian scandal; now it was clear to everyone that the woman, jealous because her restaurant was always empty, was alluding to the contribution that the baronet required of the snobbish pigeons in order to receive them for tiffin or for an aperitif: "What with the price of meat, the poor man can't make a profit on lunch or dinner, even though we all know he has always served dog in mayonnaise … " Now, waving their arms, teasing a tinkle out of jewellery that had not yet been pawned with the Banco Bilbao or the Banque de Detroit, as glasses filled to the brim spilled over onto the floor covered with carpets, the old haberdashers and the old grocers could argue about the commissions they would have given to the old duchesses of the *medina* in the event of a sale to a pigeon of an embroidered caftan, a case of liquor, or a few grams of stuff to smoke, raising their voices until they were shouting, the faces red with rage or yellow with jaundice, insulting one another, harping on about past dishonesty, late payments, and even the loan of a hat or the gift of a cheese that had gone off: " … and in any case you were starving, you ingrate, you could see, those sticks you have instead of legs wouldn't hold you up any longer."

Now, before those dead stags that were the sole witnesses, they tried to reach an agreement on how the summer booty was to be carved up, exchanging information about the pigeons' bank accounts and sexual preferences: blackmail schemes were planned, traps were engineered, plots were hatched, atrociously malignant things were said without any need to lower the voice or to smile, and both absent and present were slandered with the same ease. *A souk.* Near the door, the guests who had waited on the path surrounded Lady Weathergood, who was getting a little air with the aid of a feather fan. Not far away, Irene was still talking with Jaima. But Luca was no longer afraid that the Levantine woman might have said to her: "Our little gardener! Did the cops subject you to the ultimate outrage?"

Harold, the painter, his hair still erect like the crest of a crowned crane, but violet, no longer golden, gave him a pat on the shoulder: "Gordon was telling me that you have gone to pieces, that you have given yourself over to irises and young boys. Poor, poor Gordon ... such clichés are acceptable when you're under twenty, you will agree. But to take them back to the country with him ... "

Irene was holding a goblet of champagne. She was conversing with Perla Lytton and another two ladies. Jaima was no longer to be seen. Suddenly, a silence fell upon the room. It lasted a few seconds, then the conversations picked up again, but in low voices, a hum rising to a crescendo like the sound that comes from the audience when a show is late in starting. Harold gestured at Luca to look behind him, in the direction of the door.

"My old friend! What a surprise!" Priscilla Weathergood had shouted: "How sweet of you, to make me this lovely surprise!" Freeing himself from her embrace, emerging with difficulty from those metres of muslin and the feathers of her fan, the man faced the public with head held high. His rigid, aquiline profile was that of a Roman emperor on a coin. But rather than a sovereign on his way to the guillotine, Isidro looked like a marionette moved by a puppeteer incapable of conferring the slightest naturalness upon his movements. All dressed in gold— a stiff full-length caftan—his hair impregnated with lacquer forming a kind of papier-mâché nimbus around his face, he strode across the hall upon which silence had fallen again—a mage king in a farce, the queen in a Sicilian puppet show. At his passing, the crowd opened up. When he got to the record player, he clapped his hands and exclaimed imperiously: "*Mussica*" with lots of esses.

"He must be on morphine," murmured a voice.

"He ought to be stopped," said someone else. "If the number is a success he'll find a gig in a cabaret for the season ... "

To the rhythm of a song by The Doors, Isidro began to dance. He held his arms folded as if he were cradling a baby, and, aware that all were watching him, drunk with the attention that was centred on him, he smiled at that image of himself who was dancing on the brightly-lit stage behind his closed eyelids. He was no longer a man. He was a ghost shrouded in his golden *syrma*, an ancient and terrible figure, a Salomé wiggling his skeletal hips and rotating his pelvis in front of guests who were more and more uncomfortable, while he called for their heads. He opened the buttons of the caftan one after the other. He slipped one hand between the two flaps of the neckline, caressed the ribs of Christ, descended to his belly, pinched the elastic of his underpants from which sprouted a tuft of hairs ...

"What you are inside sooner or late comes out ... "

"They were two adventurers ... "

" ... with the Cardinal dead as if it were yesterday ... "

The only one who was observing the scene with a satisfied look was Priscilla Weathergood, sure that this incident would have contributed to the success of her soirée. Amid murmurs and sighs that were intended to sound scandalized, but were of fear, the caftan slipped to the floor. Pale in the flickering light, spectrally thin, the insect emerged from the chrysalis. Venus was born. The old puppet-master had transformed himself into the Venus of the White City, just like the big bald man who had stripped in the cemetery. Luca saw the fat guts wobbling again, and between the dilated buttocks there appeared a hand like a spider ... a spider green with chlorophyll ... parody, parody ... His head was spinning. A voice was saying that it was a scandal, he should be thrown out, that the Princess Royal might arrive at any moment. A man tried to immobilize Isidro, who shot him a withering glance. A second man, more resolute, took a hand but the marionette slipped out of his grip. Finally, two or three waiters piled in, Luca recognized the oldest as the major domo of Dar Sultàn.

"The Señor Count was always the best dancer on the coast ...

" Isidro stopped dead. He looked at the man with wide-open, incredulous, grateful eyes, and fell into his arms. The three servants lifted him up bodily—a deposition of the Cross. Someone drew aside one of the drapes, the funeral cortége vanished beyond the door ... "I had forgotten to invite him, the poor dear." Priscilla Weathergood cast a gloating glance at her seraglio. "But no one knows his new address. Let's hope he doesn't hold it against me."

Luca approached the lady of the house, who was explaining to her stalwarts that the long-awaited funds were on the point of arriving. The Generals had finally understood that her museum would have added lustre to the fame of the White City, by attracting quality tourism. In a junk shop she had found the manuscript of poor Marie-France's book on the Isis cults ... yes, the one dedicated to Janie, which those awful publishers had rejected ... Dolores nodded, gravely. Perla Lytton nodded, as did the old lady who had done it in her pants, and as did the one in silver chiffon who had improvised a dance on the path. Faced with this assembly of wrinkled, goitred nymphs with their plunging necklines and turbans, their eyes veiled with fatigue and their idiotic mouths half-open, Luca understood: the chrysalides and the moths of his sleepless nights had ended up in the display cabinets of a museum like the one Priscilla had been talking about: " ... beside the fossils Maria left me, beside her Palaeolithic or Neolithic axes, the ammonites, the stuffed platypus and the Tibetan shawl that her grandson had promised to send me from Toronto ... " He could observe with a blend of attraction and repulsion their cocoons, the complicated designs of their wings, the neuration of their tissues, the ridges, the veins, the fuzzy hair on the bodies, the broken antennae ... but they were fragile as dried irises crumbling in the pages of an old herbal, they were dead. All the Jaimas of this earth, all the monstrous creatures that had dominated his premature ejaculator's fantasies, the whales, the chimaeras, the sphinxes, the octopi, the iguanas, the bitches, the goats—the mothers—had shrunk, had been sucked down into the formaldehyde, sealed in glass jars through which they stared at him with the wrinkled little faces of foetuses, a Noah's ark all of whose guests were stuffed ...

He needed to breathe, he needed Irene. There was a detonation. A second bang. A third. All eyes turned to the windows. But the moonlit sky was not furrowed with the wakes of fireworks. Silence plunged down. Luca noticed that all the waiters had vanished. The guests had begun to decamp. Lady Weather-good, absorbed in her tale, had noticed nothing. Her most faithful devotees did not dare betray the fact that they were longing to flee, and pretending to listen to her they cast looks all around in which doubts and suspicions had already given way to fear. But then the lady of the house saw Isabel and Hassan, because the woman's staggering, the ponderousness of her gait encumbered by her dress, and the dimensions of her turban, made it impossible for her to go unobserved. "Going already?" she asked from a distance. Isabel held back her husband. She raised her head, and her face bloated with alcohol opened in a grimace that looked like an imitation of a lion roaring, but it was a yawn. "It's time to run for it, dear Priscilla," she shot back from that distance, so that all might hear. From the city the wailing of a siren rose up, different from those of the ferries coming into the roads, sharper and more lugubrious, pro-longed. But Lady Weathergood was not the type to let herself be discouraged for so little: "You are right, Fatima dear," she yelled above the siren, and no insult could have been more offensive than the name her old friend had taken by marrying a native. "You look awful, you're devastated." The lights went out. In the flickering light of the guttering candles, for a second it seemed as if the dusty stag-heads were grinning, as if savouring a revenge that they had awaited, cunning, since the days of the hunts in which they had fallen. "Thanks for the grand finale, Priscilla. If you had given us something to eat it would have been a perfect last supper." And the couple left.

Then the guests who until then had been restraining themselves began to crowd around the doorway, shoving, jostling, tripping over the carpets. As soon as they were outside, they set to running as best they could, the old women's heels making them trip on the gravel, the *Oncles* panting, cursing, all dogged by terror, heading for the motor cars that would take them to their villas, to their apartments, to their hovels, where they would grab and carry to safety something—what? was the general thought, what?—property deeds, bearer passbooks, the American shares inherited from a Laredo Toledano or Benchimol great-aunt? The banknotes hidden in the Pierre Loti they had never read and never returned to the library of the Cervantes Institute? Mummy's silverware? Estrella's topaz? The photos of a boy now married and grown fat?—only to pour like rats leaving the sinking ship into their consulates— Chile, Uruguay, the Azores, Andorra, Paraguay—or to dash down to the harbour, where they knew someone, where they had done someone a favour, to board a sloop, a patera, and away in dream, away forever from this powder keg that had exploded . . . Luca managed to reach Irene, who looked at him, nodding in sorrow. Jaima, vanished. Almost at the same moment, a hand came to rest on his shoulder. "Dear boy, you look awful", said Priscilla Weathergood. "Is that villainous old woman still ravishing you?" Luca dragged Irene away without replying. "Invite me to see the garden one of these days!" shouted their host. "Even if just for tea or a drink! Gordon tells me it's paradise!"

They were outside. The breeze was agitating the leaves of the trees and from time to time it carried from the city a murmuring, a mechanical sound of tracked vehicles. The air smelled of burnt rubber. More explosions. Again, the siren.

"Luca." Irene clutched his arm.

Towers of smoke rose up in the clear, moonlit sky. Black the bay, down there, black the city, where all the lights were out. Here and there, however, wells of light opened out. Illuminated by the fires, certain districts, certain buildings, seemed incredibly close to them, the slant of a roof, a terrace on which tiny figures scurried to and fro, the castle of the casbah, Dar Sultàn, a minaret or a bell tower, the bell tower of the Anglican church in flames, alongside the wall of the old cemetery . . .

Without saying a word, they went back up through the garden

illuminated by the moon, because the kerosene for the torches
had run out who knows how long before. In a garden a peacock
emitted its lugubrious cry; another one, closer, replied. Isidro
was lying on a bench under the portico at the back of the house.
He was snoring, and moaning. The servants had abandoned
him there in his underwear, the caftan at his feet. Picking it up,
Irene covered him with it: "He was without a shroud," she said,
returning to Luca's side.

"Let's go home, Luca."

The road was deserted, but Luca drove carefully. The beggars
who usually slept stretched out below the eucalyptus trees had
disappeared. No nocturnal football match in front of the
neighbourhood grocery store, always lit up by a street lamp
that was now out. Empty, unguarded, the villas whose gates
were preceded by flights of steps on which, until the previous
evening, the watchmen had talked and smoked *kif* with the
fishermen, and the kids played marbles, or drank beer, talking
of football, whores, money, and of how to escape and get across
the Strait, as they watched the *nazrani* coming home in their
cars. The headlights picked out a black silhouette at the side of
the road. A truck. A beam of light dazzled them. Luca turned.
Irene's profile was waxen. Her eyes wide open, her mouth
hard.

"Take it easy. We're foreigners."

Luca handed his licence to the soldier, a young man who
shone his electric torch on it, then dazzled him again as he
checked his features, then he looked at the photo again.
"Who's the *chica*?" "The lady is my wife, Señor." The boy
asked them where they were headed, then he stood there thinking. Another soldier got out of the jeep. The two discussed
things for a few minutes. Finally, the first one gave him back his
licence: "Get out of here, go. There's the curfew."

Irene sighed. And as the car was moving off: "Not even in
Durrell's *Quartets*, I assure you ... " But her voice betrayed the
efforts she was making to control herself. She laid a hand on his
leg. Then, having clutched his hand, she pressed it to her belly.

They were in the garden. The frogs, who had ceased croaking

on their entry, started up their concert again: it normally sounded like they were scolding the dogs in heat, but this evening it was a comment on the bursts of gunfire coming from the city. Without any need to exchange a word, they went down to the servants' lodge. It lay empty in the lunar light. Hand in hand, they went back up to the lawn that separated the two pavilions. From the street there came a hum, voices, a chant that was getting closer: "*Nazrani afuera! Nazrani afuera!*" Then, this time in the district, shots. They embraced. "I've been to bed with a couple of guys," Luca said.

She smiled at him: "You'll just have to make do with me, tonight."

He slipped a hand into the neckline of her blouse. He caressed her flat chest, her martyred boy's breasts.

" ... that Señora Martinez ... " Irene whispered.

"*Nazrani afuera! On est chez nous! On est chez nous! Nazrani ... afuera! On est chez nous!*"

Shots, closer. He whispered to her not to be afraid. "I'm not afraid. I can't be afraid anymore. I want us to adopt ... " His gaze moved away. It alighted on the only bare flower bed, on the still life of a man who had to possess the body of the ghost in order to discover ...

"It's you who's afraid of me, spider."

They were naked, but they were not at the bottom of the garden, they were not lying on the grass made luxuriant at a cost of a great deal of water, of toil: they were on the bed, in their room. Two bodies that had found each other again, and heedless of what was happening around them they sought each other to bloom and to fade one inside the other ... a knocking rang out on the front door. They separated. Luca jumped to his feet. "I'll come too, spider." No. She was to wait there, next to the telephone. "Is it working?" he didn't reply. He gave her a hasty kiss, the knocking was even fiercer, they were going to break down the door, only after he went into the bathroom did he realize that his bathrobe had been stolen. He went out naked, closing the door behind him, and ran down the stairs and across the lawn. He stopped. They were out there. He would see the boys awakening after a sleep of centuries in their suburbs with no sewers and in the countryside throttled by drought, he would see them laugh, waving their sub-machine gun, pointing it at him: "*Nazrani afuera! nazrani afuera!*", or perhaps they would be grown men, fathers, old men with beards, and as they shot they would brandish the Koran: "*On est chez nous, on est chez nous.*" Then he would see the wizened head of a nanny-goat, Marta's face, and with that in his eyes he would enter another unreality. The thought of Irene shook him. The smell of mushrooms, the parched tuft: "Careful, spider."

He opened up. Gentlemen, *vous êtes chez vous.*

The old Mercedes was moving off. She was there. Dishevelled, in her dressing gown, small, black. The supreme iguana. Africa goggling at his nudity. Then, almost immediately, the cannibal, marvellous smile of one who knows everything. Beside her there was a dusty cardboard suitcase tied up with string: "Hurry up, *cabrón*, give me a hand. There's a bit of a shambles in town. I thought I would have been easier here with you two. Come on, take the suitcase ... wait ... don't be *loco* ... wait, *maricón*. Close the door ... I could be ... wait *niño* ... your mother ... yes ... like that ... *así mi niño* ... yes *niño* ... yes".

PART FIVE

AFTER SHE LEFT the boulevard, Marta, with the white bathrobe under her arm, went down the street that leads to the Grand Socco, a square shaded by linden trees and surrounded by elegant cafés in which Viennese orchestras and gypsy bands played until dawn. The other days she had felt uncomfortable walking past those ladies who looked at her with indifference, devouring shrimps and waving their lace fans; it had intimidated her to walk under the gaze of the pomaded loafers who spent the afternoons sitting at those tables, having their shoes shined by the native boys and commenting on the girls as they passed by. (A costume drama? No, too out of focus and too low-budget: the only surviving clip from an old amateur film—a document.) This evening, instead, despite the usual looks and the usual comments, she felt calm. As if she were somewhere else. As she walked on in the light-coloured skirt with the poppy print, there was something childish and at once matronly about her gait, like that of certain poor, and youthful, neo-realist heroines.

She took the alley that led to the district in which her boarding house stood. From beside their handcarts, the soup vendors handed their customers—Spanish exiles, peasants, workers, dockers—bowls full of steaming gruel; veiled women went in and out of small shops. A pungent odour came from the sea, still in the dying light. Marta felt cheerful—the irrational cheerfulness of someone faced with something unknown, attracted, and at the same time overawed by an alien life and by its tangle of complications. The frightened excitement of the little nanny goat that sniffs too much salt. She went down calle Goya. Poor houses with wooden balconies, doorways in which sat beggars, barefoot children with shaved heads playing in the roadway ... facing a door above which there was a sign saying Chez Manolo, some Europeans already dressed for dinner were chatting cheerfully. One looked like ... "Hurry up,

Gordon!" another man called him, looking out of a window in his shirt sleeves. "It's his spitting image! Your little brother waiting for you!" All the others laughed.

Marta arrived at the boarding house. She asked the proprietrix for her key, while the latter stared suspiciously at the bathrobe. She went up to her room. Would she tell her colleagues? (In reality she had no friends.) She switched on the light, a naked bulb hanging from the ceiling. Laying the bathrobe on the iron bed, she realized that she could not think of Mortimer. It was an inexplicable feeling. Like not existing. As if it had been he who had thought of her. And, thinking about her, had invented her. Alone, Marta no longer existed.

She felt that her belly was full, even though lunch had been hours before (but she had drunk too much). What folly, this holiday! There was a bitterness, now, in the nubile and already wooden movements with which she undressed, folding her skirt over the only chair, taking her night-dress from beneath the pillow. A din rose up from the alley. She opened the shutters. It was a little procession of negroes in costume. One, dressed in red, was distributing coins from a saddlebag to a throng of children. From the roofs of the neighbouring houses the women sent up their cry of *you-you-you*, but it was guttural, almost aggressive. Carried by four bare-chested men, so wide it could barely pass through the alleyway, came a palanquin, swaying. On it lay … Marta recognized her. She smiled, enchanted. It was she, the millionairess who was always in the glossies! Even slimmer, even blonder, and indifferent to every-thing, dressed in an Indian sari and glittering with jewels. Now the nanny goat was happy. She had spent her meagre savings well. She would be able to tell the story for months, for years, to her acquaintances and friends (she had loads of them, at this moment), of the appearance of that goddess who had already had six husbands—and she had already vanished.

Having closed the window again, she went towards the bed. Even after her shower, she still felt dirty. But in this boarding house they distributed water in the mornings only, one basin in front of each room, too little for her, with her mania for

218

hygiene. What would she do, if she were pregnant? The boss would fire her; if she lost her job, she would have . . . she needed water. Trying at every step to overcome her fear and shame, Marta, barefoot, went back down the stairs. The owner was no longer there. In her place, behind the counter, there was the cleaning woman, a dwarf of indeterminate age who looked like a reptile, an iguana. Marta was on the point of running away. But the other, in a kind voice, asked her if there was something she could do for her.

" . . . If it's no trouble . . . a little water, please."

The dwarf weighed her up through narrowed lids. Then she got up and trotted away through the courtyard, where she vanished, leaving Marta alone, her naked feet on the little mat adorned with garlands of roses and violets, beside the leather armchair on which a cat lay sleeping, right under the gilded wooden shelf held up by a swan, which in the light of the two lanterns sent out a bright gleaming . . . there was the sound of water running. The dwarf returned with a zinc pail, one of those the peasants used for milking. She brought it to Marta, full to the brim. "Thanks. Thanks very much indeed . . . "

"Goodnight, *niña.*"

Squatting over the pail, Marta washed herself. The burning of her vagina reminded her of Mortimer, then something, from inside . . . she pulled out a clot, thinking it was blood. She looked at it in the light of the lamp. Now that it opened up, now that it was falling apart in her hand . . . with an upsurge of profound shame, she recognized the remains of the flower that she had plucked from among the stones. In her mind's eye, she saw what he had done, his whim. But as she was reconstructing the scene, rather than humiliated, she felt powerful, very powerful, as if that young gentleman, by indulging in a passing impulse, had in reality obeyed her order, her will . . . she was certain of that. As she continued to rub her vagina with the mashed petals of the lily ("mourning iris", Mortimer had called it, or that's what she had understood), she knew she was pregnant. Someone was knocking at the door. The knocking continued. Marta got up, letting her night-dress slip back down, and opened the door. It was the dwarf. She felt like asking her to leave, but the other woman's smile—and in a few seconds she had taken in the pail, the wet hem of her night-dress, the drops on the floor—reminded her of something, someone, she had seen before ... "Have you finished? If that harpy doesn't find the pail in its place tomorrow morning ... is everything all right, *niña*?" Marta burst into tears—nothing made sense to her anymore, how had she ended up here, alone as a dog, in this horrible city, in this boarding house?—and, without realizing, she threw her arms around her. The dwarf, who stank of sweat and garlic, shoved the door to behind her with her foot: "Don't cry, *niña*, don't do that, everything's all right ... who is the *cabrón* who did this? ... if we women don't give one another a hand ... " And as Marta clung to her (her face hollowed by scrimping and furrowed with tears is now in close up, it fills the screen): "Don't worry, you can't see anything ... this city is full of opportunities for a pretty girl like you ... listen to me, don't cry, we'll fix him up even if it's a little boy ... princes, sultans, lords ... don't cry or you'll ruin those pretty eyes ... I know a duke who'd be just right for you ... the duke of Mainville ... Bébé de Mainville ... do you like the name? ... do you like nice names? ... then listen, listen to my story, *niña*."

EDUARDO BERTI

Agua

Translated by
Alexander Cameron and Paul Buck

The year is 1920, and Luis Agua, an agent
for an electricity company, arrives in Vila
Natal, an inhospitable village in Portugal.
His objective is to convince the inhabitants of
the benefits of artificial light. Before long Agua
learns that the village and the castle that pre-
sides over it hide dark secrets. The beautiful
widow, shrouded in mystery, who never
leaves her castle, a will that is both puzzling
and cruel, a pioneer of aviation, an epidemic
and a breathtaking finale unite the themes of
love, revenge, humour, death, greed, heroism
and courage in the modern world.

"There is no doubt that Eduardo Berti must be
considered one of the most original, most accomplished novelists writing in Spanish today."

From the Afterword by ALBERTO MANGUEL

PUSHKIN MODERN

ISBN 1-901285-42-1 • 160pp • £10/$14